Books by J. B. Priestley

FICTION

Adam in Moonshine
Benighted
The Good Companions
Angel Pavement
Faraway
Wonder Hero
Laburnum Grove
They Walk in the City
The Doomsday Men
Let the People Sing
Blackout in Gretley
Daylight on Saturday
Three Men in New Suits

Bright Day
Jenny Villiers
Festival at Farbridge
The Other Place: short stories
The Magicians
Low Notes on a High Level
Saturn Over the Water
The Thirty-First of June
The Shapes of Sleep
Lost Empires
Sir Michael and Sir George
It's an Old Country

PLAYS

The Roundabout
Duet in Floodlight
Spring Tide
Mystery at Greenfingers
The Long Mirror
Jenny Villiers
The Rose and Crown
The High Toby
Bright Shadow

Dragon's Mouth (with Jacquetta
  Hawkes)
Private Rooms
Treasure on Pelican
Try it Again
Mother's Day
A Glass of Bitter
Mr. Kettle and Mrs. Moon

COLLECTED PLAYS

Volume I

Dangerous Corner
Eden End
Time and the Conways
I Have Been Here Before
Johnson over Jordan
Music at Night
The Linden Tree

Volume II

Laburnum Grove
Bees on the Boat Deck
When We Are Married
Good Night Children
The Golden Fleece
How Are They at Home?
Ever Since Paradise

Volume III

Cornelius
People at Sea
They Came to a City
Desert Highway
An Inspector Calls
Home is Tomorrow
Summer Day's Dream

ESSAYS AND AUTOBIOGRAPHY

Talking
Open House
Apes and Angels
Midnight on the Desert
Rain upon Godshill
The Secret Dream

Delight
All About Ourselves and other Essays
  (chosen by Eric Gillett)
Thoughts in the Wilderness
Margin Released

CRITICISM AND MISCELLANEOUS

Brief Diversions
The English Comic Characters
Meredith (E.M.L.)
Peacock (E.M.L.)
The English Novel
English Humour (Heritage Series)
The Balconinny
English Journey
Postscripts
Out of the People
British Women Go To War

Russian Journey
Theatre Outlook
The Olympians (opera libretto)
Journey Down a Rainbow (with
  Jacquetta Hawkes)
Topside
The Art of the Dramatist
Literature and Western Man
Man and Time
The Moments—and Other Pieces

It's an Old Country

It's an Old Country

A NOVEL BY

J. B. PRIESTLEY

An Atlantic Monthly Press Book

LITTLE, BROWN AND COMPANY · BOSTON · TORONTO

LIBRARY OF CONGRESS CATALOG CARD NO. 67-14448

FIRST AMERICAN EDITION

ATLANTIC–LITTLE, BROWN BOOKS
ARE PUBLISHED BY
LITTLE, BROWN AND COMPANY
IN ASSOCIATION WITH
THE ATLANTIC MONTHLY PRESS

PRINTED IN THE UNITED STATES OF AMERICA

It's an Old Country

1

On the Friday of the week following his mother's funeral, Tom Adamson had dinner with the Wentworths, Andrew and Madge. They had a big top-floor flat high above the coloured neon and glitter, the guitars and synthetic folk songs, of Sydney's King's Cross. They could afford it because they had no children. Andrew was now an assistant professor in the Eng. Lit. department of the University (where Tom taught colonial economic history), and Madge had a pretty good job with the Australian Broadcasting Commission. And they liked to live well. Their long sitting room, which Tom had never seen before without a party crowd, now combined bright yellow with sepia and a lot of abstract art. A table for three had been laid in a kind of alcove.

"Nobody else, you see, Tom," said Andrew, bringing the sherry Tom had asked for. Andrew himself was drinking whisky; he was always drinking whisky, to protect himself, he told everybody, from the deluge of beer that was washing Australia's brains away. He and Madge were English; it was only three or four years since they had left the old country. And this was really the chief reason why Tom had accepted their invitation, though of course he hadn't told them so. "Just us, mate," Andrew continued. "That's what you wanted, isn't it?"

"Yes, Andrew, it is — that is, if you insist on hearing what might turn into a long and boring story —"

"Just try to get away without telling it, mate. Look — you dropped a queer hint to me. So I dropped one even shorter and queerer to Madge, so now of course she's half out of her little mind with curiosity —"

"Shut up and take this." Madge had marched in with a tray. "It's time I started boozing. First course — cold — *oeufs-en-gelée*. Where's the gin?" She shook her dark cropped locks at Tom. She was a small vivid sort of girl, who always looked and sounded angry but wasn't. "Tom, lay off that sherry — it's terrible." She looked him up and down. "My God, you're the only attractive man I've seen round here for weeks and weeks —"

"What about me?" said Andrew, returning from the alcove.

"Too short, getting too fat, and beginning to look crummy," she told him. "And here's Tom Adamson — tall, dark, handsome, and just starting to get that ravaged look which we all find irresistible."

"Gertcha, woman! He'd never talk you into anything —"

"No. Unlike you, you devil. Talked me into your sweaty bed. Talked me into living in Birmingham — a basement in Edgbaston. Talked me into coming umpteen thousand miles to listen to *strine* fourteen hours a day, you little fat fraud."

"What a tongue and what a cow!" cried Andrew, beaming at his wife.

"Come on, boys, let's eat." After they had sat down, she turned to Tom. "When is it you're going home?"

Tom smiled. "I'm not, Madge."

"Why, Andrew told me —"

4

"Oh — I'm flying to London next Wednesday. But I'm not *going home*. I'm leaving it. I've lived here ever since I was three — thirty-three years."

"My mistake," said Madge. "The point is, you always *sound* so English —".

"Neow, he ain't neow pommy bastud, girl," Andrew told her, and he was ready to try harder in this vein if she hadn't shut him up.

"If you want me to explain," said Tom, "you'll launch me into my long story —"

"No, no, no, you must save that until after dinner. Until I've dished it up and we've eaten it, I won't be able to understand anything properly. And as you've been told already, you're here to satisfy my curiosity."

"That's how it is, mate," said Andrew. "So save it. Start shaping the narrative in your mind. Don't be afraid to abbreviate, to cut a passage here, to shorten one there, to distil —"

"You open that Château Woolaboolanoola or whatever it is," Madge commanded. "And then collect these plates while I go and dish up the *navarins*." And off she flew across to the kitchen.

"Madge takes her cooking very seriously."

"So do I," said Tom. "I mean hers, not mine. She's a hell of a good cook, Andrew. You're lucky. Oh — I don't mean just about food —"

"Quite right, mate. I *am* lucky. Too many wives are amiable outside and prickly inside. Madge is the opposite. She bosses me and insults me all the time but is really a honeypot. Try this imitation claret, Tom, because I'm sticking to whisky. All right? Good-o, mate. And let me give you a tip for when you get to London, which is full of girls looking for blokes like you, if only to get away from the three other girls they're sharing a flat with in Earls Court — and all those stockings and panties drying in the bathroom. Keep your eyes open for one who's prickly outside like Madge, and beware of all those smooth-faced, smooth-tongued, hardhearted bitches. What's she yelling about now?"

"Something about plates, I think." Tom got up and handed him a couple.

"No, no, it's all under control."

And really it was, and a very good dinner too, as Tom told Madge when they finally moved out of the alcove to take their coffee round the long low table. But when he sat down, and smiled lazily but gratefully across the table at them both, he felt himself to be invaded by a certain dark melancholy. Unusual couples like these Wentworths, who really were happy together and were not just pretending to be, couldn't help making him feel shut out, moving away on some lonely orbit, unable to do or say anything that could mean very much to them. So it wasn't modesty or a fear of boring them that made him reluctant to begin talking about himself. It was the feeling that however curious they might pretend to be, however much friendly concern they might show him, they would feel relieved and happier when he had said his piece and had gone. The point being that they didn't need — and so didn't want — anybody else around.

"Now then, mate, let's put the little woman out of her misery," said Andrew, who was now smoking a cigar that looked like a badly wrapped firework. "You're going to England to find your father. Right?"

"Right."

"Good," said Madge. "And from now on, Andrew, you shut up. Tell us what it's all about, Tom ducks, and don't rush it — take your time."

Tom hesitated, then plunged in. "I'll start with my father, Charles Adamson. Born 1897 in Surrey, second son of

6

the Reverend Cyril Adamson, schoolmaster. Served 1915 to 1919, Northumberland Fusiliers, ending with rank of captain. Had one year up at Oxford, then went on the stage. Turned painter as well as actor, then divided his time between painting and acting."

"It's been done," said Madge. "Was he any good — I mean, as either?"

"I can only make a vague guess. And you'll soon understand why. My guess is that with both he was neither very bad nor very good — somewhere in between but exactly where, of course, I don't know. He married my mother in 1928 and they lived in London. They had two children — my sister Joan, born 1929, then me, born 1930. I'm sorry about this *Who's Who* style, but I'm trying to give you the bare facts. And I think the dates are important. In the spring of 1933 he left London to join a woman he'd been having an affair with — just went and left us flat. My mother knew where he was and wrote to him several times, first begging him to come back and then reminding him that the little money she had was running out and she had herself and two children to keep. He never replied to these letters. She never had a single word from him."

"My God — what a stinker!" This was Madge.

"I thought we were shutting up," her husband told her. "Go on, mate."

"My mother came from a Cotswold farming family called Carpenter, but she'd trained as a nurse and that's how she came to meet my father in London. Incidentally, she was six years younger, born in 1903. She had a brother eight years older than she was, James Carpenter, who'd come here to Australia in 1913. He was a good sheep and cattle man, very tough and a hell of a hard worker, and by 1933 he was running his own station in Western Victoria, not far from the Hopkins River, back of Warrnambool. And this

7

was where I was raised, folks, because later in 1933 that's where my mother took us, at the invitation of my Uncle James. Perhaps I ought to add that although Uncle James behaved conscientiously and decently from first to last, making sure I got a good education when he saw that's what I wanted, I never really liked him and he never really liked me. He was a bachelor, and my mother kept house for him until she joined me here in Sydney four years ago. Of the three of us my sister Joan was the one he was really fond of, and she finally married another sheep man called Coram and they moved in with Uncle James and now that he's dead — he died two years ago — the station's theirs and they're happy as Larry. And now you're asking *So what?*"

"One of us is, mate," said Andrew. "Madge can take miles and hours of this stuff, how a lot of people she's never set eyes on met and married and had children and died —"

"You be quiet, Wentworth," said his wife. "If you were as sensitive as you pretend to be, you'd realise Tom's proper story hasn't started yet. We haven't come to the *crunch*, have we, Tom?"

"Not quite but we're nearly there, Madge. Now of course as soon as Joan and I were old enough to be told things, we learnt that we could forget about our father who was a thoroughly wicked man, best forgotten. My mother was a fairly hard, embittered sort of woman, and my Uncle James was harder still and the kind of man who'd have hated an actor-painter brother-in-law even if he'd behaved well to his family. Sometimes I couldn't help wondering — after all, I could just remember him and he wasn't my idea of a wicked man at all — but the other three had no doubts of any kind. And indeed, when I talked to Joan after the funeral and then on the telephone yesterday, she still hadn't any doubts at all and thinks I'm a soft idiot to want to spend any time and money even enquiring about our father. She hopes he's dead, rotten and forgotten. And this was after I'd explained what my mother had said to me during the last days of her illness." He stopped and when Madge held up the coffeepot he passed over his cup.

"I don't know why — and I'm not claiming anything," said Andrew softly, "but I knew — I just *knew* — your mother was going to wonder if she'd been right about him. I did. I saw it coming."

"What?" cried Madge. "After he'd simply walked out and left her stranded like that — and with two kids? Well, I must say —"

"Hold it, girl, hold it. Your mother suddenly had some doubts of her own, didn't she, Tom?"

"Yes. Right at the very end. But it was all confused, and nothing came out clear and certain. There she was in hospital, with an inoperable cancer, suffering a lot of pain, and there were days when I couldn't see her at all, and other days when I could see her but she'd been heavily doped and her mind was weak and wandering. Just as I thought she was going to tell me something, she'd doze off or the nurse would tell me I had to go. It was a bad time. I wasn't all that loud and clear myself. You can imagine what it was like."

"Andie doesn't have to," said Madge. "He went through it too, just before we came out here."

"I certainly did, mate. And while we're in the interval, what'll it be — whisky or brandy?"

Tom chose brandy and drank some before beginning again. "She'd had a letter from somebody in England — Joan had sent it on — telling her my father hadn't been as much to blame as she thought, that it had been all a mistake. Mind you, I never saw this letter. When she read it she was having a bad bout, and she'd torn it up and dropped the pieces into one of those trash buckets they're always taking out and emptying. But later when she was calmer, probably full of morphine, she began thinking over what she'd read. Then she felt she might have been wrong about him all those years — over thirty — and she begged me to go and find him. In fact she made me promise I would. And that's why I'm flying to London on Wednesday."

"Good for you, Tom!" cried Madge. "Probably she never really stopped loving him. Cursed him but couldn't forget him as she stared at all those bloody sheep for thirty years."

"But look, mate, how much do you know about him now? I mean, it's been a long time — with a big war in between, turning everything upside down and inside out." Andrew leant forward and filled Tom's glass with brandy. "Do you know where to start?"

"No, not really. He'd be only sixty-nine now, but of course he may have died years ago. Or he may be alive but not living in England any longer. Or he may have changed his name. And what he certainly hasn't done is to *make* a name either as a painter or as an actor. I've never heard of a Charles Adamson. Have you?"

They both thought a moment and then said they hadn't. "But that doesn't prove anything," Madge added. "There must be hundreds of painters and actors who are doing all right that we've never heard of."

"And he may be doing something quite different now," said Andrew. "I think that's the wrong approach. Didn't your mother tell you anything about his relatives and friends?"

"She tried to but then it was too late," Tom replied, not without a touch of bitterness. "She did her best in a vague rambling fashion, but over thirty years had gone by and her memory was going anyhow. All I've got — half a name here, a possible address there — doesn't fill a page of a small notebook. And of course I don't know anybody. I've never been back to England."

"*What?*" They stared at him.

"Well, don't look like that. After all we're in Sydney, Australia, now, not in Glasgow. How many people here *have* been to England?"

"Off the point, mate. They're not on the staff of the University either. But I'm surprised because I was distinctly under the impression that you'd moved around —"

"So I have. I did a postgraduate year at Berkeley, and of course I went down the coast — San Francisco to Los Angeles. I even took a look at Mexico —"

"But you never went to England," said Madge, "and I know why. Because your mother didn't want you to go there — hated the very idea of it — right? But now you have to go to find your father."

"I know — it seems ridiculous —"

"No it doesn't. Not to me, anyhow. That is, if you can afford to go."

"Oh — that part of it's all right. I had some leave coming. And even if I'd thrown up my job, it wouldn't have worried me financially. My Uncle James left most of his money to my mother, and now I get half hers, so I'm really rather well off."

"Then I wish I was going with you," cried Madge.

"To do what?" her husband demanded darkly.

"Not what's running in your head most of the time. But here's Tom — innocent as an egg really, for all his lectureship and ravaged look — about to drop into huge, bewildering, wicked old London —"

"And walk the streets crying *Father, Father!*" said Andrew. "I'd better go with him."

"All you'd do is to go from pub to pub. He needs me. Or,

failing me, some other woman. We're the real amateur detectives — the ferreting-out sex. We could pick up a dozen clues while the first one was still staring you boys in the face. Haven't you got a girl, Tom?"

"I had," he replied quite calmly. "But we called it off. She was tall, handsome, very dignified — even at times when dignity wasn't demanded. Now I'm going to look for a small fierce one, like you, Madge." He hesitated a moment, and then, with an obvious change of tone: "I can see I may be going to make a fool of myself. I don't know England. I've got nothing but a few vague and doubtful names and addresses, dating back over thirty years. Probably nobody will take me seriously. But however bloody ridiculous this may seem to other people, it's terribly important to me. As I told you earlier, I'd always wondered about my father. Somehow I never quite believed I'd been given the full story. And my mother was already dying — every word meant an heroic effort — when she made me promise to try to find him. And I have a feeling too —"

There he stopped, not because he didn't want to tell them what he felt but because he wasn't sure he could describe this feeling adequately.

"You feel it's a kind of challenge, don't you, Tom?" said Madge. "And perhaps you also feel that so far you haven't been much of a challenge-answerer. Or am I being unfair?"

"No, you're not. And the challenge idea is right, though I suspect I see it as something much bigger and tougher, more of a make-you-or-break-you thing. But I also feel that as I owe my existence to this marriage, I have to do my damnedest to find out what really happened to it, and what sort of man my father was and perhaps still is."

"I'd feel exactly the same," said Madge. "Good for you, Tom."

"Quiet, woman, he wants to say something else. Out with it, mate."

"I may feel a fool over there, going round asking about a father I haven't seen for over thirty years. But don't imagine it's also a way out. I've reached a dead end here — work, personal life, the lot. I *need* this journey and whatever happens at the end of it."

Madge looked hard at him. "I think you do, Tom. I think you've got to find yourself as well as your father. London — England — an old country," she continued, but then stopped. She shook her head, as if at herself and not at him, and then flashed across a grin. "For God's sake don't stay on over there and never write so that we never, never know if you ever found him. You won't do that to us, will you, Tom? Right. Well now, what can we tell you that might help?"

"Dam' little, I'm afraid," said Andrew. "I've been wondering about that. *Cudgelling* my poor, beaten-up brains. But get your notebook out, mate. Then Madge first. I'm just a provincial scholar. She's more the artistic metropolitan type."

But though he stayed until well after midnight and sometimes all three of them were talking at the same time, all a bit stoned, he found he couldn't fill half a page of his little notebook. And five days later, while both of them wanted to take him out to the airport, neither of them could, because of work. He went alone.

2

During his first few days in London, Tom Adamson could have almost believed that his plane had not landed on the bright surface of the earth but somewhere far below it. He seemed to be wandering in some subterranean kingdom, perhaps in a city at the bottom of the sea. The days — it was now early July — were warmish but had no sunlight in them. There was a thin haze spread over everything, taking both the exact shape and most of the colour out of it. This midsummer city was almost ghostly. Yet at the same time it was all thick, with an atmosphere these Londoners might have parcelled and labelled for export, it was all so thick.

Some of this thickness came of course from what he remembered of history and literature. All the rich and heavy centuries seemed to press down on him. He felt he could take a bus to the legendary, an underground train almost to mythology. The city might be one huge mess of snarled traffic, rather dingy trading, and people by the million who mostly looked as if they had something the matter with them that National Health couldn't diagnose; yet somewhere in this mess, in the next square, down that side street, between bus stops, what really belonged to a fairytale might be happening. Tom was not a fairytale man but an economics historian. On the other hand, he was no ordinary academic tourist. After all he had spent his earliest childhood here in London, and increasingly now he remembered what he had noticed as a child of three, living in a magical country. Therefore, though he gave it no encouragement, the sense of magic, of infinite possibilities beyond reason, remained with him, lighting as it were the whole gigantic confusion, at once thick and ghostly, from within. And then of course there was something else, setting him apart from all the tourists. He was here in London, in England, to find his father.

Though he couldn't resist spending most of these first days sightseeing, he kept his search steadily in mind. Actually he made his first move not five minutes after he had unpacked, in his rather stuffy little single bedroom. It had a telephone but no directory, so he went below and commandeered the section A-D, which offered him well over fifty Adamsons. And there, staring him in the face, making all his mystery-mongering about his father look silly, was — *Adamson Charles, 3 Ashtree Place, S.W. 3*. Of course this might be another Charles Adamson, but then again it might not. His father might be living almost round the corner, and as he rang the number he didn't know whether to feel glad or sorry. After he had prepared himself for a most intricate and elaborate search, picking up a wisp of a clue here, a faint trail there, this possible father-round-the-corner, probably comfortable and prosperous, seemed a kind of insult. However, there was no reply to his ringing. He tried the number six times during his first two days, but always with the same result. The girl on the hotel switchboard might have thought him a bit of a pest but somehow she didn't. Indeed, she began to sound sympathetic, as if he might be the victim of unrequited love.

He had been booked into this hotel by the travel agent in Sydney. It was a rather small and old-fashioned place behind Brompton Road. It didn't seem to be in London at all but somewhere in Ireland. Most of the guests appeared to be either pious elderly ladies, tottering to or from the Oratory, or Roman Catholic priests, plump and rosy, chuckling in pairs. And the staff was Irish. The chambermaids were either very old and given to muttering or very young and bewildered, straight from some remote village in Donegal. The manageress, Mrs. O'Shea, was tall and terrifying, a kind of Yeatsian ruined beauty, who when she really opened her eyes, which were usually half-closed against cigarette smoke, seemed to reveal a blue sky on fire. The headwaiter, known to all as Michael, was also tall, and very dark and mysterious, as if he lived in an atmosphere of espionage and counter-espionage. He could take an order for mulligatawny soup and roast mutton, repeating it with his lips nearly closed, as if it really meant a couple of bombs for the I.R.A. The elderly head porter, Fergus, was never actually drunk but never seemed quite sober either; he was one of those irritating characters who are eager to do everything for you so long as you don't mention any particular thing, always an exception, very hard to do, probably impossible.

On Sunday, Tom postponed any attempt to find anybody. He went out to Hampton Court, where the sun was shining at last but on far too many other people. It was on Monday morning that he began his search in earnest, making a start by ringing Charles Adamson's number again. This time his call was answered, by a woman who said she'd come in to clean and tidy up, and that Mr. Adamson was away and had been for the best part of a week. Mr. Adamson was an oldish man, Tom supposed. The woman said that he supposed wrong and couldn't have the right number, Mr. Adamson being no more than about thirty-five and not likely ever to be an oldish man, the way the place looked some mornings. So now 3 *Ashtree Place, S.W. 3,* was evidently a dead end. Tom told himself he had never expected it to be anything else.

Without leaving his room he spent the next half-hour staring at his notebook and the vague sketches of names and addresses his mother had given him. One half-name, Ben-something Bel-something, the best his mother could do, though she was sure he was one of Charles's actor friends, took him to the theatre advertisements in *The Times*. And there the man was, playing in the successful comedy at the Haymarket: Benson Belgrave. He was in the telephone book too.

"Mr. Belgrave, my name's Tom Adamson. I've just arrived from Australia to make some enquiries about my father, Charles Adamson. I believe he used to be a friend of yours, Mr. Belgrave."

"Rather a long time ago, I'm afraid. And I haven't the least idea where he is now." He sounded mildly amused but ready to ring off at any moment.

"I don't want to be a nuisance, Mr. Belgrave, but I've come here to find him — or at least to discover what's happened to him — and I know so little about him that I really don't know where to start. Could I come and talk to you, please?"

Belgrave must have caught the rather desperate note in Tom's voice, and now he no longer sounded amused. Gravely courteous, he explained that he had various engagements during the day, and finally suggested that Tom should come and see the play that night — he would have a ticket left for him at the box office — come round to his dressing room and then have supper with him at his flat. "Could you do that?" he continued in his carefully modulated actor's tones. "Good! And if you're wondering why you should have to see the play in order to talk to me, let me say it's mostly sheer vanity on my part, though I'll be genuinely interested to learn what a newly arrived Australian thinks of our play. Tonight then, Mr. Adamson."

Abandoning the search for the rest of the day, Tom went sightseeing in a rather absent-minded fashion, finding it impossible to forget for more than a moment or two that soon he would be going to the Haymarket and then, during or after supper, talking to one of his father's old friends. He had often been to theatres in Australia, of course, but he was unprepared for the elegance and charm of the Haymarket. On the other hand, the audience, entirely without elegance and charm, a giggling, nudging, whispering lot, might have been imported straight from Sydney. The play was a drawing-room light comedy about an impoverished earl, played with authority and distinction, with a restored elegance and charm, by Benson Belgrave, happy to share his enjoyment of a dream earldom. The best of the others was an old actress who played the earl's sister, an ancient cackling monster; and next to her, better than the young men, a girl with a delightful voice and a delicious nose. All the performers seemed to regard the play as an amusing little toy to be tossed from hand to hand; and Tom thought they were right. When the actors took their calls — with Belgrave bowing with a humility that had something ironic and mocking in it — Tom was left with a feeling of vague sadness that he didn't try to understand.

Belgrave was sitting in front of his dressing-room mirror, wiping cold cream off his face. Now he looked quite different from the earl, rather old and tired. Tom accepted a whisky and soda from the dresser, and then sat in a corner, trying to appear small, harmless, no trouble to anybody.

"I can see a resemblance," said Belgrave, when he had finished with his face. "But you're bigger all round than your father as I remember him." He got up and took off the faded old dressing gown. "Did you enjoy our play?"

"I enjoyed your performance enormously, Mr. Belgrave. I've never seen acting like that before. Everything was so beautifully controlled, economical, pointed. It was you — and one or two of the others — who held me and fascinated me, not the play itself, which seemed a bit empty, if you don't mind my saying so."

"Not at all. Quite agree with you." Belgrave was dressing now. "It's what we used to call a vehicle. But being a vehicle, at least it takes the actors somewhere. The new plays by the new young men have more in them, no doubt, though a good deal of what they have in them doesn't seem to me theatrically effective. And a lot of the direction and acting seems to me quite horribly bad — sloppy, messy, undisciplined, never properly focussed. They make me feel they need another couple of weeks' more rehearsal, under some old-fashioned director who knows what he wants and imposes some discipline until he gets it. But I'm out of date, of course, not 'with it.' That doesn't matter. But the trouble is, the real Theatre, the effective and attractive Theatre, is almost out of date too. These sloppy and lazy young men, who are always making arrogant statements, have ten times the publicity my contemporaries ever had but only about a tenth of the public. They've created a wide black gap into which most of the Theatre is fast disappearing. And you don't improve the situation by chucking a lot of public money down the same hole. However, you don't have to believe me, Mr. Adamson. After all, I'm getting on, feeling rather tired and very hungry. Let's go, shall we?"

In the taxi, Belgrave said, "I hope you'll like this little house of mine. Really quite tiny, though I do share it with a friend. But he's away just now, filming on location. I bought it just before the war, when you could still buy a little house in Chelsea without robbing a bank — or the public. We have a Spanish couple taking care of us — quite stupid but willing. Have you ever enjoyed yourself decorating and furnishing a house you're fond of?"

"No. And I wouldn't know where to start," Tom told him. He didn't add that this seemed to him a woman's job. There was nothing obviously effeminate about Belgrave, but Tom realised now that there might be a good deal of woman in him. The house turned out to be as elegant and charming as Belgrave's earl, but was rather too cramped and carefully arranged, like a tiny museum, to please Tom, who liked big careless rooms. After he had had a wash, Belgrave, now wearing a black velvet jacket, led him into an exquisite doll's-house dining room, where Sancho Panza in a white coat served them with pâté, grilled soles and green salad and cheese and a chilled white wine that Belgrave said was a Traminer from Alsace. It was all very pleasant but Tom couldn't escape the feeling they were having supper on the stage at the Haymarket. With his grey hair and long fastidious face above the black velvet, Belgrave looked fully as distinguished now as he had done as the earl, and as they ate and drank he offered a splendid performance as a delightful host, asking questions about Australia. Tom shrank from dragging his father into this easy chitchat, and began to wonder uneasily if the evening would contribute nothing to his search.

However, after the coffee had arrived in what Belgrave firmly called the drawing room, where they settled into two handsome easy chairs, upholstered in black leather, Belgrave gave him a sharp look, took out the cigar he was smoking and said, "I suggest you explain why you're so anxious to find your father, my dear fellow."

Tom did, as briefly as possible but omitting nothing of any real importance. "I knew before I came here that it wouldn't be easy to find him," he said in conclusion, "but now it's beginning to look really difficult, perhaps impossible."

"Surely not. Your father must have had relatives. So you start with them." He sounded rather impatient.

Tom felt some impatience too. "For thirty-three years my mother refused to tell me anything about him, except that he was a very bad man. Then when she changed her mind and asked me to find him, she was already close to dying and not able to concentrate and search her memory. All I could get out of her about my father's relatives was that he had an elder brother — she thought his name was Louis — but where he lived, what business he was in, she couldn't remember. She was equally vague about his friends. I had only half your name, and if I hadn't seen that Haymarket advertisement, I wouldn't have been able to appeal to you. And I *am* appealing to you, Mr. Belgrave. I realise you've been very kind — but don't stop now, please."

"My dear fellow, I'll do what I can. Charlie Adamson was a friend of mine once — though a long time ago, mind you — and I want you to find him. That is, of course, if he's still alive. Let's see — how old will he be now?"

"That's something I *can* tell you. Sixty-nine."

"A year older than I am. And what's that nowadays? Though of course there was the war. And I must warn you that I've never set eyes on him, never even heard his name mentioned, since 1940. But let's be practical for a minute or two, my dear fellow, before I wash you away on a flood of reminiscence. Now Charlie alternated — as I never knew anybody else to do — between acting and painting. Very well then. He was certainly a member of Equity — our actors' trade union — when I knew him. So call there and ask if they know anything about him. But of course he may have stopped acting years ago. He preferred painting, though when I knew him he couldn't make a living out of it. Perhaps he can now. So why don't you go round to some of the galleries?"

"I will," said Tom, bringing out his notebook. "But aren't there a hell of a lot of them?"

"Yes, but most of them have sprung up during the last ten years. Try the older ones — the Leicester, Tooth's, the Adams, the Lefèvre, and so forth. You may be wasting your time, but it's worth a try."

"Of course. Thanks very much." Tom made some hasty notes. "How good was he — as a painter or an actor?"

Belgrave removed his cigar and stared at it for a moment or two. "He wasn't really good in either capacity, when I knew him. But he wasn't bad either. He had some good parts in the later twenties and early thirties, mostly based on looks and charm. The women always liked him."

"Did you?"

"He was good company, Charlie Adamson. He was also very selfish. But then so am I. The truth is, nearly all actors are. We feel so insecure, so uncertain of ourselves, we've no time and energy to spare for any serious consideration of other people. Not everybody of course, but most of us. We're lazy too, once we're established and have our own reliable technique. I don't say Charlie was lazy, dividing himself as he did between the stage and his easel, but then he was still fairly young when I knew him. By the way, I can just remember your mother. She didn't like actors and never ought to have married one. Perhaps Charlie told her he'd be soon out of the Theatre. He was a great promiser. Not a cold-blooded liar but one of those fellows who believe all their promises at the time they're making 'em. The ironical thing was that when he *did* leave the Theatre, he also left his wife and lived with another woman —"

"Oh — then you know about that —"

"Yes — and I'll tell you about it. But let me explain first about Charlie and the Theatre. He was out of it for about a couple of years, perhaps a little longer. It must have been about 1936 when he turned to acting again. And he'd missed his chance. He was nearly forty then, no longer a juvenile lead, and managements weren't particularly interested in him. Oh — he got parts, mostly character, but instead of fifty pounds a week they'd offer him twenty or fifteen, and, though he hated touring, soon he had no option and was probably down to twelve or even ten pounds a week. The truth is, my dear fellow, he was steadily drifting downhill right up to the time the war broke out. And, if you ask me, that's why he joined the army, though already into his forties."

"He was in the army, then?" Tom tried not to sound too excited.

"He was during the summer of 1940. That's the last time I ever saw him. I was playing the lead in a little comedy at the old Royalty, and Charlie, who was on leave, had seen the play and came round to have a drink with me. I don't remember what branch of the service he was in, probably he never told me, but I have an idea that he'd just got a commission and so was wearing a brand-new uniform. I seem to remember chaffing him because he looked too old to be a subaltern. And that's all, and I'm afraid not much use to you, my dear fellow."

"No, a dead end, I imagine. But what about the woman he went to live with, after leaving my mother? Did you know her, Mr. Belgrave?"

"I did indeed. She was an actress — a leading lady for many years — called Elinor Coping. She was Nelly to most of us. And there were lots of jokes, usually dirty, about Coping. I never liked her acting myself. It was both coarse and uncertain. But she'd a powerful personality, always got plenty of publicity, and had a sexual aura as strong as a fish market. She pretended to be our age, I mean Charlie's and mine, but she was already a leading lady when we were just beginning, and I'd say she was about ten years older. If she's still alive — and that's something I don't know — she must be getting on for eighty now, and I'll bet a horrible old bitch. Just a minute, I'm going to look her up in Who's Who in the Theatre, which is generally reliable." He went across to the bookcase, took out a fattish volume, and peered at several of its pages. "Yes, well you see, she has no entry now among the biographies of living actors and actresses. That's because she hasn't acted for a long time. On the other hand, her name's not in the Obituary section, which is very carefully edited. It's at least ten to one then that Nelly Coping's still alive, giving somebody hell somewhere." He returned to his chair.

"Well, that's something, isn't it?" said Tom hopefully. "Though I suppose she mightn't still call herself Elinor Coping."

"Not a chance, I'd say, my dear fellow. She married some rich man in the late twenties. I've forgotten his name but I have a notion he was much older than she was and some kind of industrialist from the North. She left the stage, after a bad flop, about 1930, and I think her husband died about two years later."

"And then the next year, 1933, somehow she persuaded my father to leave his wife and family. She is the one, isn't she?"

"No doubt about it," said Belgrave cheerfully. "Mind you, they'd had an affair before then, and for all I know it may never have been really broken off. I don't think Charlie was ever in love with her, but he was strongly attracted — she was that kind of woman. If you thought yourself a bit

24

of a dog, she was the bitch in heat. Even so, that's not why
Charlie went to live with her. And I'm not guessing now. I
know because he told me. He'd had enough of the stage
and wanted to paint. And she'd plenty of money, a big
house somewhere in the country, and there he could paint
his head off. Fun in bed, lavish living, and a chance to paint
— and she probably told him she'd put up the money for a
big one-man show — so of course he couldn't resist it."

"And what about his wife and children?" Tom demanded bitterly. "I know you think he was selfish, but
surely he couldn't have been so callous. What was my
mother supposed to do while he was living it up with his
rich mistress?"

"No, no, my dear fellow. Now you're going back on what
you told me earlier, that he couldn't have behaved so badly,
that something went wrong. After all, that's why you're
here. Now Charlie Adamson may have had enough of his
wife — they just couldn't get along — but I can assure you
he was extremely fond of his two children and was a bit of
a bore about them. He'd no intention of leaving you
stranded, I'm certain of that. But he was living with Nelly
Coping, a ruthless bitch if there ever was one. Now you say
your mother wrote to him several times and never had a
reply. But suppose he also wrote to her several times and
never had a reply — um?"

"But you don't know that."

"Yes, I do, because he told me. That was when he'd
broken with Nelly and come back to the Theatre. He told
me his wife had never replied to his letters, but, without a
word, had taken herself and the children straight out to her
brother in Australia. My dear fellow, it's my belief that
Nelly Coping destroyed all those letters coming or going.
And then somebody who'd had a hand in it — a maid perhaps — finally wrote to your mother and told her more or

less what had happened. I know it sounds a plotty sort of business, rather like the plays we used to do in the twenties, but that was Nelly Coping's kind of atmosphere. If any one person was responsible for that complete break between your parents, then that person must have been Nelly Coping."

Tom was angry. "I'd like to wring her neck."

"My dear fellow, I don't suppose she has a neck now. She was putting weight on over thirty years ago. By the way, don't ask me where she lives or what she calls herself nowadays, because I haven't a clue. She married again, perhaps twice. But I haven't a single fact that might help you. Sorry!"

"You've been extremely kind and helpful, Mr. Belgrave," said Tom, getting up. "Here's the address and phone number of my hotel. If you do remember or learn anything I could use, please let me know. And just one last thing. Mr. Belgrave, you are *sure* you never saw or spoke to my father after the summer of 1940?"

"Positive, my dear fellow."

"But you might have heard or read something about him —"

"I might, but I don't think I did. In fact I'm almost certain —" but there he checked himself.

"You've just remembered something, haven't you?" said Tom.

"No, it's not as simple as that — it really isn't. I've not remembered the actual something but only the idea that there was — or is — a something I ought to be remembering. No, it's too vague, too elusive. Sorry! Don't forget I'm getting on and I've had a long day —"

"Yes, of course." But Tom stared at the actor's face as if it were a faded page of print in a language he barely understood. It was a curious face, superficially looking ten years

26

younger than it ought to have done, as if the nightly cold cream smoothed out the lines of experience, and yet, after the first glance, appearing old, very old and desolate. And then Tom knew that Belgrave was lying, that what he had suddenly remembered was not something too vague, too elusive, to be caught, held, described, but something quite definite and probably discreditable, which he was keeping back either because he didn't want to hurt Tom's feelings or because he was tired and felt he had talked long enough.

"Shall I try to call a radio cab for you?" said Belgrave.

"No, thanks. I'll start walking — I have a street map — then pick up a taxi if I need one."

Once out in the warmish dark, Tom felt again — and even more strongly now — that he was wandering in some subterranean kingdom or in that city at the bottom of the sea. There was little to be seen or heard, for it was late, but everything he did see or hear was meaningful in some odd, hidden way, containing a secret significance, like an incident in a huge play or film that he couldn't quite understand although he knew that whatever happened in it was important. In one square, a Rolls-Royce stole up, a chauffeur opened a door, and a tall elderly couple, starched and glittering in full evening dress, mounted the steps to their front door, as if to a march by Elgar. Further along, under a street lamp, four long-haired young men, two of them carrying guitars, were swaying and singing something obscene, all of them drunk. A bedroom window opened and a voice told them to be quiet and go away. "Get stuffed, Dad," one of them shouted. Then in the next street, near a lamp, Tom saw a little car drive up, and out of it came a fair youth in a dinner jacket and a girl, even younger and fairer, in a long white dress. The girl left him at the bottom of the steps up to her door, but then she turned and laughed as she saw him still waiting there, and she floated down into his arms, so that they might have been Aucassin and Nicolette. And Tom walked on, not really knowing what he felt, carrying a kind of burden of confusion, in which elation, hope, melancholy, despair, were bewilderingly mixed.

They didn't keep late hours at Tom's hotel, and the night porter, a surly old character, had obviously gone to sleep some time before Tom arrived, so that he had to ring for several minutes.

"All ri', cock. No need to wake the whole bloody place up." The old man was still half-asleep.

"Sorry, but I can't stand out there all night."

"I was dreamin', see. Then that bell comes, knockin' 'ell out of my dream."

Tom decided to be amused. "What were you dreaming about?"

"Can't remember. But I know it was a bloody sight better than this."

3

Next morning there was a slight but persistent drizzle so that the London atmosphere seemed thicker than ever. Over his sludgy coffee and tired sausage and bacon, Tom stared at his little notebook. He soon realised that the first thing he must do, following Belgrave's sensible advice, was to make enquiries at Actors' Equity and then at some of the older picture dealers'. And as he felt that this was no day for finding his own way about London, just before ten he took a taxi to Equity.

A stern middle-aged woman, not one to be confided in, regarded him dubiously. "Charles Adamson? I don't remember that name, and I've been here over twenty years. Is it important?"

"It is to me," Tom told her. "Nothing to do with the Theatre, I'm afraid. Purely private. But he's a relative, and I know he used to be on the stage. In fact, last night Benson Belgrave, who used to be a friend of his, told me he'd been a member of Equity."

"Well, Mr. Belgrave ought to know. Did he suggest that you come here? He did? Take a seat, then, and I'll see what I can find out. Charles Adamson, wasn't it?"

After about ten minutes she returned, bringing with her a slip of paper that she carried as if it were a tablet of stone.

"Charles Adamson was a member of Equity throughout the thirties. His membership lapsed during the war, when he was no longer acting, probably in one of the services. There's no record of his having rejoined after the war, so it's more than likely that he never returned to the stage. And I'm afraid that's all I can tell you. The last address we have, going back to 1939, wouldn't be much use to you, I imagine."

"No, it wouldn't. I suppose it's safe to assume that if he didn't rejoin Equity after the war, then he never went back to the Theatre?"

"I think it is, yes. So, I'm sorry, but we can't help you."

"No, of course not. But thank you for trying." Tom hardly felt any disappointment. In some obscure fashion he had known all along that his father had long ceased to be an actor. It was far more likely that he had started painting again after he had left the army, and that even now he might be earning a living, even if it was only a very modest living, as a painter.

So he spent the rest of the morning and, after a snack-bar lunch in a crowded pub, all the afternoon going round the older galleries. Whether his enquiry was answered by oldish women with Central European accents or youngish men as sleek as wet seals, he drew the same blank, and a very blank sheet too: nobody was interested; he began to feel like a displaced person asking for a country. However, at the very last gallery he visited, the Cadogan, something different happened.

The place was in a confusion of unpacking and hanging, and in the centre of this confusion was a shaggy elderly man smoking a fierce little pipe. "Now what?" he cried as Tom approached him. "Now, now what?"

"I'm sorry to bother you —" Tom began.

"So am I. If you've come to buy a picture, you can't. Not

30

until Thursday. If you've come to sell one, give it up. Anyhow I'm not the boss here. Just a dog's body. John Edgar Ridley — dog's body," he added bitterly.

"Well, Mr. Ridley, I don't want either to buy or sell a picture. I want to ask you if you know my father."

"That's a change. Haven't met anybody for years who cared a damn about his father. Goes for my lot too. Feel like King Lear half the time. Like a cup o' tea? Pauline — George," he shouted. "Keep going. Taking my friend into the office for a cup o' tea." He motioned Tom to follow him, and they went round the corner at the far end, arriving in a very untidy little office. The tea must have been made some time before and came out of the pot almost black. "Put plenty of sugar in, my boy. That's right. Tell you the truth, I need a change from Pauline and George and that muck we're hanging in there. Half of it's just pretentious bosh. You couldn't give it to me. But on Thursday morning that room'll be full of long-faced, solemn-eyed donkeys who couldn't tell a picture from a horse's arse. I know about painting. Used to run my own gallery. Now I'm a dog's body for all these charlatans. What did you say about your father?"

"I'm trying to find him. His name's Charles Adamson. He was both a painter and an actor."

"So was Sickert at one time," Ridley began. But then he stopped. "Now wait a minute. Let me think. Charles Adamson. Charles Adamson." He relit the fierce little pipe, then spoke through a cloud of smoke. "Yes, I remember him. Bought three or four pictures of his — oh — at least thirty years ago. But I doubt if I'd have remembered him if I hadn't mentioned Sickert. He tried to paint like Sickert — broad low-tone — same palette — but of course he couldn't pull it off. Promising though, specially for an actor. Yes, Charles Adamson. Good-looking fellow. And he's your father, is he? Well, what happened to *him*? Still painting, is he?"

"I don't know." Tom tried not to sound exasperated. "I was hoping you'd be able to tell me, Mr. Ridley."

"Me? Look — I can't work miracles, my boy. I've just remembered him after thirty years. Three or four pictures — about twenty-five pounds apiece. And I think we'd one drink together. You must admit that's not bad —"

"It's very good. But I was hoping you might have seen him since then —"

"Dammit, he's your father, not mine. You're being unreasonable, my boy. When did you see him last?"

"In 1933 —"

"Oh — it's like that, is it? Well, I'm sorry, but I've never seen him nor heard of him for about thirty years."

Tom got up. "Well, thank you, Mr. Ridley." Then he hesitated. "Did you like him — I mean as a man, not as a painter?"

Puffing away, Ridley thought for a few moments. "Trying to remember. Yes, I think I did," he said carefully. "Otherwise we wouldn't have had that drink, would we? He wasn't *important*, you understand. I didn't need to *handle* him. No money in him. No future as a painter. Never saw him acting. Never liked going to the theatre. I probably bought those pictures because I liked him — pleasant attractive sort of fellow, I'd say. And that's more than I'd say about *my* father, who was a dictatorial bad-tempered old bugger. Died years ago, of course. For that matter, yours may be dead by this time."

"I know," said Tom as they moved out. "And I can't prove he isn't. But somehow I have a feeling that he's alive somewhere. But where, God knows."

They were now back in the main room. Ridley stopped at some large pink, yellow, brown blotches. "Look at this.

Fugue in B Minor. Three hundred pounds. And some-body'll pay it. All a lot of balls. Sometimes I think I'm going out of my mind. Well, wish you luck, my boy. Re-member me to him if you find him — John Edgar Ridley."

It was raining hard now. There were no empty taxis to be seen; the buses were filled to capacity; there seemed to be no handy Underground station. Tom walked and arrived at his hotel wet and disappointed.

"There's no messages for you, Mr. Adamson sorr," said Fergus across his desk. "Not a one, sorr."

"You surprise me," Tom muttered. He had a long hot bath and read a paperback detective story in it. He had several historical works waiting to be read, but somehow, perhaps because he was in search of clues himself, he found himself continually reading paperback detective stories. He took some time drying himself and then dressing, partly be-cause he felt listless but also because, while sitting on the edge of the bed half-dressed, he drank some of the duty-free whisky he had brought with him. So it was rather later than usual when he felt ready to dine, and though he disliked both the hotel dining room, with its sad old ladies and chuckling priests, and the food it served, he decided not to go out.

"I'll tell you what, Mr. Adamson," Michael, the mysteri-ous headwaiter, whispered, "you could have chickun." He spoke as if the fowl had just been discovered in Patagonia and specially flown over. "I can recommend the chickun. Maybe with a nice half-bottle of white wine. Something to cheer you up, Mr. Adamson, all on your own on a night like this."

The magnificent manageress was also dining alone, in the corner near the entrance from the kitchen, and it may be that Michael told her that Mr. Adamson ought to be cheered up. What is certain is that Tom, who finished dinner after she did, found Mrs. O'Shea on the lookout for him when he wandered out of the dining room, wondering what to do with himself. She invited him to take Gaelic coffee in her sitting room, which was behind the door marked *Private* to the left of the cashier's desk. It was a fairly large room, which began as an office, with a desk and a hard chair and a little frosted window that could be opened into the cashier's department, but then turned itself almost violently into an O'Shea sitting room, with two big easy chairs, a lot of crimson and metallic green cushions, little tables for ashtrays and Gaelic or any other coffee, and larger tables bristling with photographs of innumerable O'Sheas. The lady herself was as usual dressed in black, but to show that she was now off-duty she was wearing a scarf so dazzling that it appeared to be fluorescent, phosphorescent, and possibly radioactive. And above it, looming out of mythology, was the great beautiful ruin of her face, larger than life, belonging to the widowed queen of Cuchulain or somebody. The smoke from her perpetually smouldering cigarette did not force her down into this world but suggested some ancient and unimaginable sacrifices. As she squinted at him through this smoke, from the other easy chair, she seemed amiable enough, but Tom still found her terrifying.

After they had sampled the Gaelic coffee and Tom had praised it and thanked her, she said, "It's a pleasure to me to be entertaining a fine tall young man like yourself, Mr. Adamson. I'm wearied to death of all these priests and sad old women." She must have been well into her sixties herself, but spoke as if she were about half the age of her guests — which in spirit no doubt she was. "There's no life at all in this damned hotel, though I shouldn't be grumbling, because if I'd stayed where I was in Ireland I'd be looking after a place full of Germans and Japs. And in the name of

God, who wants them? You're some kind of scholar your-self, aren't you, Mr. Adamson?"

Tom explained that he lectured on colonial economic history at the University in Sydney.

"You have the brains for it, I can tell by your manner and looks, Mr. Adamson. So you'll be over here — oh we've had a few of 'em — on a what-d'you-call-it — a sabbatical — isn't it? And every day going to the British Museum, wearing out your eyesight — no life at all for a fine young man like yourself — sitting alone in there, wishing you'd a girl to take out —"

"No, it's not quite like that, Mrs. O'Shea. I'm not over here doing research. As a matter of fact, I'm looking for my father."

She opened her eyes wide, giving him their full blue blaze. "Are you telling me you've come all the way from Australia looking for your Dad? Well, for God's sake! You'll explain that or never speak another word to me."

He began with no intention of telling her everything, but she asked so many questions that it all came out. "And though I've only just started," he said finally, "I'm begin-ning to think I've reached a dead end already."

"And that's why you had such a long face on you in the dining room, isn't it? Shame on you, Mr. Adamson! As you say yourself, you've only just started. I've put in more time and trouble finding a pair of bedroom slippers. You men you've got no proper perseverance. Before you've hardly begun, you faint by the wayside. My man, Cap'n O'Shea, was just the same. Which reminds me now — will you take a drop of the same Irish we had in the coffee? You will? And so will I."

"I've always been a fairly obstinate character up to now," Tom told her as she brought out the bottle and glasses.

35

"I've never been told I gave up too easily. I think the trouble is, Mrs. O'Shea, that while I really do want to find my father — it's serious and important to me — I also can't help feeling a dam' fool going round asking questions about him. After all, a man's supposed to know about his own father."

"And there's many a man thinks he does when he doesn't," she said, with a cackle that came out of ancient feminine malice. "You won't want any water with this, young man. It's too good to have any water near it. Now then — we'll drink to your father, the poor man, because I'm already taking his side in all this." After an interval for the drink, she went on: "I've the same feeling you have, and I come from a family famous for such feelings, always true in the end though impossible to explain. I say he's alive and maybe wondering at this very moment where his fine grown-up son might be. And all you need to do now is find him." She gave him a great blue triumphant look. "Isn't that right now?"

Working hard to give her the smile she expected, Tom agreed that it was. "But how do I set about it?"

"I'm coming to that. Now for a start you don't waste any more time and trouble enquiring among actors and picture dealers and the like. You're on the wrong tack altogether there. It's so out of sight, out of mind, with all that lot." Here she stopped because there was a buzz on her telephone. She listened impatiently for a moment or two to her caller and then cut in sharply. "No, he can't stay here. I told him last time never to set foot in this hotel again, and I meant what I said." She came back to her easy chair, drank again, rather fiercely this time, and lit another cigarette from the smouldering ruin in the ashtray. "That was about a wild Belfast man who was here last year. He can't hold his drink and at two in the morning he was banging up and down the second floor landing calling deadly insults on the Holy Father and a priest behind every bedroom door. But talking about him won't help you find your Dad. Where'd I got to?"

"You said I was on the wrong tack —"

"So I did. Actors and the like. No good at all. It's as true today as it was hundreds of years ago when it was first thought of — that blood's thicker than water. So it's relations you want. *Relations*, Mr. Adamson. Mother of God! — I've had second cousins of O'Shea's that I'd never seen nor heard of coming here and asking for reduced rates. Now tell me again what your father had in the way of relations."

"All that my mother could tell me was that he had a much older brother, Louis, who probably died years ago, and that this Louis, she seemed to remember, had a daughter about ten years older than I am, and, she thought, a son about my age. But if she ever knew their names, she'd forgotten them. And of course the daughter probably married years and years ago, and I don't know what her married name is. The best bet — well, the only one really — is the son about my age — my cousin. If he's anywhere around, he probably knows all about my father. And, as I told you, there is this Charles Adamson in the phone book I thought might be my father, but then the cleaning woman who told me he was away also said he was only in his thirties. So there might be just a faint chance —"

"Quiet now," cried Mrs. O'Shea, with such authority that he stopped at once. A gigantic soothsayer now, she sat up straight but closed her eyes. Tom kept quiet, watching her and feeling a bit silly. After a few moments of this oracular performance, she opened her eyes wide. "I have a feeling — it's one of my strong feelings — that this is the man you want. Now get me the number — the phone books are on my desk there — and I'll ring him myself, to keep the luck going."

Five minutes later she was through to Charles Adamson, 3 Ashtree Place, S.W. 3. But not to the man himself. "Well, find him, find him," she was saying impatiently. "Tell him it's urgent — life or death. Listen, young woman, I don't care if it's a party and he's *stoned* as you call it, I want him at the other end of this telephone or there'll be trouble." Still keeping the receiver to her ear, she turned to Tom. "It's my opinion we're on to a wild one. If he's not giving a party, then he's running a night club. The girl I talked to sounded as if she was swimming in liquor. She could fall flat on her face before she gives him my message. No, no, this is him." Now she shouted into the instrument. "You're Mr. Charles Adamson, are you? . . . Okay, so you're always called *Chas* — just *Chas*. Now, listen. This is very important and might be greatly to your advantage. Was your father Louis Adamson and did he have a younger brother, Charles, who used to be an actor and a painter? He was? He did? That's all I wanted to know, Chas. You get back to your party before they kick the sideboard into firewood." As she put down the receiver she gave Tom a huge triumphant glance. "I knew it. I told you. That's your man — your very own cousin, *Chas*. Don't forget he likes to be Chas, not Charles. So off you go in the morning and pay him a call, though not too early, I'd say, because he'll have a terrible head and mouth on him."

"Mrs. O'Shea, that's wonderful — really it is. And I'm very, *very* grateful."

"It's been a pleasure, Mr. Adamson. But I've a feeling you'll have to watch that one. If he's a decent quiet young fellow like yourself, my name's not Peggy O'Shea. So be careful. Just remember you're new here, straight out of the egg, and you're in a wicked old city in a wicked old country."

"The wife of a colleague of mine in Sydney, an English girl, said something like that to me —"

"And I'm glad to hear it. Always listen to women, Mr. Adamson, unless of course they're after deceiving you, which half of 'em'll be doing half the time. But we've found your cousin Chas for you. A drinking man, no doubt — a wild one, I'd say — but he'll be the right man to tell you all about your poor Dad. You can't beat relations."

"Blood being thicker than water," said Tom, smiling. He nearly added something about "reduced rates" but then thought he'd better not. They chatted for another quarter of an hour or so, and then he went up to bed. He felt a curious excitement, quite different from anything he had felt since leaving Sydney, a sense of strange possibilities, which kept him awake, not quite thinking, not quite dreaming, for at least the next two hours.

4

THE next morning Tom found that the drizzle of the day
before had been warmed and transmuted into thin layers of
mist, which a Londoner might never notice, a haziness that
turned streets and squares into watercolour sketches of
themselves, a steamy thickening of the air that caught and
held every smell, from the fragrances of the little flower
shops to the reek of deep frying oil from the back doors
of restaurants. He passed these back doors because he spent
an hour idly exploring the complicated territory between his
hotel and his cousin's Ashtree Place. Remembering what
Mrs. O'Shea had said about not calling upon Chas too
early, he had decided to arrive there about eleven, but he had
found it impossible to stay in the hotel. The curious excitement of the night before had come rushing back a moment
or two after he had wakened and had then remembered
where he was and what was about to happen. So to pass the
time and to enjoy his street map — Tom was a map man —
he avoided main roads and streets, where the traffic was
already beginning to build up and quiver with impatience,
and turned down side streets or into those odd Mews places
where, instead of horses, there were young wives, often very
pretty, opening or shutting scarlet or primrose doors. There
was nothing historical, no guidebook stuff, in this region;

but on this particular morning, with its haziness, its melting watercolour vistas, its occasional gleams of sunshine lighting a window box or a polished door-knocker, the whole urban conglomeration seemed magical. He felt as he had never felt since childhood that it might suddenly reveal a life of infinite unimaginable possibilities. The opening of a door, which needn't be painted primrose or scarlet, might work the miracle.

Ashtree Place, not easy to find and not very far, he concluded, from where Benson Belgrave lived, consisted of two short rows of houses facing each other across some railed-in grass and several trees. Tom didn't know much about architecture, but these houses seemed to him to be Georgian on a rather small scale. They were arranged in pairs, with the front doors of each pair close together, sharing a portico and three pillars, with four steps leading up to them. There was a railed balcony outside the tall first-floor windows. Number Three looked older and shabbier than its neighbours because it hadn't been painted recently. On the left of the faded-green front door were three bell pushes: the top one was labelled *Chas Adamson*; the middle one had a card over its original label, and on it was written *Countess Helga Lebork*; and the bottom one said firmly *Basement — Dr. Firmius*.

Tom rang Chas's bell and then went straight in, the front door being unlocked, crossed a dingy and neglected hall where there appeared to be a lot of unwanted pamphlets lying about, and began climbing some stairs covered with threadbare and stained carpeting. It was obvious that the owner of 3 Ashtree Place had not been spending any money on it for some years. At the top of the second flight of stairs was a small landing dominated by a door that badly needed repainting. It had no bell but it had a large brass knocker with some metal letters above it — *CH S ADA S N*. As he had rung from below, Tom was hoping that this door would be open, with his cousin standing there to welcome him; but it was most inhospitably closed. Disappointed and rather annoyed, Tom used the knocker vigorously. Nothing happened. He banged away even harder.

The voice seemed to come from the opening to the letter-box inside. It shouted somewhat hoarsely, "Will you — for Christ's sake — *go away?*"

"This is Tom Adamson — your cousin. You said I could come and see you this morning," he shouted back.

The door opened slowly, only a few inches, to reveal a very dark eye, alight with curiosity.

"I rang at the front door, you know," Tom told it.

"That's the trouble," said Chas as he opened the door properly. "Nobody I know does. And I must keep all the other bastards out. But welcome, welcome, coz!" And he led the way into quite a big sitting room furnished with a kind of shabby grandeur — there were two of the largest sofas Tom had ever seen — but looking now like the shore on which a party had been wrecked, with empty bottles, glasses, messy bits of food, cigarette ends, all over the place.

"The old shambles, eh?" said Chas, grinning. He was wearing nothing but some flat slippers and a striped silk dressing gown that had had too much greasy stuff spilt on it. He was rather shorter than Tom but sturdily built, and he had black curly hair beginning to retreat from his forehead, very dark eyes set in an odd way, rather like those of an animal, and a wide and curling mouth, not thick and loose-lipped but rather thin. Staring at him with frank curiosity — they were now in fact exchanging stares — Tom told himself that this was a chap who didn't give a damn; and as he knew he had given too many damns himself, never having had the courage to tell his mother he would rather live alone, to try his luck with some of the wilder girls he had met at the Wentworths' and elsewhere, to be as openly defiant of his university seniors as Andrew often was, Tom couldn't help regarding his cousin with a reluctant admiration in which there might be some envy.

"I did a nice little deal with a pair of nits in Manchester two days ago," said Chas, grinning again. "So I felt I had to throw a party. But two of the silliest sods who came and talked big and spewed around are going to pay for it. By the way, got a cigarette? I'm clean out. Thanks." After he had lit the cigarette, he gave Tom a long look that began narrow and hard and then opened out into a sparkling matiness which had a curious energising effect on Tom. "Well, well, well, so you're Uncle Charlie's son Tom from Australia — um? Delighted to see you, coz! No, really I am. Dee-lighted!"

"And I you, Chas. Now, can you tell me about my father? He's not dead, is he?"

"Dead? Of course he isn't dead. Why should he be?" Chas spoke as if nobody had died for years.

"Then where is he — do you know?"

"Haven't the foggiest at the moment, coz. Been out of touch lately. But just say the word — and I'll find him for you. Too easy. I've hundreds and hundreds of contacts. Have to have. So you say the word, I pass it on, and Uncle Charlie's found. How's that?"

"Fine, Chas. The word's now been said. After all, I'm here to find him."

"Then stick around, Tom boy, keep in close touch, and you'll soon have him on a plate. Good old Uncle Charlie!"

A girl came out of a doorway on the left, carrying a cup of coffee. She was a blonde with rather stringy hair and a crumpled face, and all she had on was a slip. Without taking any notice of them, she padded across to a door on the right, back to the bedroom where she belonged.

"Not installed," Chas explained. "Just one of the party leftovers. I'll tell her to piss off. Do it now." And he did, throwing open the bedroom door and telling her he was too busy to take any further interest in her.

"What's that one — a tart?" Tom asked when Chas came back.

"Tart?" Chas was horrified. "What — pay for it? Look, cobber, if there's any paying to be done, they can start paying me. And anyhow that bit probably earns more than you do. She's a model. What *do* you earn? And what d'you do?"

Tom explained what he did and said that he probably earned what would be in English money about fifteen hundred a year.

Chas looked and sounded horrified again. "Man, you're just droning for peanuts. Isn't there any real money in the family out there?"

"A certain amount," said Tom cautiously. Chas might be already having a heady effect upon him, but he was still able to feel he would have to be careful about money with Chas. "Tell me, Chas, what do *you* do?"

"I'm a kind of promoter. Tried shipping one time — in a small way, of course. Then cars. Then I'd an interest in a couple of night clubs. But if I wasn't there, I got robbed. If I was there, to look after my end, I went half out of my mind through sheer bloody boredom. Then the two nits I was in with sold out to a very hard character. But we'll save that story for a better time and place, *camarade*. As I told you, I've a lot of contacts. If I hear of anything going cheap and I think I know a possible customer, I do a deal. Small profits but a quick turnover, and no bloody great overheads. Take this little Manchester deal. Ten secondhand fruit machines — the old one-arm bandits — and now my only worry is that the fellow who promised to let me have them cheap was properly stoned at the time. Incidentally, though

44

I don't look it — I own this house. My old man left it to me, together with a bundle of shares I played around with before kissing 'em goodbye."

"But you have tenants below, haven't you, Chas? A Dr. Firmius in the basement. A Countess Helga Something between you and him."

"Dead right, Tom boy. But the maisonette's really let to some people called Morgensten who are in the States. And they've sublet it to the Countess, who's a hell of an eyeful — you wait — but better kept away from. Old Firmius below gives no trouble except that he's more than halfway round the bend. But look, boy, why don't I get dressed and then we can go round to our local, the Swan and Lily? Right? Right."

Before he reached the bedroom door, the girl came out, dressed now in a tubular yellowish frock and a lot of lacy stocking, and carrying a hatbox. She marched straight past Chas without so much as a glance.

"Till next time, dearie," he called to her.

"Not if I see it coming." But she stopped to look Tom over. "And who are you?"

"I'm Chas's Cousin Tom from Australia."

"My God — watch him — or you'll be on your way to the cleaners, big boy." And out she went.

"Give me ten minutes," said Chas.

Tom felt it would be easier to begin tidying up the room than to try to sit at ease in it. He had cleared away the bottles, glasses and most of the plates by the time Chas returned, looking quite trim in a dark flannel suit and one of those striped ties that suggest exclusive cavalry regiments.

"Tom, d'you happen to have a spare fiver? Looks bad in the local if I can't stand my round. Thank you, thank you, thank you! I don't know about you, but I'm in dire need of strong cool drink. Lead on, coz."

The Swan and Lily, only just round the corner, was a longish low building that looked very old. The saloon bar, into which Chas led the way, at once delighted Tom. It was not really a small room but it was so narrow and low-ceilinged, had so many dark beams and so much ancient worn woodwork in it, that Tom felt he was ordering gin-and-tonics in another but cosier Mermaid Tavern. True, the girl who served them was hardly an Elizabethan type; she was very thin and had lacquered short hair and a dead-white face with a lot of green round her eyes, and might have just come out of a horror film. And now and again a pink and golden youth of about forty-five looked in to hiss something at her, like a disturbed goose. But Tom was able to ignore them, he liked the place itself so much.

"Such a marvellous atmosphere," he told Chas. "This is what we don't get — and can hardly imagine — in Australia. How far do you think this room goes back?"

"Three years," said Chas. "Reg and Percy had it done — a nice plastics job — just after they took the place over. That's Percy who keeps popping in. Reg'll be supervising the cold snacks, very fancy and cost the earth. A pair of queens, of course. Another of 'em did this room. Did a job for me once — night club. He sold me a seashore motif — with bloody great lobsters coming out of the wall. So as soon as the customers were fairly stoned, just when they wouldn't care what they were spending, they took one look at the wall and hared off." Now Chas turned from the bar and glanced down the room, which was still almost empty. "Ida dearie," he called to the unusual barmaid, "who'll be coming in this morning that I know?"

"Couldn't say, Chas. And anyhow — the point is, will they still know you?"

"Another crack like that, Butch," said Chas with a cold concentrated fury that surprised Tom, "and one wrist'll be out for the rest of the day." His face was as white as hers was, but all anger. And as Tom looked at him he was astonished to find in himself an entirely unexpected impulse, quite outside his normal experience, to hit and hurt the girl himself.

Then, hastily recovering himself, he said, "Chas, what about your sister?"

"What about my sister?" As if he had no idea what Tom meant.

"Well, you have a sister, haven't you? And she might know something about my father."

"Oh of course — quite right, quite right, cobber!" His colour had returned and with it his grin and dancing look. He finished his drink. "Better order two more. If I do it, that bitch'll pretend not to hear me. Yes indeed, our Uncle Charlie. Well of course Leonora hasn't my contacts, but she just might have heard something I've missed. It's worth a try. But leave the arrangements to me, Tom boy."

"Glad to. But I don't want to be a nuisance, Chas."

"You and I," said Chas with great deliberation, "are going to find your father, my Uncle Charlie. It's Number One on the programme. Highest priority. And no time, trouble and expense spared. As I told you, I'll have him on a plate for you — and long before you'd know where to begin to look on your own. But of course we'll see if Leonora knows anything."

He said no more because at that moment a young man with long fair hair and a black open shirt pushed his way between them, crying, "Glass of bitter, Ida." Then he gave a very different cry and said to Chas, "What do you think you're doing?"

"I'm stamping on one of your dirty feet, cock," Chas told him coolly. "And I'm going to stamp on the other unless you get out of our way. Bugger off."

Again Tom felt that sudden hot impulse to do something violent himself, perhaps to put a hand on the young man's back and give him a huge shove that might send him sprawling. However, after a moment of Chas's menacing stare, the young man went muttering to the other end of the bar. Relieved that he had not had to obey that strange impulse, Tom asked Chas to tell him about Leonora.

"Leonora? Well, she's been married for years and years and years to a fellow called Dudley Corris, who's a contractor, though he doesn't do much now because he's a Tory M.P. And even in the House, which is full of stupid old sods, he's known to be one of the stupidest. So they gave him a knighthood. And my old sis is now Lady Corris. She enjoys this, and it's about all she does enjoy. One son, the apple when younger, but now a sad disappointment. Christened Edward but insists upon being Ted — won't answer to anything else. Plays the guitar and might be the twin of that rude twerp over there. As for Leonora and her Dudley, they're like a pair of stuffed horses just taken out of the deep freeze. I haven't spoken to Sir Dudley for about four years. And Leonora and I don't hit it off. In fact, you're more likely to get something out of her if I'm not there. But I'll go down to their place with you. They'll be in the country now — or at least she will. House called Bushworth Lodge — other side of Oxford. Oh — now then — hold it — I've an idea —"

But then he noticed three men and two girls who had just arrived and told Tom he must have a word with one of the men. Left to himself Tom edged nearer the end of the bar, to leave more room for newcomers ordering drinks. After a few minutes, when Chas had still not returned, Ida had nobody else to serve and she drifted towards Tom's corner.

"Listen," she began, coming close to him, "did I hear you say something about Australia?"

48

"Why yes. I've just come from there. And Chas Adamson is my cousin."

"Then perhaps you don't know him very well — um?" And without waiting for his reply she began to repair her make-up.

"No, I don't."

"I thought not," she said between peerings and puffs and dabs. "Well, I'm broad-minded. Have to be — doing this job here. But now I'm telling you to keep well out of his way. He's a bloody villain — the real thing. Sooner or later they'll have him inside. Up to now he's been lucky. But it can't last."

"But why — what does he do?"

"Anything but work and go straight. There's a bookie comes in here —" But then she checked herself and moved away. Chas was back.

"Fellow there owes me seventy-five quid," he announced. "He used to admit it, without paying up, of course. Now he says he doesn't owe me a cent. If we'd been alone I'd have shaken him till his false teeth dropped out. Let's have a short drink, then find something to eat. Large pink Plymouth for me, cobber. Then I'll tell you my idea. You'll love it. But we ought to have a car. Got to be mobile to find Uncle Charles — um? And it's bloody silly to hire a car. Thing is to buy one cheap — a good car, mind you — from somebody who never ought to have bought it in the first place." He picked up his pink gin. "Chap over there, just come in, probably has one he can't afford any longer. How much can you run to — three hundred — four — ?"

"Well, I don't know. I haven't thought about it, Chas —"

"Don't start then, cobber. Just leave it to me. Shan't be long."

So Tom was left alone again, this time for quite a spell. The place had filled up now and he was gradually pushed back from the bar counter until he found himself closely ringed round by men and girls, nearly all talking hard. They were wildly different in appearance, ranging from the slovenly to the excessively smart, but they were all alike, it seemed to him as he listened to them, in being on the edge of things. They were nearly doing a television series, almost about to have a play done at the Arts, just missing a commission to photograph Sicily for a coffee-table book, possibly writing two songs for a new musical, being asked to try again for that super modelling job. They used so much professional jargon — if only to prove they were really "in" and not wandering round the edges — that it was often hard to understand exactly what they were saying. And while they might be all well on their way towards ultimate disillusion and misery, just now they were gay and excited, full of enthusiasm for themselves, their work, their enchanting style of life. Tom had met a few men and women of great and widely recognised talent, large personalities a long way from these edges, people bang in the centre, and they had displayed little or none of this enthusiasm, often seeming dubious, disenchanted, melancholy, weighed down by the sense of responsibility a great talent and reputation bring. But these types, with fuzzy little talents at best and with only the faintest glimmer of reputation, were still enchanted — at least at this hour with drinks in their hands. And not for the first time, Tom wondered about the drinks, which demanded a constant passing of pound notes. Nobody he had overheard so far appeared to have earned any money recently, yet here they were buying double gins and whiskies. Thank God he hadn't to lecture on the economics of arty boozing!

Chas, a ruthless way-maker, ready to push the girls' bottoms or bounce off their breasts, to tread on men's toes with a glare and no apology, arrived to say it was time they went into the next room to have some food.

"It's in the bag, Tommy-me-lad," he announced as soon as they had served themselves at the snack bar.

"Just a minute, Chas." And Tom looked at him without smiling. "If we're going to spend some time in each other's company, then there's something I must tell you. I don't like this 'cobber' and 'Tommy-me-lad' and the rest of it. Just call me Tom and leave it at that."

"Right you are. Anything to please, Tom." And he grinned, in no way looking or sounding abashed. It was impossible to imagine him feeling abashed; his cheeky self-confidence was yards thick.

"Thanks, Chas. Now what's in the bag?"

"The car, the car we need. That chap Monks I was talking to is as broke as I am. He has an Allerton-Fawcet I can get for as little as three-twenty-five if I dangle the notes in his big fat face. You know the Allerton-Fawcet, don't you?"

Tom said he'd never even heard of it.

"Where've you been? It's a smallish sports type, very powerful, very fast, tremendous acceleration, just the kind of car I like to drive."

"Speak for yourself, Chas. I drive just to get from place to place, that's all. I don't imagine myself winning some *grand prix*. I like to tootle along in comparative comfort and safety."

"That may be all right in Australia, Tom, but it's no bloody good here. Wait till you've spent half the morning trying to get in front of an overloaded lorry. You need a fast car here just to overtake all these bastards crawling along the roads. The Allerton-Fawcet was made for this good work. Monks has only had his a couple of years, and of course he wasn't going to come down to three-twenty-five.

But if I show him the lovely money he'll never be able to resist it. And when we've found your poor old Dad and you don't want to take a car all the way to Australia, I'll bet you anything you like I can sell that Allerton-Fawcet for more than you gave for it. And we need a car for this week-end I've been planning — the idea I mentioned to you —"

"Has it anything to do with finding my father, Chas? That's why I'm here, don't forget."

Chas halted his attack on the very large piece of veal-and-ham pie he had chosen, a savage attack up to now, to stare in apparent amazement. "Come off it, chum, come off it! Didn't I tell you as soon as you'd explained that I'd find him for you? What happens is this. You ring up my sister Leonora in the country — I'll give you the number — and say you're driving down Saturday morning to see her. She'll ask you to lunch if she isn't going out. I'll drive down with you — I know the way and it's a bit tricky — but you drop me at a rather good pub called the Crown and Lion, where we'll spend the night —"

"Do we have to spend the night?"

"Just let me explain before you start pulling a bloody long face, Tom. This pub's at a place called Anglefield which is about halfway between Leonora's house, Bushworth Lodge, where I'm barred, and the vast bogus mansion owned and occupied by one Lady Ellowstone, who will be giving one of her notorious Saturday dinner parties."

"But do I want to attend one of this lady's notorious Saturday dinner parties, Chas?"

"You do but you don't know it. The old girl's very rich and quite barmy — been well round the bend for years. And her great thing — well, never mind about that now, I'll explain it later, when I've arranged for us to be invited. The point is — we need a car, and Monks's Allerton-Fawcet is a hell of a good buy and I want to nail him while he's still in the next room and half-stoned. You can put your hand on three hundred and twenty-five pounds — cold cash — can't you, Tom?"

Tom had to admit that he could. His usual cautious practice was to spend weeks trying to decide about a car — and even then it would be a staid dependable sort of car, no roaring and raffish Allerton-Fawcet — but once again, in spite of certain doubts, he found his caution vanishing in the curious atmosphere his cousin created. It was as if Chas could effortlessly reveal to him an underside, long buried, of his own nature, a hidden Tom Adamson, a reckless, extravagant, disreputable fellow. And it was this fellow — though not without some doubts and protests from the sensible Tom Adamson — who found himself the new owner of a longish, low-slung, vermillion sports car upholstered in leather now very much off-white with all manner of curious stains — a watch-my-dust Allerton-Fawcet man — ready to overtake everything and not with a hoot but a snarl.

Not without some difficulty, for the man who answered the telephone at Bushworth Lodge didn't seem to have much English, Tom spoke to his cousin Leonora, now Lady Corris, and was invited, not quite reluctantly but with no obvious enthusiasm, to lunch on Saturday.

5

It wasn't easy to drive the Allerton-Fawcet slowly — both Allerton and Fawcet must have been against it — but Tom did his best between the Crown and Lion at Anglefield, where Chas had removed himself and their two bags, and Bushworth Lodge. Pointing out not unreasonably that it was he who knew English roads and traffic, Chas had insisted upon taking the wheel himself between London and Anglefield. Even though he was still under the curious spell that Chas put upon him, Tom had sense enough left to realise that Chas driving a car like the Allerton-Fawcet was nothing less than a monster. He did everything that Tom had always detested in other drivers. His aggressiveness and recklessness, selfishness and rudeness, were appalling. He behaved as if he hated all fellow-drivers, as if their very existence on the road was a planned insult. Tom found it impossible to enjoy such countryside as he saw and all the towns and villages he had looked forward to seeing, there was so much roaring, snarling and cursing all the way, as if they were the advance guard of some invasion by an iron empire.

Once Chas had been left behind, it was all different. Strongly resisting the Allerton-Fawcet impulse to go roaring and snarling again, Tom enjoyed the side roads he took, and the green-gold-and-white pastures, the sleepy villages, the vague hills, what seemed to him now the whole dream landscape of Oxfordshire. He was rather sorry when he arrived at Bushworth Lodge, a fair-sized mock-Tudor house among rose-beds and borders of the tall blazing flowers of high summer. His cousin Leonora herself was tall but far from blazing. She bore no resemblance whatever to her brother Chas, and their close blood relationship seemed incredible. She was a thinnish wintry sort of woman, about fifty, who appeared, like a few other Englishwomen he had met, to have cast herself, perhaps forced herself, into an aristocratic role without having the energy, confidence, ease and charm it demanded, like an actress in an inferior repertory company.

She explained at once that lunch would be rather late. Her husband was working with another M.P. — Bob Nokes, a Labour man — on a joint committee report, which they were anxious to complete before lunch as both of them had engagements later in the afternoon. So if Tom had no objection, she would give him a glass of sherry in the garden and then, while they were alone, he could tell her what it was all about. So he settled as best he could into a complaining cane chair. The sherry was brought by the man who must have answered the telephone, a kind of Neapolitan sketch of an English butler, and it was very pale, very dry, too thin — rather like Leonora herself. However, she listened carefully to his brief account of himself and to his longer explanation of how he came to be looking for his father.

"I wish I could help," she said when he had done. "I really do, Tom. It seems odd to be calling you Tom, a complete stranger, but after all we *are* first cousins, aren't we?"

"Yes, Leonora." He said that just to break his bit of ice.

"But I'm afraid I'm going to be useless. You see, your

father and mine saw very little of each other. They didn't get along at all. I remember meeting him a few times when I was quite young, and thinking him amusing and rather attractive. On the stage and all that — rather fascinating to a girl in her teens. But of course that's a long time ago. I haven't the least idea where he is now, what became of him —"

There she stopped. "*What became of him,*" Tom repeated slowly, looking hard at her. She didn't meet his look but tried to seem busy taking a sip of sherry, not a convincing performance. "I think you know something that you suddenly decided not to tell me, Leonora. And I think you ought, you know. Don't forget, I've come a devil of a long way to find him. And anything might help."

"I don't think this would, Tom. And I was telling you the exact truth when I said I didn't know anything about him — don't even know if he's still alive. So why should I hurt your feelings?"

"Because I have to *know*. And don't worry about my feelings."

"Well, it was all very embarrassing. It happened a year or two after the war. I can't remember the exact year. Dudley and I were married during the war, and somehow your father, whom I hadn't seen for years, found out my married name and where we were living. He came — and I must say looking rather shabby and dissipated — to borrow money, not just a few pounds but, I seem to remember, several hundreds. He was quite desperate, he said. He didn't explain why because Dudley came in then and was very curt with him — Dudley didn't like the look of him, and anyhow he hates people who try to borrow money — and there was an embarrassing little scene between them, and that — well, that was the end of it. I never saw him again."

He gave her another hard searching look. "You never saw

him again, no. But did you ever *hear* of him again, Leonora?"

"Why do you ask me that?"

"Because I think you did. And I *must know*."

She hesitated a moment, then began hastily, "Dudley always looks at a lot of newspapers. And one morning — a few months after your father had called on us — Dudley pointed to a little paragraph in one of his papers. I don't remember the details but it said that Charles Adamson, a former actor, had been sent to prison for handing out dud cheques all over the country. I'm sorry, Tom. I didn't want to tell you but you would insist."

"That's all right," he heard himself saying. "In fact, now that I know, I'm not really surprised. I think an old actor friend of his I met suddenly remembered but then pretended he hadn't. Somehow this prison thing has been in the air ever since I came over here. I think I feel better now the truth's out."

"Do have some more sherry. These are such tiny glasses."

"Thank you." He stared at the garden, which at that moment might have been so much painted canvas, only to be lifted to reveal reality — for instance, his father being carted off to jail. And he asked himself if he really did feel better now that he knew, because he liked to be truthful with himself, and finally decided that he didn't. "I'm sorry, Leonora. What did you say?"

"I was saying that naturally you'll want to know *where* this happened. And I wish I could tell you. But I simply don't remember. It wasn't in or near London, I'm sure of that. Somewhere in the Midlands or the North, I fancy," she concluded vaguely.

"I can try to find out. But it's years and years ago, and what's happened to him since, where he is now, God only knows." He sounded gloomy; he felt gloomy.

"Well, you found *me* out, didn't you, Tom?" She was being a bit sprightly, perhaps to cheer him up. "That was clever of you. How did you manage it?"

"That was easy. Your brother — Chas — told me."

"Oh!" And there was plenty of meaning in it. "Yes, of course — Charles. You're in touch with him, are you? Then I can tell you what's happening. He's told you he'll find your father for you in no time. And you're already discovering that it's all going to be rather expensive. Am I right?"

"Quite right. I take it, Leonora, you don't approve of Chas?"

"I don't — no. I've been quite long-suffering with Charles. After all, he was very much the young brother, spoilt by everybody at home. Now for years he's been quite impossible. I never see him if I can possibly avoid it. And Dudley absolutely refuses to have him either in this house or in our London flat. You must understand, Tom, that Charles is utterly devoid of any scruples of any sort. You can't believe a word he says. He refuses to do any decent honest work. He's beastly with women. He never stops lying and cheating —"

"Yes, I know."

"Oh — you *know?*" She was really feeling surprised. "But if so, why do you have anything to do with him? Don't believe for a moment he'll really help you to find your father. All he'll do is to spend your money and probably land you into trouble. So why have anything to do with him? You're obviously not his type at all. Unless I'm very much mistaken, Tom, you're a quiet, sensible, conscientious person, just the opposite of Charles —"

"But that's the point, I think."

"What is? I don't see what you mean."

"It's not easy to explain, Leonora." He waited a moment. "In order to find my father, I'm having to turn my life upside down. And I suppose what fascinates me about Chas — or Charles, if you prefer it — is that he's anything but quiet, sensible, conscientious, so entirely different from what I am — or was. He's myself upside down, so to speak. And of course I know very well — I may be a bit naive but I'm really not a fool — that Chas would never spend even half a morning really trying to trace my father. I also know already that he's an expensive chum to have around. That car you saw me arrive in was entirely his idea. Even so — and this is the hard part to explain, Leonora — I can't help feeling that it may be through Chas — me-upside-down — that I may find my father if I'm ever going to find him. You're looking puzzled. I don't blame you. Perhaps it's something any woman would find it hard to understand —"

There he had to stop because Tweedledum and Tweedledee, smelling of whisky, joined them. Tweedledum turned out to be Leonora's husband, Sir Dudley Corris, Conservative Member of Parliament, and Tweedledee Mr. Bob Nokes, Labour Member of Parliament and a trade union leader. Sir Dudley was rather pinker and smoother and better-dressed, and the Nokes eyebrows and moustache were rather larger and fiercer; but there really was very little difference in their appearance; and though Sir Dudley enjoyed his vowels and almost ignored his consonants, while Nokes stressed his consonants and cared little for his vowels, what they actually said was almost identical. Yet all the way into lunch and then at the table, they insisted upon the huge dark antagonism between them. And Tom, who after all had spent some years lecturing on political and economic subjects, did not propose to stand any nonsense from them.

"Coming from Australia," Sir Dudley told him, "you'll never believe, I dare say, that Bob and I are really at daggers drawn."

"No, I won't," said Tom coolly. "Because I don't believe you are."

"Ah, that's where you're wrong," said Nokes triumphantly. "Oh — on a little matter like this joint committee, we can work together all right, just as we've done this morning — eh, Dudley?"

"Quite right, Bob."

"I don't say we can't be friends outside the House. We can. It's a matter of pride that we can — not like in most countries where the parties are at one another's throats, day and night, anywhere and everywhere —"

"They've never had the parliamentary experience we've had in this country," Sir Dudley remarked with some complacency.

"Or of course there may be some real differences between them," Tom told the politicians. They stared at him with almost as much surprise as they would have felt if one of the characters in the hunting prints on the wall had suddenly addressed them.

"I'm sure somebody would like another cutlet," said Leonora. "They're quite small." And they were too; it was a meagre lunch. Tom, who was hungry, hoped that this mysterious mad Lady Ellowstone, if she invited him and Chas, would have a less frugal notion of dinner.

"Don't you be misled by appearances — er — Tom — isn't it?" Sir Dudley was rather patronising. "No doubt it all seems rougher and tougher in Australia."

"I'll bet it does," Nokes told them. "I was there a few years ago. Fairly rough and tough. A real democracy."

"It's only Australian journalism and manners that are rough and tough," said Tom, determined now to assert himself. "Politically it's really a timid country — has been for years. Academic people, university teachers — and, re-

60

member, I'm one — seem to me far bolder here, altogether
more independent, than they are over there."

"Isn't that interesting?" said Leonora, appealing to nobody in particular and without any sign of interest in her
voice.

"I understand you haven't been here since you were a
small child," Sir Dudley said to him. "How does this country strike you?"

"I've not had a chance to look at it properly yet," said
Tom. "But so far it seems one part garden to three parts
rubbish heap."

The Nokes eyebrows moved down. "Hard to please,
aren't you, young man?"

"Probably, Mr. Nokes. But aren't most people too easily
pleased? They are in Australia."

"I've always wondered," Leonora began. But then she
stopped, and on her face was an expression Tom hadn't
seen on it before. It suddenly made her look fully alive,
though not entirely happily, for it was not without a certain
apprehension. She was looking at somebody who had just
entered the room, behind Tom's back. "Edward — Ted —
you're shockingly late, you know. Mr. Nokes — Tom — this
is our son, who is Edward but likes to be called Ted."

Tom had seen him before, though he didn't say so. Ted
was one of the four very noisy young men he had encoun-
tered that night walking back from Belgrave's house. In
fact Ted was the one who had shouted up to the bedroom
window, "Get stuffed, Dad." Now he looked just the same
as he had done then; evidently he made no concessions
when staying with his parents, and his faded jeans, leather
jacket, and hair-do seemed monstrously out of place in that
primly conventional dining room.

"I'm not shockingly late if I didn't come in here to eat,

am I?" Ted muttered to his mother. "Just looked in to say I'm off to London and don't know when I'll be back — not before Monday, that's certain." He didn't look at his father, who also seemed to avoid looking at him: they weren't even on looking terms, Tom decided.

"Your — what-is-it? — combination — group," said Leonora, forcing a smile of sorts out of what must have been a dreadful mixture of love, fear, misery, "has engagements tonight and tomorrow, has it?"

"A bit dicey but I'm hoping so."

"I bet you play a guitar, don't you, young fellow?" cried Nokes jovially.

"Yes, I do. What do *you* play?"

"Solo whist when I get a chance. And that's not often. I'm too busy helping to keep this country going."

"Going where — for Christ's sake? No, don't tell me. Just save it, Dad."

Sir Dudley jumped up, scarlet with fury. "Shut up and get out."

"Suits me." And Ted went out. With a cry that might have meant anything, his mother hurried out after him.

"I'm sorry, Bob — talking to you like that —"

"Don't mention it, Dudley. They're all alike — idle and impudent young buggers. You get 'em in Australia too, I expect, Mr. — er —"

"Oh — yes, Sydney's full of 'em. I've even got students who look and talk like that."

"I'm told they're everywhere now." Sir Dudley almost groaned it out. "What's going to become of 'em? What kind of a world is it going to be?"

"Don't you worry," Nokes told him. "They'll soon settle down and then take their share of responsibility. They seem to want plenty of sex, so their girls will see to it they settle down. Isn't that so?" he asked Tom.

62

"I don't know. One disturbing thing is — and several teachers have told me this — that some of the brightest and most promising lads turn aside from everything to enjoy this beatnik lark. And while it doesn't much matter what games you get up to when you're twenty, it does matter what you've made of yourself when you're forty. The trouble about being young so much, dismissing everything, a whole world of knowledge, culture, experience, just to *be* carelessly wonderfully *young,* is that soon you stop being young — and then what?" Tom offered them a rueful grin. "Sorry! I seem to be starting a lecture. Bad occupational habit, I'm afraid."

"Don't mention it," said Nokes. "Sir Dudley and me, we spend half our time listening to speeches a dam' sight longer than that. Eh, Dudley?"

"And most of 'em come from your lot, who don't know what they're talking about. Let's have our coffee in the garden. I'll tell the man — and find a cigar for you, Bob. What about you, Tom? Cigar? Don't smoke 'em? I'm delighted to hear it, the price they are now."

The Tweedledum-Tweedledee battle, chiefly for his benefit, Tom felt, was resumed in the garden. Sir Dudley was all for private enterprise, proper rewards for initiative, no encouragement of idleness, no interference from the state; and Nokes rattled away about the public ownership of the means of production, the elimination of the profit motive, the strength and glory of the trade union movement; and they seemed to Tom like an alternating pair of gramophones or tape-recorders. Their voices gave them away: mind and heart weren't in them; better a drum for each to beat. The afternoon wasn't hot by Australian standards but it had a sleepy weight, still new to him, and soon he began to yawn. He needed better talk and stronger coffee to keep him awake. Leonora didn't reappear, and he guessed that

63

after catching up with Ted, adored but feared, and trying to remonstrate with him and trying equally hard to explain his father's outburst and trying even harder still to persuade him to tell her where he would be going and what he would be doing, she had upset herself so thoroughly that now she was lying on her bed, clutching a soaked handkerchief. Having built up a kind of wintry pseudo-aristocratic resistance to everybody and everything else, she was vulnerable only in this one place, but there she was stabbed repeatedly. Or so he was guessing now, in a dreamy fashion. He was almost asleep when the two politicians left him for their afternoon engagements; and then — and then . . .

He seemed to be waiting outside some prison gates for his father. Several faceless sorts of men came out, then at last his father. Tom knew at once this was his father. But then, as the figure came nearer, Tom also knew that his father had borrowed most of his face from Fergus, the never-quite-sober elderly head porter at the hotel — a very silly thing to do, though he didn't feel he could say so to his father . . .

"Did I awaken you? What a shame!" Leonora was giving him as good a smile as she had in stock. She was now looking quite smart in a garden-party kind of way. Obviously she was expecting guests. And indeed the operatic Neapolitan butler and a woman, probably his wife, were setting out tea things on various small tables.

"Sorry about this," Tom said, struggling out of his chair. "I ought to have cleared out. I'll do it now."

"No, please don't, if you haven't to be anywhere else in a hurry. I have to entertain a county Conservative Women's group and they'll all be much happier if they find a good-looking young man passing them things. I really mean it. You'll be doing me a favour, Tom." Before he could reply, she had turned away. "No, Alfredo — not there. Let Lucia finish here while you get ready to answer the door. And you'd like to wash, wouldn't you, Tom? Alfredo will show you."

Half an hour later, he was toiling away among the assembled ladies, all middle-aged to elderly. They all seemed to talk about gardens. One of the first arrivals, a fierce-looking old woman, to whom he was offering a cucumber sandwich, had said at once, "You garden?"

"No, I don't." Not expressing any regret; he didn't have to be barked at like that.

He had often read — and rather wondered at — *Humph!* in print, but now he actually heard it, with a sort of snort somewhere inside it. He was dismissed, even as a bringer of sandwiches.

When they stopped talking about gardens, they talked about sons or grandsons at school or in college. No girls ever seemed to be mentioned. Nor for that matter any rebels like Ted. Just an undeviating male line of succession. And not a word from anybody about business, exports and imports, the state of the country, the state of the world. Tom felt he might have suddenly been pushed back into 1866, with a not-to-be-mentioned Gladstone introducing a Reform Bill. Did these women ever tell themselves, even when suddenly awake at three in the morning, that their whole style of life, rose-beds and lawns and schools and all, might easily collapse? Were they brave or utterly damned stupid? Leonora, for instance. There she was chattering away, probably, he imagined, with thoughts about Ted still gnawing away inside. Why, for God's sake, did she have to pretend she had never known anything but this country-house, landowning life, when in fact she had merely married a contractor who had made money and got himself into the House and had been knighted for his docility? And then, just when she had fitted herself neatly into the long-established pattern, she had found herself facing Ted.

And Ted came back into the picture. This was when he found himself offering a piece of chocolate cake to the only young girl at the party. She looked about eighteen, and had a rather weak, china-doll prettiness. She insisted upon detaining him. "Where do you come into this?"

"Well, I'm Leonora Corris's cousin from Australia. I was lunching here and then stayed to make myself useful."

"Where's Ted?"

"He went to London."

"Oh — blast! I ought to have known he would. I think Ted's rather fab, don't you?"

"Not exactly, no. But I'm a square type."

"Well, I suppose you have to be — at your age. Though if you were young, I can see you being rather fab too. God — I wish Mummy'd stop yapping with these dreary hags so we could go home. At least I could play some records. How do you like England?"

"I don't know yet."

"As a matter of fact, I don't. Sometimes, when I can get away from the family and go to London, it seems absolutely fab, the most. But then when I'm stuck down here, dragged into things like this, I begin to feel I'm going up the wall. What time is it?"

Yes, indeed — what time was it?

The last of them went about half-past five, and then he told Leonora he ought to go too.

"Sit down a minute, Tom. You've been so kind and patient, I really am very grateful. Would you like a drink now? Sure? Well, do sit down and let's talk seriously for a little while."

"What about?" he said as he stretched himself out in the

66

low cane chair again. "Family affairs? My father? Your brother? Ted?"

"Well, I know you've other things to do — but I was wondering if you could help me with Ted."

"No, I couldn't, Leonora. Not because I've other things to do — though of course I have — but simply because it would be quite useless. Youngsters like Ted can't be got at. They seal themselves in. Until they're ready to come out, they have to be left alone. Don't forget, I've known dozens of them. If you try to put any pressure on them, they'll be worse not better, go really wild. And — you won't like this — it might be better for the time being if he didn't even try to spend part of his life here —"

"Oh — no, then I'd never see him, never know what was happening to him. I couldn't bear it."

"You could try. It's very difficult for youngsters who are confused anyhow to go in and out of two quite different worlds. That scene in the dining room — no, Leonora, don't start apologising. It isn't necessary, and I'd much rather you accepted my point. At home he has to fight hard to be the Ted Corris he wants to be just now. We're all most desperate — at our cruellest — when we're trying to preserve a life-illusion. Oh hell — I'm getting pompous. Sorry, Leonora!"

"I'm still wondering if I ought to have told you about your father going to prison —"

"And I still say yes. It may help me to find him, if he can be found. And I have a feeling that he can."

"But please don't believe you can do it through Charles. I hate to talk like this, Tom, against my own brother, the only one I have. But Charles isn't just lazy and extravagant and wild — he's *wicked* — *really wicked*. And his wickedness can't help you or anybody else."

"If this worries you, Leonora, I wish you'd remember what I said earlier —"

"That upside-down business? I'm afraid I didn't understand what you meant, Tom."

"I'm not sure I do — yet. But anyhow I'll try to be careful — No, I won't say that. Perhaps I've always been too careful, and that's why I had to meet Chas. Now I must go, Leonora — and thank you for having me here." As they skirted the house and came in sight of the Allerton-Fawcet, he handed her a card. "The address and phone number of my hotel. It's just possible you might remember something else about my father. And you could ask your husband if he remembers anything. I'd be deeply grateful if you'd let me know — the sooner the better, please. Right."

"Yes, of course, Tom. But I hope you'll come down here again —"

"I'd like to, but I don't know where this father business may take me —"

She gave him a cousinly peck on the cheek, and then looked at him. "Tom, if Edward — Ted — should get into trouble —"

"If there's anything I can do, I'll do it. But don't think of him as if he were already a lost soul. The lost souls don't wear their hair long and play guitars. They have crew cuts, trained minds, sign on for research in biological warfare, and don't give their parents a moment's worry."

6

At the Crown and Lion, Anglefield, Chas, half-undressed in his bedroom, was drinking whisky and sorting out a pile of full-dress evening clothes, orders, decorations, ribbons. "You owe me two quid, Tom, for your share of this lot, so hand them over."

Chas already owed him a great deal more than that, but Tom decided not to mention it at this moment and gave him two pound notes. "What's it all about?"

Chas grinned. "I'll explain later. But we ought to get a move on now. We're due there at eight. I've had to guess your size in tails and everything else, but I don't think I'll be far out. Now as orders and decorations must be worn, I'm giving you this lot. You're getting the Imperial Service Order, then St. Michael and St. George, a Knight Commandership of the British Empire, and this very tasty Order of the Golden Eagle — Roumanian, I fancy, I've bagged the Bath —"

"But, for God's sake, Chas —"

"I'll explain on the way there. And when I said the 'Bath,' I meant the Order of, not the bathroom, which is all yours. But get a move on, Tom. If we're late, we miss half the fun —"

"But I can't wear —"

"Yes, you can. Everybody's in the gag except the old girl herself and she's completely barmy. Come on, chum, be a sport. Here you are." And he dumped all the stuff on Tom and almost pushed him out of the bedroom.

As he changed, Tom reflected that only Chas, with his upside-down values, his gusto, his curiously hypnotic quality, could have induced him to take part in such a masquerade. Once away from Chas he began to feel dubious and uneasy, but interest returned, and indeed rose to excitement, when at last, wearing everything Chas had given him, he stared at himself in the looking glass. He was not a vain man and, unlike so many men he knew (who proved the feminine contention that man is the vainer creature), he had never spent time and money dressing himself up. But now, astonished and then delighted by what the looking glass showed him, he was almost a peacock. If this crazy Lady Ellowstone wanted to see him like this — then why not? God's truth! — he'd never before done justice to himself. He began to imagine a career that would entitle him to look like this at least once a week. Not Power but this Glory.

"As I told you," Chas said as he sent the Allerton-Fawcet shooting out of Anglefield, to the despairing envy of the Saturday Night lads hanging about the streets, "Lady Ellowstone — Gladys — is well round the bend, has been for years, but she's allowed to keep and to spend quite a large packet of the millions her husband left. He was a shipping man. They say she was originally a barmaid but that's never mentioned. Most of the time she lives quietly in this dam' great house, but she insists upon giving these Saturday night dinners, when orders and decorations must be worn. She has a secretary-companion, Miss Trask, who of course is in the know. But the man who really runs these dinners is an artful old sod called Bassenthwaite, who's really an old character actor who functions as her majordomo-cum-butler. He keeps a room at the Crown and Lion where he hires out these rigs and decorations. Half the guests are out-of-work actors and actresses, and the rest are odd balls like me — and you, for that matter, chum. By the way, I'll be Lord Ashtreeplace —"

"Not very inventive there, are you, Chas?"

"No, but it serves. You'd better be simply Sir Thomas Adamson —"

"No cover there, Lord Ashtreeplace."

"You don't need any. Of course rumours go floating round, but Miss Trask and Bassenthwaite sit tight on any publicity. And Bassenthwaite has a pal called Crike, who's a private detective. A few months ago, a gossip man from one of the Sundays bribed his way in, but Crike soon knew too much about him and killed his story. Crike'll be there tonight. He comes as a bishop. If I get the chance I'll ask him about finding your old man." Here Chas broke off to tell a fellow-motorist, whose particular lapse Tom failed to notice, that he was an idle clumsy clot. After that the Allerton-Fawcet went roaring and snarling well on the wrong side of the road, and it wasn't until they were back where they belonged that Tom felt like talking again.

"I'll admit I rather fancied myself when I saw how I looked as a fraud," Tom said, "but even so I don't see how you and the rest find this charade worth the time and trouble. And don't tell me, Chas, you've taken pity on the poor old lady."

"Hell, no! But it's a giggle. And then old Bassenthwaite, who knows about food and drink and hasn't to count the pennies, lays on a bloody marvellous dinner — you'll see. And though there are never as many women as men, it's a bad night when there aren't one or two juicy willing birds, full of champagne, who'd rather explore the house with you than stay yapping in the drawing room. So if there's one you fancy, just give me a sign, because I can tell you where to take her. Oh — and if she's Lady Betty or the Honourable Phyllis Blueblood, don't tell her she isn't. We all agree to keep the game going at all times. Part of the giggle."

"I'll try to remember. But look here, Chas, this bloody marvellous dinner has to be cooked and served —"

"Not to worry. They're all in the know of course, but Trask and Bassenthwaite have it all sewn up. And don't forget that as soon as we're in that house, I'm Lord Ashtree-place and you're Sir Thomas —"

"And Crike the Private Eye is a bishop. What's he Bishop of?"

"Can't remember. Parkhurst perhaps. Now we take this next turning, and we'll be there in ten minutes."

The drive must have been half a mile long. The vast house that rose up through the green dusk seemed to be something between a mansion and a belated castle, with terraces below and turrets above. In the courtyard half a dozen cars, ranging from a gigantic old Rolls to a three-wheel bubble, were already parked, and there were two or three more arriving behind the Allerton-Fawcet. Men obviously of the highest distinction were moving up the steps that led to the main entrance, with here and there a gleam of silk or satin. A charade or giggle it might be, but Tom couldn't help feeling, as he and Chas climbed the steps, that this was easily the grandest party he had ever attended. A multitude of lights had been turned on; there were two footmen in uniform just inside the immense hall; and as Tom, guided by Chas, crossed it and then turned to the right, there, standing between the open double doors, wearing some kind of uniform in black velvet and a gold chain and holding a large gilt-edged card, was one of the most impressive figures Tom had ever seen.

"Good evening, Bassenthwaite," said Chas in a condescending Lord Ashtreeplace manner.

"Good evening, my lord. And good evening to you, Sir Thomas. I'll announce his lordship first, Sir Thomas."

Bassenthwaite then moved forward several stately paces, produced a cough that was an apology of the utmost dignity, and then announced in a magnificently rich tone, "Your ladyship — Lord Ashtreeplace, Knight Grand Cross of the Most Honourable Order of the Bath, Knight Commander of the Royal Victorian Order, Officer First Class of the Ancient Latvian Order of the Bear."

Tom then heard himself announced: "Sir Thomas Adamson, Knight Commander of the Most Distinguished Order of St. Michael and St. George, Companion of the Imperial Service Order, Knight Commander of the Most Excellent Order of the British Empire, and Paladin of the Ancient Order of the Golden Eagle."

He moved towards a blaze of jewels and then found himself bowing over the hand of their wearer, Lady Ellowstone, who appeared to be stoutly built but yet had a very thin face. Her head wobbled constantly, almost indignantly — as if it wanted to be somewhere else. The company he now joined looked extraordinarily distinguished. Sherry and various cocktails were being offered, accepted, and disposed of at a rate perhaps rather uncommon in the highest circles. The drawing room was very big, and everything in it seemed to be very big too: settees that could make six giants comfortable; pots that four men would have to lift; indoor plants that would not have looked out of place in a primeval forest; and lights sufficient for an airport. This overall bigness, together with all the coloured sashes, stars, orders, medals, suggested that a curtain would soon rise in one of the world's larger opera houses: all that was lacking was the sound of an eighty-man orchestra playing the overture, though music of a sort was coming from somewhere. Tom, anxious not to feel nervous or foolish, and keeping drinking time with the company, swallowed three powerful dry martinis, and after being introduced by Lord Ashtreeplace to a Countess, a Dame, two rather pretty girl Honourables, and several assorted peers and an Admiral who was already more than half-plastered, began to feel a little drunk himself. Crike, a large slack sort of man with one eye that drooped and ran, was there as the Bishop of Murchester. In his most magnificent manner, Bassenthwaite anounced to her ladyship, their excellencies and lordships, etc., etc., that dinner was served. The procession across the hall moved at about the speed of the *Meistersingers.*

There were place names at the dining table, the longest Tom had ever seen and really a wonderful sight. Chas had been right about Bassenthwaite as a caterer. The menu opened with caviare, smoked salmon, pâté de foie gras, dallied delicately with consommé, then forged ahead with salmon-trout and a green sauce, saddle of lamb with new potatoes and garden peas — it was written in English, not French — and offered more wines than Tom knew. He was sitting between one of the pretty girl Honourables, the one with a snub nose, greenish eyes, and a dangerous tendency to giggle, and a certain Lord Shutter, blunt-featured and blunt-mannered, a kind of rough-diamond peer, though splendidly decorated. (Unlike most of the other men, he was obviously not an actor, and Tom decided he was probably Bassenthwaite's cousin from some Northern iron foundry.) Grace was said by the Bishop of Murchester, and Crike, in spite of that drooping, sceptical, cynical eye, made a neat convincing job of it. Tom added iced vodka, with the first course, then sherry, with the soup, to the torchlight procession of the dry martinis below. He soon felt there was something absurd but delicious about his sitting there, in-

stead of trying to find his father. Lord Shutter took time off
from eating and drinking, at which he combined methodi-
cal efficiency with speed, only for a few grunted monosylla-
bles. The pretty girl Honourable, whose name was Dora,
poked around with her forks and took indiscriminate sips
from her various glasses, trying the vodka again after the
hock and claret, and then seized Tom's hand under the
table and squeezed it hard, she said, to keep her from giggling. The courses and the wines came and went. Then the
Admiral, who was still only a little more than half-plastered, proposed a bluff old seadog's version of the Loyal
Toast. Lady Ellowstone, wobbling harder than ever, took
the ladies away. Lord Shutter helped himself to four cigars.
Tom rejected port but accepted brandy. From a Most Illus-
trious Order of St. Patrick and a Most Exalted Order of the
Star of India he heard two dirty stories that he remembered
Andrew Wentworth telling much better. Then they joined
the ladies.

Lady Ellowstone was holding court in the drawing room
— which was fair enough, however dotty she might be,
after that magnificent dinner. Sir Thomas Adamson was
surprised to notice that his relative Lord Ashtreeplace was
closely in attendance there, though he also noticed that his
lordship was even closer to the other pretty girl Honourable. He found Dora drifting around the far end of the room.
She was pretending to examine several immense dark-
brown pictures.

"All the animals in these pictures have eyes like people,"
she said. "They're giving me the willies. What is there to do
now? I've never been here before."

"Neither have I. It's a warm night. We could go out on
the terrace."

"Yes, let's," she cried. "We could do a bit of snogging. I
was thinking that during dinner. But nothing else, mind.

75

No rough stuff. I don't know who you are, it isn't safe, and I don't want to ruin this dress — it isn't mine."

So out they went, and it was very pleasant on the long paved terrace, where they talked as they strolled but did a bit of snogging when they arrived at each dark end. Dora refused to keep up the dinner charade and explained how she'd had a few small parts in films and was now playing a depraved secretary in one of those television series about spies, so elaborately plotted that she herself never knew what was supposed to be happening, and how — this was after she'd started crying in the final bit of snogging — she'd fallen in love, was still in love, with a stinker who was absolutely adorable. They must have been out there over an hour — and a few people were already leaving — when he heard his name being called and then saw Chas in the light coming from the drawing room.

"You'll have to excuse me, Dora. My cousin seems to want me for something. We came together and perhaps he thinks we ought to go."

"Well, I'm going anyhow. And thanks for being so nice to me. You're sweet." And she gave him a quick kiss and hurried indoors.

"You're looking rather dishevelled, Lord Ashtreeplace."

"I know. I just had a wild short time upstairs. That's why I wanted to get hold of you. Here — let's move out of the light." Chas stopped after they had gone a few paces. "Quite simple, Sir Thomas. Seem to have lost my handkerchief, so I want to borrow yours for a minute — just for a quick tidy up."

After doing some rather vague work with the handkerchief, Chas grinned. "Never worn tails before, have you, old boy? Well, you never keep a handkerchief in your trousers pocket. It's low — bloody low. You pop it into the pocket in the tail — like this. See?"

"Well, now that's settled, what about going? I'm ready, Chas."

"I've had all I want except a drink or two for the road. But I have to see Bassenthwaite for a minute or two. Don't know why, but I like to keep in with him. He has a little room of his own just off the dining room. Stick around, Tom. Give yourself a drink. There's an old malt whisky in there that's bloody marvellous."

"I might risk one with plenty of water. But what about our hostess? Don't we thank her — and so forth?"

"Vanished, I think, chum. In a tizzy about something, somebody said. Well — Bassenthwaite now. See you later."

Tom was enjoying the old malt, standing alone near the grog tray, when suddenly he found himself staring at the drooping moist eye of the Bishop of Murchester, who then filled and emptied a whisky glass so quickly that it seemed like a conjuring trick. As soon as he had done this and had turned to Tom, he seemed to rid himself of any ecclesiastical suggestion and become Crike, private investigator.

"Finish your drink, if you don't mind, Mr. Adamson," he said in a hoarse low tone, "because, if it's all the same to you, I want you to come outside and walk along the terrace as far as the dining room. Okay?"

"If it'll amuse you, Mr. Crike," Tom whispered, "but what's the point of it?" However, he finished his drink.

"Tell you when we're outside." Then, when they were walking along the terrace, he went on: "From outside the dining room I can see the door to Bassenthwaite's pantry. He has your cousin in there now. That's right, isn't it — cousin? I thought so. Well, when Bassenthwaite's done with him, he may — or may not — want to see you, Mr. Adamson. And he'll give me a signal. So that's why we're here."

"Yes, Mr. Crike," said Tom, more amused than annoyed,

77

"but you're not explaining what it's all about. Bassenthwaite may want to see me. But do I want to see him? That seems to have been taken for granted."

"I don't think you'll object as soon as Bassenthwaite has explained. Ah — your cousin's coming out now. Very jaunty. You keep back a minute, just till he gets out of the dining room." Then, after a pause: "All right now, and Bassenthwaite's given me the signal. So in we go, Mr. Adamson."

Bassenthwaite was in his shirtsleeves, smoking a pipe. It was a large pantry and Bassenthwaite had turned it into a kind of sitting room. He pointed to one comfortable chair and took its companion himself. This left Crike standing, but apparently he wasn't staying. "I'll look in again in about ten minutes — eh? I take it our friend had nothing to hide. Didn't expect he would have. Too fly. I'll go and circulate." And off he went.

"Well, Mr. Bassenthwaite, you gave me a superb dinner, so if there's anything I can do in return, tell me what it is."

"I'm glad you enjoyed it, Mr. Adamson." Even in his shirtsleeves, smoking a pipe, Bassenthwaite still had a weighty dignity. But now the butler had vanished and in his place was the old actor — and he must have been about seventy — who had played so many noble Romans and great Renaissance princes that something of their manner and weight remained with him. "And all I want you to do in return, as you put it, is to turn out your pockets for me." And clearly he wasn't joking.

Tom stared at him. "I think you'll have to explain why. Am I supposed to have stolen something?"

"Crike and I believe somebody has. It's an emerald bracelet that Lady Ellowstone was wearing. The clasp must have given way — we've had trouble with it before — but exactly when and where we don't know. But the bracelet's gone — and somebody has it."

"Is that why Chas was in here? Well, I'll turn out my pockets for you." Tom stood up. "But I must point out that, apart from the moment when we shook hands, I was never anywhere near Lady Ellowstone either during dinner or afterwards, when I was out on the terrace with a girl."

Bassenthwaite nodded. "Crike pointed that out too. Even so — just humour me, will you, Mr. Adamson?"

"Certainly. And it won't take long. All I have in this suit — look — a wallet, some loose change, and a box of matches —"

"No handkerchief?"

"Oh yes — of course — it's in some mysterious back pocket that Chas discovered for me." He pulled out his handkerchief, but there was something else there, and he pulled that out too. And in the tiniest fraction of time before his fingers actually touched the thing, he had known what it would be.

"Thank you, Mr. Adamson," Bassenthwaite said as he took the bracelet. "Quite small, as you can see, but a very nice piece — beautifully matched stones — and her ladyship's very fond of it. She may be vague about titles and decorations and the kind of people who have 'em — and now and again she's given me a look as if to say she knows it's only a show I'm putting on for her — but she isn't vague about her jewellery. I'll send her maid up with this, shortly."

"I hope you don't imagine I took that bracelet —"

"I'm sure you didn't. In fact I'm sure you didn't know it was there. Even if you could have taken it, you're not that good an actor. I've seen too many in my time trying to act

79

astonishment. No, our friend Chas took that bracelet —
Crike says he'd plenty of opportunity just after dinner —
and then he popped it into your back pocket —"

Tom couldn't deny it. "But it was just one of his idiotic
jokes, you know, Mr. Bassenthwaite. A joke against me as
well as you —"

"Might have been, might not." Bassenthwaite looked
hugely dubious: he had the face for it. "Ugly bit of work,
I'd say. And he doesn't come here again. Of course you may
think this whole dinner business on the ugly side — a lot of
people pretending to be what they aren't and dressing up to
deceive a silly old woman. But it makes her happy for an
hour or two. And if it was all the real thing, would it be
much better? Might even be worse, taking itself seriously
and not making anybody feel happier." He put down his
pipe, got up and struggled into his uniform coat. "Have to
get back on the job. Ah — this'll be Crike. Come in, Mr.
Crike."

"By the look and sound of you, I'd say you've found it.
Planted?"

"Planted in Mr. Adamson's tail pocket. He thinks it was
just a joke, so we'll leave it at that, though of course Chas
Adamson doesn't come here again. Now I must get back on
duty, also send this bracelet up to her ladyship. But if you'd
like to stay and have a word with Mr. Adamson about his
father, you do so, Mr. Crike."

"What's this about my father?" Tom asked as soon as he
was alone with Crike. "How did you know I was looking for
him? Did Chas tell you?"

"He told Bassenthwaite, who told me. Now Bassenthwaite knew your father when he'd stopped calling himself
Adamson —"

"When and where was this?"

"Hold on, Mr. Adamson. I'm a private investigator —

that's my living — so I sell information, I don't give it away."

"But this was Bassenthwaite's —"

"And he let me have it. I could please myself about passing it on to you. After all — and I'll say it again — I make my living selling information. Now I don't know how you're fixed financially. Could you afford my services?"

"I imagine so," Tom told him rather stiffly.

Crike waited a moment. "Aren't you going to ask me what my terms are, Mr. Adamson?"

"No, I'm not, Mr. Crike. I came over here to find my father myself, not to employ somebody else to do it. And I must add that I resent your refusal to tell me what Bassenthwaite told you."

"I've already explained that, Mr. Adamson. As for finding him yourself, I doubt if you've a hope in hell of doing it — that is, without competent professional assistance. It isn't even the needle in the haystack, because once a man's been in prison and has changed his name, you might say he's trying to stop even looking like a needle. But here's my card, Mr. Adamson. Go on, take it. You might easily change your mind. It's my experience that people are always doing that about my kind of work."

"Possibly." Deciding now that he didn't take to Crike, Tom was stiff with him. He was equally stiff with Chas on their way back to the Crown and Lion. When asked what had happened in Bassenthwaite's room, he was coldly curt. "Bassenthwaite knew at once you'd planted that bracelet in my back pocket. I told him it was one of your idiotic jokes. He was dubious. But then, so was I. You'd have kept it, wouldn't you, Chas, if you could have done?"

"Certainly. Why not?"

"That makes you a thief."

"Don't be such a bloody prig. The old dottypot has more

jewellery than she knows what to do with. And she can't live much longer, anyhow. I can, and I'd have done nicely for the next few months on what that bracelet would have fetched."

"I still don't like thieves."

"Oh — turn it up, for Christ's sake!"

They went in silence to their bedrooms. When Chas came down next morning, after Tom had finished his breakfast, he announced that he hated Sundays in London and had rung up some friends who didn't live too far away and were picking him up in a car in time for lunch and had asked him to stay the night. So Tom returned to London alone in the Allerton-Fawcet, taking a picnic lunch and doing a certain amount of exploring down side roads, which for the most part turned out to be extremely dull. And Sunday night in his hotel was even duller. He went to bed early and read a paperback about an American private detective who took no exercise, few proper meals, an astonishing amount of neat whisky, and yet, after being knocked out at least once a night, could run, jump, climb, fight and make love without feeling even slightly dizzy.

7

MANY people dislike Monday morning, but Tom had been prejudiced in its favour for years. And this Monday morning was mistily fine and quite warm. But what was he going to do with it? Over breakfast he began to wish he had stayed somewhere in the country. In terms of finding his father, London now seemed a dead end. And it was maddening to remember that on Saturday night, because he had been so grand and pernickety with Crike and Bassenthwaite, he had thrown away the chance of knowing what his father had done after being in prison and — more important still — what he had decided to call himself. The name his father had adopted then might very well be the name he was still using. And here was Tom the idiot son, he reminded himself while taking more than his share of marmalade, not knowing what move to make next, a blank day in front of him, and no longer knowing his father's name. "You don't happen to know an elderly Charles X, do you?" he could almost hear himself saying. So now what? He looked at the popular daily that the hotel gave him, but found it impossible to share the editor's excitement because some young actor had just been dropped from a television serial.

However, there was a letter for him. It was from Belgrave. *You may remember,* he wrote, *that I promised to let you know if by any chance I discovered the present name and address of Nelly Coping — the actress your father went to live with — the one who undoubtedly worked all the mischief. She is now Lady Truskmore, a widow and a very old sick woman, and unless she has now been carted off to hospital, she lives at the Manor House, Littlewold — a village in the Cotswolds, roughly somewhere between Winchcombe and Broadway. If you decide to go there — and it is delightful country — I am told that a car would be better than the train. I doubt if my name would be any use to you — Nelly Coping and I were never on friendly terms — but you are welcome to try. Don't bother to acknowledge this but don't forget to tell me if and when you have definite news of your father.*

This was something to do, somewhere to go. He had a good road map and now he spent a happy quarter of an hour with it, finally deciding to go by way of the Oxford bypass, Witney, Burford, Stow-on-the-Wold. He left about ten o'clock and it was just after one when he parked the Allerton-Fawcet outside the Swan Inn at Littlewold. Most of the journey had been unpleasant, filled with the grinding of gears and decisions about overtaking lorries and vans that seemed to enjoy frustrating an Allerton-Fawcet. Part of the trouble was that Tom, a cautious driver with no desire to release his aggressions with the clutch, was simply not an Allerton-Fawcet man. It demanded a Chas and shook with impatience because Tom was now in control of it. There might have been a lot of things worth noticing between London and Witney, but Tom, lost among the machines, never noticed them. Sometimes he had the feeling that he and all the other drivers were not going anywhere but simply fleeing from some mysterious catastrophe.

Then from Burford onward it was all different. He drove

at ease into an enchantment. The green hills and the old stone walls belonged to some dream of England. It was a tiny world, which no doubt at any moment might be taken to pieces and exported in plastic containers, that seemed to have been created by and for shepherds and craftsmen, pilgrims and lyric poets. The slumbering rows of houses looked as if they were turning centuries of pale sunlight into walls of honey. They had doorways waiting for Piers Plowman to return. Tom felt it was all wrong to be driving a car — especially this Allerton-Fawcet — through these villages. He ought to be walking, ready to stop, to turn aside, to explore and to wonder — best of all with some girl he had never met and probably never would meet. He wasn't given to vague thoughts and longings of this kind, but this seemed nearer Eden than he had ever been before, and a man needed Eve by his side.

Littlewold, when at last he found it, seemed one of the smallest and sleepiest of the villages. When he got out of the car, in front of the inn in the little square, not for the first time but with more force than ever before he realised what is wrong with motoring, which keeps us in the atmosphere of the cities we have left behind, boxed in with the fume and fret of them, still unable to breathe untroubled air. Now, out of the car at last, he could smell, taste, savour Littlewold and all its ancient, pale-golden companions. And he felt it didn't matter if he never set eyes on Lady Truskmore, once Nelly Coping, who anyhow shouldn't be living here, the wicked old bitch.

Even so, the saloon bar of the Swan was a sharp disappointment. Unlike the exterior, which was perfect, it had recently been brought bang-up-to-date. It was a plastic job, chairs, little tables and all, in metallic shades of green and purple. On the walls, insulting the ancient stones somewhere behind their glossy finish, were bright trend-setting advertisements of new drinks that were bad imitations of older and better drinks. The bar had been tarted up, and so had the barmaid, herself a kind of plastic job. Two young men, elaborately casual in dress and loud in manner, were chaffing her over their gins-and-tonics. Nevertheless, all three spoke with a regional and rural burr that belonged to the rounded hills and the old stone walls and revealed one ancestral link that still hadn't vanished; Tom could have clapped his hands at the sound of it. If England, he felt, ever succeeded — with television screens in every huge comprehensive school — in finally flattening out all her regional accents, she would be ruined forever.

There were some pork pies at the end of the bar counter, and Tom asked for one of them. He also asked for a pint of beer, and was told rather sharply that only bottled beers were served in that room. If he insisted upon a pint, then he must ask for it in the taproom, "through there." So he took his pork pie into the taproom and found himself back in wonderland. It was low-ceilinged, not very big, and rather dark, having only one small window. It was all wood, and very old wood at that, with tables and seats polished by unending use. An oldish man in shirtsleeves was behind the bar, and two other oldish men, sitting close together and muttering as if in some conspiracy, were the only customers. Nothing was being advertised; not a single device for making people spend more was in sight; the place was a hundred years behind the times and might be condemned any day now; it was wonderful. Tom ate his pie and drank his beer very slowly. The clock he could hear ticked so deliberately that it might have belonged to some other order of time: Australia had probably not yet been discovered.

He sauntered round the village and poked and pottered until it was nearly three o'clock. The Manor House, he knew because he had asked, was only just beyond the vil-

lage, but his car had been standing long enough outside the
Swan, so he drove as slowly and quietly as possible across
the square, up the road, and then into a drive with roses on
one side of it and tall flowers like sentinels, hollyhocks and
delphiniums and the rest, on the other. The house was old,
long, lowish, with an odd confusion of roof levels and chim-
neys. The front door was open; all was dim and silent
within; the whole place and everybody in it could have been
asleep. He hesitated before pressing the bell, finding himself suddenly and sharply divided between the feeling that
the house was waiting for him, just for the pressure of his
finger, to tell him the story he wanted to hear, and the con-
trary feeling, which most sensitive people know at all such
moments, that he was on the wrong track altogether and
about to make a fool of himself. The warm and drowsy afternoon, its hazy sunlight still seeming strange to him, had
an unreal quality that encouraged the negative feeling, the
impulse to walk away before he turned into an ass. But the
positive took command; nothing venture, nothing win; and
he rang the bell.

As soon as the tall elderly woman, angular and severe,
appeared in the doorway, he knew at once — and would
have bet money on it — that she was the woman who had
written to his mother. But her intuition wasn't keeping
pace with his. "We're not buying anything, if that's what
you want, young man."

"And I'm not selling anything. My name's Adamson —
Tom Adamson. I've just come from Australia. I'm trying to
find my father, Charles Adamson. And I have an idea it was
you who wrote to my mother about him."

"Good gracious me! Yes, it was. Come in, then, Mr. Adamson." She led the way across a rather small panelled hall
and showed him into what was obviously an unused drawing room, shuttered, dim, with its furniture all shrouded,

87

and thick with a musty smell of decay, like a seashore from which the tide had ebbed forever.

"This is where I ought to bring you, I suppose," she said dubiously, "but we might do better in my kitchen."

"I'm sure we would. You lead the way, please."

"My name's Agnes Williams," she said as they returned to the hall, "but then you know that if you read my letter —"

"No, I never actually saw your letter, never mind why for the moment —"

"Well, I was going to say that if you call me anything, then just make it Agnes. That's what I'm used to."

"And I'm used to Tom."

"Certainly not, Mr. Adamson. I know my place if hardly anybody else does nowadays. Well, here we are. Just a kitchen."

"But much, much better, Agnes, than that dead drawing room. Air, sunlight, life still going on. Where shall we sit? Here?"

They sat on small hard chairs, facing each other across a scrubbed kitchen table. There was a smell of hot jam that took Tom back to his childhood; not for a long time had he been around when jam was being made. In the clearer light he saw that while Agnes had a long and rather ugly face she had unusually fine eyes, a kind of burning hazel and wonderfully expressive, so that whatever was being said they offered their own performance, like beautiful twin actresses.

"I'll explain first about the letter, Agnes," he began gently, and told her about his mother's last weeks and how he had promised to find his father. Then, being careful to avoid any suggestion of reproach, he said, "Now I think you must tell me what was in the letter and how you came to write it when you did."

She nodded, then waited a moment or two. "In the war I

got converted, and it turned me into a different woman. But in those days when Mr. Charles Adamson, your father, was living with her, I was nearly as bad as she was. I knew she was doing a wicked thing with those letters — not posting the ones he was writing to his wife, and pretending none had come for him — but I didn't care. I had a conscience — we all have one, always — but I didn't choose to listen to it. Then years afterwards I did. And I was full of remorse. And there were some pieces of wicked business I did try to put right, as far as somebody in my place could. But by that time I didn't know where your father was, Mr. Adamson, because by then he wasn't having anything to do with her. And all I knew about your mother — and she was the important one — was that she went to Australia. So years went by and there was nothing I could do. Then — and of course it's only a few months since — I got this letter from my niece, Maureen, my brother's youngest." Here she stopped and looked at him, her eyes wide and brilliant, her long plain face wearing them like jewels.

"I expect you think everything's a muddle, Mr. Adamson, all just a matter of chance — I know I used to. But now I'm sure it isn't. Everything's *meant*. It only *seems* higgledy-piggledy. Because my niece, Maureen, married an Australian and went to live somewhere near Adelaide, she heard something about your mother. Because she wrote to me and gave me some sort of address for your mother, I wrote to your mother telling her about that wicked business with the letters, years ago. And because I wrote to your mother —" She hesitated.

"Just before she died she begged me to come here and try to find my father," Tom said rather hastily, to save her any embarrassment. "And here I am."

"Yes, and because you're here — I don't mean in this house but here in England — then —"

"Then *what?*" And he smiled.

But she didn't return the smile. "I don't know. I'm not a fortune-teller. But because you had to come here, looking for your father, *then — something —* something important so you'll never be the same as you were before, Mr. Adamson." She waited a moment. "Do you think you're going to find your father?"

"Sooner or later, if he's still alive — and I have a feeling he is —"

"You trust that feeling, Mr. Adamson. It's part of what is *meant*. But how far have you got?"

"I know that he was in the army during the war and that a year or two afterwards he was sent to prison and that after he came out he changed his name. I learnt most of that only two days ago. It's not going to be easy from now on, when I don't even know his name and he may have taken all kinds of miserable little jobs and not stayed anywhere for long. Now, Agnes, tell me frankly what *you* thought of him."

"Well, Mr. Adamson, if he was sent to prison, that would be through carelessness not real wickedness. He was never downright wicked, like somebody I could mention. He was more like a big silly boy, not meaning any harm to anybody, but so easy and careless he thought if he left things alone they'd always work out all right for him. This meant there'd probably be a woman to do it, like leaving clothes all over a bedroom, feeling sure somebody like me would fold and tidy them and put them away. But of course he might be quite different now, specially after being in prison."

A bell jangled on the wall, giving Tom something of a shock. Somehow he had come to think they were alone in the house.

Agnes got up. "That's her ladyship, telling me she's

awake and wants something. Her heart's bad and she's put
on a lot of weight, and now she never leaves her bed except
when I take her to the bathroom. There's a woman comes
to do the rough work and to stay here while I'm out shop-
ping. Otherwise I'm on my own and do it all. Very different
from the old days. But then, so is she. She's starting her
punishment in this world in preparation for what she'll get
in the next. Now she can't live and is afraid to die." All this
was said without any suggestion of rancour, just calmly
stated. The bell rang again.

"Just one thing, quickly," said Tom as she was about to
go. "Are you going to tell her I'm here? Is there any point in
my seeing her?"

"Yes, so long as you don't count on getting any sense out
of her. She might understand who you are — and she might
not. Her mind comes and goes. Now I wouldn't sit waiting
here for me, Mr. Adamson. I may be some time. Have a
look round."

He spent a few minutes in the garden, not very large by
English country-house standards, now untidy and obviously
neglected but riotous with flowers. Then, seeing a french
window open, he went indoors again, finding himself in the
dining room, no more in use than the drawing room but not
so closely shuttered and musty. A picture above the fire-
place at the far end of the room caught and then held his
attention, and he went along there to take a closer look at
it. A woman in a striped summer dress, pink and pale green,
was lolling and smiling in a long garden chair, shaded from
the strong sunlight behind her, an impasto of orange and
bright yellows. There was nothing masterly and distinguished about the painting; it was not the work of a man of
great talent; it might easily have been something of a fluke;
but just as it had caught and held his attention across the
room, now, as he stood before it, staring, it seemed to catch

and hold all that a man had seen and felt on a long-lost summer afternoon. And he knew who that man was before his eye found the *C. Adamson* 1933 in the bottom right-hand corner. For a minute, two minutes, three or five minutes — he never knew — he remained there, fixed, as if all that he had ever felt about life in this world, its joy and hope, its anguish, its despair, its mystery, had descended upon him like a weight he could bear only without moving.

"Yes, that's her as she was then," said Agnes, startling him. "Not the best likeness I'd say but the one that was always her favourite as a picture. Well, Mr. Adamson, I'll take you up if you like. She's all ready for a visitor."

"She may be ready, Agnes, but am I? Even if she understands who I am —"

"And that I can't guarantee, Mr. Adamson. I told her, but her mind may have slipped away by now."

"Well, even supposing it hasn't, do you think it's possible she knows anything about my father that I might find useful?"

"No, I don't. If she'd know, then I'd know — and I'd have told you. They had some bitter quarrels — chiefly her doing, though he couldn't forget he'd lost his family — so they were off and on for a few years, before they broke properly. Then it was all up, finished. And this was before the war, mind. No, she'll tell you nothing useful. I don't know," she added sardonically, "that she ever did tell anybody anything useful. Even so, after coming all this way, you might as well go up and say something to her. It'll make a bit of a change for her."

Tom made a face. "It would if I told her what I really thought of her."

"Oh — she's had plenty of that in her time. But it's too late now. Shall I take you up then, Mr. Adamson?"

"All right. And I'll just be a polite visitor."

She was lying, seemingly mountainous under the clothes, in a big four-poster. The room was cluttered up with everything from television and radio sets and a portable gramophone to open chocolate boxes, magazines and paperbacks, jigsaw puzzles, photograph and press-cutting albums, dolls, and bottles of every known size and shape. Its air, which had been there far too long, was suffocatingly sickly-sweet with some taint of corruption and decay, some suggestion of the mortuary and the graveyard. Her features weren't large but the face surrounding them was, and might have been moulded out of bluish lard. The mere notion of telling her what he thought about her now seemed ridiculous. Time had forestalled him, and had been more ruthless than he could ever have been.

"This is Mr. Tom Adamson, your ladyship, the one I was telling you about." Agnes used a false bright tone that Tom had heard before in hospitals and had always hated.

"Shut up, Agnes. Go away." The enormous woman had a high childish whisper of a voice. She looked at Tom now. Her eyes, not large with all that fat round them but still very dark, were more alive than the rest of her. "Hello!"

"Hello!" And Tom wondered what else he would ever find to say. Agnes, who might have prompted him, had gone.

"Who did she say you were?"

He could at least answer this question. "I'm Tom Adamson. You used to know my father — Charles Adamson."

"Did I?" Then she produced a strange sound. Laughing, was she? Apparently she was, for when he made no reply, she said with something of an effort, "Don't — make me laugh — you silly man."

It was useless, of course, but he felt compelled to tell her that he wasn't trying to make her laugh.

"Just another — silly bloody man."

He didn't respond to that one.

"Tell you something. Come closer." As he did — and he was still standing — she closed her eyes as if she'd already forgotten about telling him something. But she hadn't. She opened her eyes, got him into focus, and went on: "Tell you a secret. Never liked men — not really. Started badly. Only fourteen — and he must have been forty. Hurt me and frightened me. Always reminded me afterwards. Made 'em all pay. Who you said you were? Painter?"

"No, my father did the painting. I'm Charles Adamson's only son. Charlie Adamson, you remember? There's a picture of his — you sitting in the garden — hanging in the dining room downstairs. You're wearing a striped dress — pink and pale green."

The features huddled together on that mound of lard now rearranged themselves, and he saw what he had least expected to see — not only a smile but one apparently brought unchanged from another world, a dazzling, almost bewitching smile. And when she spoke now, she was more coherent and animated than she had been before. "Yvonne made that dress. She had a little place in Brook Street. I used her whenever I could in the Theatre. She wasn't French — but her husband was — a stupid little man but she adored him. I ought to have had her and then kept her — instead of bad-tempered buggers like you, Adamson."

"You never kept me, Lady Truskmore," he told her firmly. "And now I won't keep you any longer. Good afternoon!"

"Tell Agnes I want my tea. And don't believe a word she tells you — always lied like the devil."

When he rejoined Agnes in the kitchen she had just made tea. "I didn't think you'd be long up there, Mr. Adamson. Wasn't much use, was it?"

"No, it certainly wasn't."

"Don't say I didn't warn you."

"She asked me to tell you she wanted some tea —"

"She can wait. You have yours. I fancy you'll have earned it. Did she say anything about me?"

"Her very last words were that I hadn't to believe anything you told me." And Tom grinned.

"I'm not surprised. Have some sponge cake, Mr. Adamson. I make it myself. But then I do everything in this house except the washing and the rough work."

"You must be almost a prisoner here, Agnes."

"I am. And waiting on her hand and foot as well as everything else, knowing all the time what a wicked woman she is!"

He drank some tea and then looked at her after putting down his cup. "There's something I meant to ask you earlier. Why did you stay on — to put up with all this — once you felt she was a wicked woman? I imagine somebody like you could have easily found another job."

"Of course I could. Even at my age. Half the hours, twice the money, and no insults and temper and dirty childishness. Have another cup, Mr. Adamson. I'll just attend to our tea, then I'll explain how it's been."

A few minutes later, after the kettle, the teapot, the cups, had been dealt with, she settled herself down opposite him, in a rather formal way as if she might be about to give evidence, and began: "Until I was converted — I belong to Christ's Witnesses, Mr. Adamson — I was nearly as bad as she was. I hadn't always been. I'd had a proper strict bringing-up. But she did it. Her and the Theatre. I was her dresser — if you know what that means — yes, of course you do. There every night except Sundays. And Wednesday or Thursday and Saturday afternoons, there from about quarter-past one till nearly midnight. And I can't explain what the Theatre did to me — I've never worked it out ex-

95

actly — but somehow it made me nearly as bad as she was. There's something about all that dressing-up, painting your face, pretending to have feelings, just so that people will clap you, that eats into character, decency, real goodness. And the harm it does spreads to everybody backstage. I used to laugh at narrow-minded old-fashioned people — Quakers and Methodists and suchlike — who'd have nothing to do with the Theatre. But now I don't. And I'll tell you this, Mr. Adamson, without meaning any offence. It wasn't being a painter but being half an actor that did the mischief to your father — poor man! But he was never wicked like her, just careless."

Tom nodded. "But, Agnes, you haven't explained why, after you were converted, you didn't leave her."

"I saw it was the cross I had to bear, Mr. Adamson. And I'll bear it till either she dies or I do. And now, if you'll excuse me, I'll take her tea up."

He thanked her for his and said he must go. He left Littlewold at once, but, still under the spell of this Cotswold country, he decided against going straight back to London. He passed two or three hours in bemused exploration, falling in love at first sight with Chipping Campden, wishing again more than once that he wasn't alone, dined fairly early at Burford, then headed for London on roads far emptier than they had been in the morning. They gave him time to reflect. His thinking and feeling were richly confused. In any practical sense he wasn't an inch nearer his father than he'd been when getting out of bed and wondering what to do with himself. But his feeling didn't support this, didn't tell him he'd had a wasted day. Its experiences, he felt, had taken him further into a world, not his at all up to now, which if he didn't try to escape from, didn't reject out of disgust or fear, would enable him to find his father. He drove into London and under the neon lighting still trying to work out this idea of the two worlds, the one where Tom Adamson of Sydney University felt at home, the other, like a submerged continent, where Charles Adamson, who'd been careless and anyhow hadn't had much luck, was living — and perhaps waiting.

8

CHAS rang up next morning, not long after Tom had finished breakfast and was dividing his attention between the paper and wondering what to do. One of Chas's earlier mornings. And Tom was prepared to be stiff with him, after Saturday night's bracelet affair, but was defeated by Chas's easy gay tone, that of a man who has forgotten Saturday night by Tuesday morning. There was no doubt that Chas had the gift of living tremendously in the present and communicating at once a sense of excitement about it. Tom was sure now he deeply mistrusted Chas, as everybody else seemed to do, and had started really to dislike him. Nevertheless, Tom found it hard to resist him.

"Listen, Tom, d'you like cocktail parties?"

"No, not much."

"Neither do I. Too much yap-yap-yap and they soon begin watering the drinks. Though you can usually do all right if you're looking for some enthusiastic little bint to start tearing her pants off. Anyhow, the point is, chum, my beautiful fancy foreign neighbour — you must have noticed her name, Countess Helga Lebork — is giving a party this evening. It ought to be good. She hasn't any money but she's half in some publishing racket, so all the drinks and food will be paid for by those boys. And you're invited."

"She doesn't know me."

"She knows me — and I know you. Besides, you're just the type — Australian university and all that jazz — they're trying to nobble."

"What's she like?"

"Unbelievable to look at — she'll knock your eye out, boy — but if you ask me, just another bloody foreign fraud. But what the hell! — there'll be plenty of other people there —"

"But they won't help me to find my father, will they?"

"They might at that. How do *you* know what might come of it? For God's sake, Cousin Tom, don't be so stuffy — and loosen up a bit. I know you're worried about your old man —"

"Who might be down and out somewhere," Tom put in, grimly.

"Okay, he just might. But if you're feeling like that about him, don't be so snooty, spend some money, and ask old Crike to find him for you. Crike might look a dead loss as a bishop — you remember him? — but he's a very knowing and crafty old sod."

"I can believe that, Chas. He told me on Saturday night I hadn't a hope trying to do it myself and offered to take the job on. But I turned him down. Somehow —"

"Yes, yes, yes, let's save that. I have to see a man. You come up to my place about half-six, then I'll take you down to Countess Helga's — and we'll get half-stoned and I'll find you some tasty little piece —"

"No, you'll be on your own there, Chas. I'm not in the mood. No, I don't mean I'm turning the party down. Wait a second." It was all something-and-nothing, one silly cocktail party more or less, yet he couldn't escape the feeling, as he hesitated, that he was about to take a grave decision, like a man facing two identical doors opening on unimaginable

99

things. He was being idiotic. Chas made an impatient noise.

"All right, Chas. Your place at half-past six."

After leaving the telephone he sat for a few minutes in the hotel entrance lounge. The card Crike had given him on Saturday night was in his wallet; he took it out and stared at it. Was he being a proud fool in refusing to employ Crike? At the moment he himself was making no progress at all, had no idea what the next independent move ought to be, whereas Crike, the professional bloodhound, already knew, through Bassenthwaite, something about his father that he himself didn't know. But the fact that Crike wouldn't freely offer what he knew only hardened Tom against him. There was a touch of blackmail about it. Tom couldn't help feeling he didn't want to reach his father by way of that rather sinister drooping eye of Crike's. Not without an effort he dismissed — for the day, he hoped — the thought of Crike, and rang up Belgrave to ask him to lunch, promising him a detailed account of yesterday's visit to Nelly Coping and the Manor House, Littlewold. Fortunately Belgrave was free, and though he ate and drank disappointingly little, he listened with unconcealed malicious glee to everything Tom could tell him. This left Tom curiously divided. one part of him, playing host and raconteur, was pleased and proud to capture so completely the interest and close attention of his elderly distinguished guest. The other part knew only shame and melancholy. He was ashamed of himself, for highlighting his account without any shadow of compassion, and of Belgrave, old enough to know better and so ruthless in his malice. He didn't tell him what Agnes had said about the Theatre. Perhaps he ought to have done.

At half-past six he found Chas looking at a lot of ties. "Got all these for thirty bob from a chap who'd been in the Special Tie trade and was getting out of it. He was more than half-pissed at the time. They all belong to various posh schools, colleges, regiments, athletic teams — you know this tie thing here? Whenever I'm tarting myself up a bit for a party, I wear one of 'em — it doesn't matter a damn which — and every time some clot comes up and says how glad he is to meet somebody from the Old School, the Old College, the Old Regiment, the Old Side, and I tell him how glad I am too — and now and again I suddenly find I've forgotten my wallet and touch him for a fiver. I rather like this one, don't you? Just right for the suit I'm wearing."

"Very natty," Tom told him. "What does it make you a member of — do you know?"

"I have an idea it's the International Lawn Tennis Club. And that's okay. Countess Helga isn't going to suggest we adjourn for a few sets of tennis. Lot to be said for the Special Tie when you're among us pommy bastards, cobber. Knew a fellow who lived for years on his wits, a Guards tie, and an old Rolls." Chas had now fastened his tie, and was looking himself over in the long mirror.

"You'll do, Chas. But don't start the 'cobber' stuff again. I've already told you I don't like it. Tell me something about this Countess Helga. After all, I'm going to her party."

"Time we went down too," Chas said, coming away from the mirror. "Otherwise, the drinks'll be watered and the smoked salmon will turn into slices of cheese. However, I can be putting some shoes on while I tell you all I know about darleenk Helga. That's how she talks — 'Ow you say and darleenk — the real old corn. She probably began as a waitress in Brooklyn." He was now bending over his shoes, red in the face and puffing a little. "She's one of these foreign mystery women, who come and go and nobody ever knows why they came or why they went. They always have some money, not a lot but enough to get by, and they never seem to work for it, not even on their backs."

"Apart from the bit about backs, that seems to me to describe you, Chas."

"Okay, but I don't want foreign female competition. These types like Countess Helga are a bit of the way into everything — publishing, theatre, ballet, art, antiques, cosmetics; you name it — but not very far into anything. They're often agents, but not for anybody you've ever heard of — maybe creatures from other planets. And as I told you over the phone, this one'll knock your eye out, but don't let her kid you — she didn't me, not from the first — there's nothing there except a waste of time and money. She's just a wonder girl in a wet dream. And don't say I didn't warn you."

Tom laughed. "Thanks, Chas, but I don't think it's necessary. I'm quite grown up, you know, and after all the type's not unknown in Australia. Ready?"

"Yes," and he began moving. But he stopped when they reached the door. He gave Tom what was for him a curiously sombre look. "Don't be too confident. I don't think you've run into one like this in Australia. Moreover, you may be quite grown up there but not here, not the same man really. I'm warning you." And he opened the door.

"But taking me to meet her —"

"It's an experience."

Down below they ran at once into that peculiar din which Tom had come to detest, so that on several occasions, hearing it, he had turned and run away, the sound — unlike any other — of human beings apparently enjoying themselves at a cocktail party. It never seemed a blend or ragged chorus of the actual voices, often familiar enough, of the people crowded together; it was more like the individual voice, never heard elsewhere, high and harsh and jeering pitilessly, of some collective monster they had created. Tom's impulse to turn and escape was stronger than ever before; but Chas had an arm across his shoulder, pushing him forward; and there were other people who had just arrived. Indeed, there was such a press of guests that he had time only for a glance at the woman, tallish and fair, who was greeting them, just inside the main room. But a glance was enough. Unless his eyesight was queer or he was going dotty, he had just been introduced to the most beautiful woman in the world. And not only that. Though he had never seen her before and even now had had only this one glance, he had recognised her — at once, in a flash that lit the room. He had been waiting for twenty years, ever since sex first troubled him, to set eyes on this woman.

"Might as well split up now," Chas muttered. "Never works starting to hunt in pairs. See you later. But if you miss me, don't come upstairs, I'll be busy."

Tom nodded, moved away, took a drink and gradually worked himself into a corner, simply in the hope of being able to take a long look at her. She would have to turn round soon, couldn't stand there much longer, welcoming these grinning idiots. Just to look at her was all he was asking. The idea of talking to her, perhaps claiming her undivided attention, was as yet too presumptuous altogether. He remembered with amazement and then scorn what Chas had said about her. Saturday night had been bad enough, barely forgivable, but this was the end: Chas must be written off — a dead loss. Except for that last thing he had said, after that odd sombre un-Chas look: *It's an experience*. And without knowing or caring what was in his glass, Tom drank to that.

Now at last she had turned round. He tried to make himself as tall as possible, to get a clear view of her above all the bobbing and nodding idiot heads between him and her. But he had to move a little because he was sharing this corner with three pieces of tin, battered and soldered together, now accepted in advanced circles as a work of sculpture. Yes, she was fair but quite unlike any English or Australian blonde. Her eyes, wide apart, weren't set in the usual boring fashion; they had a slight slant to them, like the eyes of some princess in an ancient folk tale from the North-East; and instead of slouching, as so many girls and women did now, she carried herself proudly, her head, with its darkish gold hair thickly knotted at the back, almost arched on her long firm neck. At least that's how it seemed to him then, as he dodged a little this way and that, to get a clearer view of her; but he was quite prepared to believe she might seem quite different soon, only remaining supremely beautiful, alien but magically so, a figure emerging at the end of a long vague dream of Woman.

Then he could no longer see her at all. An enormous man, with a creased neck like a baby's wrist magnified twenty times, completely hid her, probably while he slobbered and spat some cursed foreign rubbish at her. Tom finished his drink.

"It is good — what you are drinking?"

This came from an old shaggy sort of man who was sitting down so that Tom hadn't noticed him before.

"To tell you the truth, I really don't know," Tom said to him apologetically. "I haven't been attending to it."

The old man laughed. "No, you have been admiring our hostess."

"Well — yes, I have. Is she a friend of yours?"

"We are neighbours here. I live in the basement flat."

"Then you must be Dr. Firmius. I'm Tom Adamson — Chas Adamson's cousin — from Australia —"

"Ah! — so you begin at the top of the house and come down. Now you are here. Soon you must visit me — in the basement. In the mornings — no, I am working. In the af-

ternoon I walk in the park. But in the evenings I can always
be found below, until very late. Now you must see how it is,
Mr. Adamson." And he made a chuckling noise and gave
Tom a mischievous look. "At the top of the house, there is
energy, there is sensuous life. In the middle here, there is
beauty, there is sex, there is imagination. But only in the
basement will be found wisdom." He was old and his eyes
were deep-set and small, but they were as quick and bright
as drops of mercury. He looked and behaved like a friendly
troll king. Tom tried to stare at Countess Helga again but
had no luck. A wide waitress arrived with an equally wide
tray, offering them little glasses of vodka and bits of smoked
salmon and herring.

"A-ha — we are now in a Baltic world," Dr. Firmius
cried jovially as he helped himself.

A man and a girl, who apparently knew Dr. Firmius, took
food and drink off the tray when Tom did. A minute later
he found himself talking to the girl, who wore a dark green
dress and was squarely built and rather untidy. She didn't
interest Tom in the least but he felt he must be polite.

"I'm Judy Marston. Who are you?" She seemed to be
one of those no-nonsense girls. She had greyish eyes and a
low and rather hoarse voice.

"Tom Adamson — from Australia —"

"What do you do there?"

"I teach colonial economic history at the University in
Sydney."

"If you wrote a book, what would it be like?"

"Reasonably accurate — but dull." He was still trying to
catch at least a glimpse of the Countess.

"If you think it would be dull, probably it wouldn't be.
The people who are really dull mostly imagine they're
rather exciting."

"Do they?"

"You didn't look as if you'd be snubbing," the girl said reproachfully.

"I'm sorry. I didn't mean to be." Which wasn't strictly true, though he realised now he'd overdone it.

"If you think I'm pushing and boring, then I must explain why I'm here. Not to enjoy myself. I hate these dam' things and I go to four or five a week. Really I'm working. I'm with a publisher — never mind which or who as you're not interested — and part of my job, which is mostly reading and reporting on manuscripts, is coming to parties like this and scouting and touting round for books. That's why I asked you what yours would be like if you wrote one. See?"

"Certainly." He was still not looking at her but hoping for a glimpse of the Countess. "But just now I'm not thinking about writing a book."

"Then you must tell me what made you come all the way from Australia — Professor — Mr. — Adamson, isn't it?"

"Yes." Tom hesitated a moment. He didn't want to begin explaining and answering questions, because he was hoping the girl would go away. On the other hand, ever since he had arrrived in England he had made a point of telling people he was looking for his father, however silly it sounded, because there was always a chance he might learn something. So now for once he looked at her and spoke carefully. "I came here to find my father, Charles Adamson, whom I haven't seen for thirty-three years. What's the matter?"

She shook her head impatiently, then looked determined and rather belligerent, which wasn't difficult for her because she had a rather wide mouth and square jaw, obviously a tough, prickly sort of girl. "All right, I'll tell you. What you heard then was Judy Marston — *me* — trying to express sudden wonder and delight. Because for the first time since we started talking you really looked at me instead of staring over my shoulder to see if there was anybody more important to talk to. It's the usual cocktail-party thing of course, but I thought you might be different. You didn't imagine you'd find your long-lost father here, did you?"

He didn't like that, and his sharp "No, of course not" told her he didn't. But now he suddenly had a clear view of the Countess, and it seemed to him she threw a magical look in his direction.

"Oh!" the girl cried, first turning quickly and then looking hard at him. "I see now. You're not the cocktail-party type, after all. It's just her, isn't it? Have you known her long?"

"Never even seen her before this evening. Only exchanged about three words with her."

"But you think she's wonderful — um?"

"She seems to me," said Tom deliberately, "the most beautiful woman I've ever seen in all my life."

Judy Marston scowled at him and made a rude disgusted kind of noise. "That's what I think," she announced, as deliberate as he'd been. She was about to turn away, but added hastily, "And if you ask me, you'll never find your father. Better go back to Australia." And now she did turn away. "Oh — Dr. Firmius — what about the great opus — ?"

He'd been dismissed and he couldn't care less — good riddance! Now he could concentrate on the Countess. Another drink arrived, not vodka this time, some sort of wine. A few people were going already, the kind of people who always go early, never wanting to miss anything, never wanting to stay with it, people who exist to keep a diary of engagements. There now arrived the comforting thought that this magical woman, this golden witch, was giving the party and couldn't run away from it, however long it lasted. Soon, more and more people, having other engagements, would leave while he could stay on and on, sooner or later claiming her attention. Would that be difficult? Now for the first time he took a good look at all the other people there, moving out of his corner to examine more of them. There were a few wispy and hissing youths, but all the other men he could see — he didn't count Chas and anyhow couldn't see him — were older than he was and either fat, sweaty and booming or anxious and haggard. Though many a girl in Sydney had told him he was good-looking, he'd never been sexually vain, but now he couldn't believe she would prefer anybody here to him, not once they'd really met and talked.

The women would anyhow have been robbed of all bloom and promise by this one creature of enchantment, but they did seem to be mostly middle-aged and the only young woman he saw — apart of course from the cheeky and prickly Miss Marston — was a plumpish brunette in pink. She was in the next room, where a variety of drinks and more substantial food had been set out on a dining-room table, and Chas had taken charge of her. He gave Tom a wink to keep away and flicked a thumb towards the ceiling — and the flat above to which the brunette would soon find herself being conveyed. So Tom kept away from them, and, remembering that he might have to stay on and on, liberally helped himself at the table.

"Hello!" a woman cried at him. "We met at the Martin-Finches', didn't we? I adore them, don't you?" She was almost as tall as he was, and thin, toothy, enthusiastic, perhaps a bit pickled.

"I'm afraid I don't — no."

"Really? Well of course she has her off days — who doesn't? — and he can be tiresome —"

"I'm sorry — but I don't know them."

"Well, where *was* it then? God — my memory! Now — be nice — tell me where it was."

"It wasn't anywhere. I've only just come from Australia. Let me give you a slice of ham —"

"That's not a crack, is it?"

He gave her a smile, his first, suddenly realising she might be able to tell him something about Countess Helga. And the very thought lit up this dull room, this boring woman. "No, of course not. It's very good ham — spiced in some way —"

"Well, just a tiny piece, then. And a little salad, perhaps." And then she added, "Oh, you *are* kind," as if he'd driven a hundred miles to bring her ham and salad.

Well, now she had to earn it. "Is the Countess a friend of yours?" He tried to be so casual that he sounded like a half-wit.

"Oh no, nothing like that. I've met her around, of course. She's the kind of woman you can't help meeting around. What she does, what she's up to, what goes on, God knows! My dear man, you're falling, are you? Some men do, I know. Most don't, though. I'm not counting these mysterious foreign types she's always with. Their Queen Bee act with her is really commercial. They're all after somebody's money. Not mine. I haven't any."

Chas and the plumpish brunette in pink went into the other room, the larger one, and were obviously on their way to the flat upstairs. Tom had now taken a dislike to this toothy woman but couldn't decide on his next move. If he remained where he was, Helga might come in to take a look at the buffet, and then he had a chance of claiming her attention. If he returned to the other room, where she actually and wonderfully was, he might find himself lost in her peculiar entourage. What to do, then? He was not as a rule a dithery fellow but now he found himself suffering from a paralysis of will, which, as he realised later, came creeping into all his relations with Helga.

Finally, sensing his lack of interest in her, the woman broke off her bright toothy chat and announced that she was going. Tom lingered on after she had gone, trying to eat a weird salad, possibly regarded as a treat in Lithuania. Then, just as he was cursing himself for his indecision, Helga came in, having apparently dismissed her entourage. Not only that but she came straight up to him. He had vaguely hoped for this, as one does for a miracle, but he had certainly not willed it, not having any will to set to work. Helga, as again he realised later, was outside the will.

She said at once that she knew he was the cousin of Chas who had come all the way from Australia, after many years, to find his father. She also said, after some stammerings from him, that he must come and meet some of her special friends and that afterwards, when she was not so busy as a hostess, he and she might have some little talk together, if he would like that. Much later, when he was back in his bedroom but much too excited for sleep, he found that just as he couldn't remember what she looked like, it was equally impossible to remember *exactly* what she said, only the mere gist of it. Her voice, he knew, was quick and low-pitched and foreign in a special delicious way, and was as entrancing as her appearance, but that was all he did know for certain. And trying to remember exactly how she had behaved and what she had said was like trying to remember a dream. What mostly remained for memory to feed on was a figure in a golden haze, a shining magic, a spell lighter than air and terrible as a thunderbolt. He had always been of the secret opinion that the poets, so often overpraised, were given to gross exaggeration; but now, sitting half-undressed in his bedroom, he knew he'd been wrong. He also knew that after asking her to lunch with him and being told she wasn't free for lunch, he had pressed her to dine with him tomorrow night and that after some heart-shaking hesitation she had agreed and had named the restaurant — for eight-thirty. And now he saw that the great problem was how to get rid of the hours, how to shovel them into the incinerator where they belonged, until the rockets went up, to signal that life was beginning again, round about eight-thirty tomorrow night.

9

He had not been awake ten minutes next morning before he knew what he had to do not long after breakfast. He wasn't exactly abandoning the search for his father, even if in this Helga atmosphere it now seemed a drab little project, but he saw that the only sensible thing to do was to employ Crike, the professional, the expert. So after breakfast he rang the number on the card Crike had given him, only to be told that Crike wasn't there but might be coming in later, perhaps about noon. He wrote a couple of letters, full of nothing because he never mentioned Helga, and killed an hour or so with a meaningless ramble. The weather was still fine but had now lost all heat; indeed there was a wind that might have come straight from Greenland. Most of the people he saw looked discontented, as if they too were killing time but not doing it fast enough.

He was back just before noon but Crike didn't call him until nearly half-past twelve. Crike said he could be at the hotel about quarter to one, practically inviting himself to lunch. He arrived on time and Tom invited him to lunch. Out of his bishop costume and wearing an old and rather shiny black suit, Crike looked like an unsuccessful undertaker or a rather shady solicitor; his eye drooped and watered harder than ever; and Tom didn't take to him. After drinking two large pink gins, he ordered the most expensive items on the menu and devoured them as if he'd had no solid food since Saturday night.

"Don't mind me," he told Tom. "I'll admit it, I'm fond of my food. I can do without it if I have to — and sometimes on a case I may have to make do with a few sandwiches — hate the things too; curse of this country — but when there's good wholesome food to be had, I order it and enjoy it, Mr. Adamson. Not a bad fillet steak, this, not bad at all. Incidentally I've run into this headwaiter somewhere before today. And he knows it. And he knows I know he knows it — if you see what I mean, Mr. Adamson?"

"I do, Mr. Crike. But let's talk business now. What are your terms?"

"They vary. I'm very stiff with divorce people. But I'll be easy with you, Mr. Adamson. It's an interesting case — rather out of the ordinary — a bit of a challenge — and I'll take it on for fifty pounds a week plus expenses — all itemised and quite reasonable. You can afford that, I imagine, Mr. Adamson — um?"

Tom said he could, but that if the search went on for weeks and weeks it might prove to be very expensive.

"Quite so," said Crike. "And I was coming to that. In a case of this sort, a bonus is the fairest thing. If I find him by the end of the first week, you give me a hundred pounds bonus. If it takes two weeks, only fifty pounds bonus. After that, no bonus. Obviously I'd rather collect the bonus and get on with some other job than lie down on this one. Quite fair, isn't it, Mr. Adamson?"

Tom thought it was, and then asked him how long he considered it would take.

"Without any information at all — two weeks. With the start that Bassenthwaite's given me, I might do it in a week. And you'll receive a full careful daily report, Mr. Adamson.

Now I suggest we take our coffee in some quiet corner of the lounge, and if you're thinking about a cigar, I'll join you. I like a cigar after lunch."

Tom didn't, but he offered Crike one, if only as a prize for his impudence.

In the lounge, behind his cigar and over his coffee, Crike opened out. "You can consider this my first report, Mr. Adamson. Now I can tell you what Bassenthwaite told me. And we have our first bit of luck here. Ten to one it'll prove to be a Midlands job and I've had a lot of cases in the Midlands and know my way around there. I'm very hot both in London and the Midlands. Not so hot in the North, and — I'll be frank with you, Mr. Adamson — no dam' good in the South-West — the thick-cream places."

Crike contrived to grin without taking out his cigar. Tom nodded, but he was wondering where Helga was and what she was doing. The thought of her darkened the lounge, not the brightest of places at any time, and made it and Crike seem equally dingy and tedious, exiled from magic forever.

"In 1949 Bassenthwaite was with a twice-nightly Rep at Sutwick, an industrial town in the West Midlands," Crike began in a businesslike, reporting-to-client manner. "He was more or less running it because the so-called director, who'd put up most of the money, was young and inexperienced. Your father came right out of the blue and saw Bassenthwaite. They'd acted together in the West End before the war. Your father didn't try to hide anything. He'd done time in one of those first-offenders' camp prisons, somewhere between Sutwick and Birmingham. He was calling himself Charles Archer. This sort of name-changing is very common. You keep your first name because if you've had it a long time it's not easy to get used to another. You choose a surname with the same initial because you may have bags and other things with your initials on. Anyhow, he was now Charles Archer."

Tom repeated the name slowly. "By the way," he went on, "do you think he's still Charles Archer?"

"Depends on what he's been up to," Crike replied rather apologetically. "If he's kept out of trouble and he's a reasonable man, he won't have changed his name again. Much to lose and nothing to gain. I'll assume until I know different that I'm looking for Charles Archer. Now then, Mr. Adamson. He begged Bassenthwaite to get him taken on — doing anything — acting, stage management, scene-painting, anything. Bassenthwaite needed help as much as Charles Archer needed a job, but it took a lot of arguing to squeeze another salary out of that Sutwick company. In the end he was taken on at nine pounds a week, doing anything and everything he was told to do, a real dog's body, starting about ten in the morning and finishing at midnight. And he stuck it too, Bassenthwaite told me. He was still there when the Sutwick Repertory Company packed up in the summer of '50."

"I see," Tom said, chiefly because Crike, who was doing something to his cigar with a penknife, paused as if hoping for some comment. "And then what?"

"Nothing for certain, of course. That's where I start. Now Bassenthwaite, who knew what was coming, went straight off to join a company somewhere in Scotland. Charles Archer — I'll call him that to keep it all tidy — didn't know what he was going to do."

"So now he disappears."

"Maybe, maybe not. There was just one little bit of a clue Bassenthwaite could offer me. And it's lucky for us he has such a good memory. Charles Archer was very friendly — *very* friendly — with an oldish woman, a Mrs. Jones, who owned and ran a big pub in Colston, just outside Sutwick. She used to visit the Sutwick Rep every Monday, taking a night off from the pub. And Charles Archer often went out there on Sunday lunchtimes, about all he ever had to himself. That's all I've got, Mr. Adamson, but it's *something*. And I'm hoping to begin my enquiries tonight at that pub in Colston. I don't even know the name of it yet — Bassenthwaite himself never went there — but I'll soon find it. And you'll have my first report — all neatly typed — day after tomorrow, Friday morning. This address of course — um? Good! Now I've given you all I have, Mr. Adamson. I want what you've got."

"What do you mean?"

"I mean — everything you can remember about your father. I know it's a long time ago —"

"It's thirty-three years —"

"Never mind. Tell me everything you remember. I must have it."

This was reasonable enough, but Tom could have yawned in his face. However, he plodded through the next fifteen minutes, offering every detail that remained in his memory while Crike, looking stern and important now, not cunning, scribbled in a dilapidated notebook that looked as if it had figured in innumerable unsavoury divorce cases.

"And that's all?" said Crike when Tom stopped talking.

"That's all."

"Thanks very much, Mr. Adamson." Crike put his notebook away. "Might be useful. Might not. But I'll make one point — very frankly. Don't expect to see — if I bring it off — the man you've just been talking about. He's gone. A lot's happened in those thirty-three years —"

"I know, I know —" Tom sounded weary because he felt weary. He'd had enough of Crike, perhaps had enough of his lost father.

Crike got up and began brushing cigar ash off his coat. "There's just one other thing, Mr. Adamson. It's too late to get to my bank and I want to be on the move. Could you let me have a cash advance on expenses — just for convenience?"

After Tom had looked into his wallet, he hesitated. "I've about twenty pounds here, Mr. Crike. You can have them if I can be sure the hotel can cash a cheque for me. I'm giving somebody dinner tonight in a fashionable restaurant —"

"A-ha! A-ha!" Crike had instantly transformed himself into an elderly satyr. Then he waved a hand and became a man of the world, somebody in the City perhaps. "Not to worry, not to worry! They'll cash a cheque for you here — fifty cheques. But if you'll be easier in your mind, let's make sure." And he led the way to the cashier.

No sooner had Tom spoken to the girl than Mrs. O'Shea, the magnificent manageress, popped out of her office next door. Tom, who hadn't exchanged more than a quick passing word or two with her for days, gave her a rather apologetic smile.

"Come in here to write your cheque, Mr. Adamson, and if it's for the kind of money we have, then it'll be no trouble at all."

"Thank you, I'll be with you in a minute, Mrs. O'Shea." He gave Crike the twenty pounds and went with him to the door and then outside.

"I'll tell you frankly," Crike said solemnly, "nowadays I'm not as fond of moving around and interviewing people as I used to be. At least nine cases out of ten go to my two assistants. I prefer to see clients at the office and then go home, instead of looking for beds and breakfasts in all kinds of bloody awful places. I'm taking your case myself because it's unusual, it's a real challenge to an old trained investigator, and I like you and I want to find your father for you,

Mr. Adamson." Crike jammed on, a little to one side, his old-fashioned black homburg, and held out his hand to be shaken. He looked such a scoundrel that Tom felt he really must be honest.

"Read and keep my reports, Mr. Adamson, even if your mind's on other things. As soon as I'm sure I *have* found your father — ten days at the most, I'd say, possibly within a week — I'll send you a wire. Ta-ta, then!"

Tom wrote out a cheque for forty pounds, which Mrs. O'Shea passed through her little window to the cashier. As soon as she had closed the window she settled down for a gossip. "The money'll be there waiting for you, but you're not leaving this room until you've told me any news you have about finding your Dad. And who was that you had with you?"

"His name's Crike. He's a private investigator who's undertaken to find my father —"

"A Private Eye, is it?" cried Mrs. O'Shea. "Well, he looked as big a villain as I've seen for many a day, that one."

"I know. For some reason, he tries so hard to look a villain that I think he must be an honest man."

"But maybe that's what he knows you'll think, if you catch my meaning."

"The double bluff. You've been reading spy stories, Mrs. O'Shea."

"I might have at that. But have you discovered anything about your poor old Dad?"

He told her what he had learnt, prison and all.

"He's had no luck at all, the poor man. But I'll tell you this, Mr. Adamson, and I'm nearly twice your age and I've had twenty times the experience. There's many a good man who's found himself in prison. And there's many a black-hearted villain, living off the fat of the land, who's never been near a dock. So don't feel too bad because you know your Dad's been inside. Keep after him so you can be a comfort to him in his old age. Or is it all to be done now by this Private Eye?" She gave him a shrewd look.

"Well," Tom began, but then stopped. He met the look again. "When he first offered to do the job, I turned him down. But then I changed my mind. After all he's a pro and I'm not only an amateur but a stranger in this country. He can probably do more in a day than I could in a month." But he knew he sounded lame.

Mrs. O'Shea went into her soothsayer act, sitting up straight and closing her eyes. "I've one of my strong feelings — you remember them? — and it's telling me your head's full of a girl, and that's why somebody else can find your Dad for you." She opened her eyes now to their full blue glare.

"I suppose you're right — to some extent," he muttered.

"You'll be taking her out tonight. And that's why you must have money."

He admitted rather sheepishly he had persuaded this girl or woman to dine with him, and that he had an idea the restaurant she had chosen might be expensive. And under further pressure, he gave Mrs. O'Shea the name of the restaurant.

"It might be expensive, you say," she cried. "I tell you it'll be ruinous. I'm in the trade, don't forget. You'll be robbed. A pound for a bit of sole to start with. Thirty shillings for a steak. Eighteen-and-six for a helping of asparagus. Six shillings for a spoonful of runner beans. Coffee — five shillings. Nothing on the wine list — not even the *vin rosé* they buy at eighty shillings a dozen — under two-pound-ten. Highway robbery by candlelight, that's what you'll be asking for, young man. And the young woman who chose it either knows too much or knows too little."

"She's not English. She's Countess Helga Lebork."

"And you haven't known her long?"

"I met her last night at a party she gave."

"And what's she like?"

Then the dam burst. He'd been waiting all day to describe Helga to somebody. Out came the princess from the far folk-tale, the smiling enchantress, the golden witch, the woman at the edge of every dream and behind all music, now robed and crowned by his eloquence.

"And that's her," said Mrs. O'Shea coolly when at last he had finished.

He nodded, offering her a tentative smile.

"Well, I've heard about her before," Mrs. O'Shea said. "Oh — not Countess What's-it — but *her* — it's all the same. From men of course. Usually younger than you, but not always. And of course there isn't any such person. She doesn't exist — except in your daft heads. Any woman in her right mind knows *that one* just isn't there. You've made her up. You've gone down and down inside yourself to find her — instead of going out to find your father. A real woman's another person, like yourself but having trouble with her girdle, taking something for constipation, on the lookout for a bit more security and new curtains for the bedroom, if possible reduced by twenty per cent from the original selling price. And be damned to golden fairy princesses!"

"What you're really saying," said Tom sulkily, "is that men shouldn't fall in love."

"And — by God — I am not," Mrs. O'Shea shouted. "It's the very last thing you'd ever find me saying. I'll never see sixty-five again but I'm waiting and ready for a man — not any man but the right one for me — to come through that door, look me straight in the eye, and tell me he loves me." She stopped there to reach out and pat him on the knee. "You're a decent upstanding young man," she continued in a lower and gentler tone, "and if I hadn't taken a fancy to you — and the way you came across the world to find your Dad — you wouldn't be here this minute. I'm your friend. You've got it bad so now you're hurrying, time and money no object, on your way to nothing. I ask you as your friend to be careful. And to tell me what happens. And if you should come across a girl who's solidly there, a person, and she bothers you and you don't care for her very much, tell me about her too. And the sooner the better, I say. If I knew one that was right, I'd plant her in your way so you'd find yourself falling over her. And that's not meant as a dirty joke neither. Well, off you go now to get your money, for I've fifty bills, half of 'em a swindle, to look through — God save us!"

He told himself as he went that after all she was rather a silly old woman.

10

AFTERWARDS, Tom could never recollect properly, make any shape and sense out of, this Helga-time. He never asked himself to remember any of it while it was happening. Then, immediately it was over, he wanted to ignore the fact that this time had ever existed. And then, long afterwards, when he no longer felt he'd simply been a fool, when he really wished to know what he'd done, thought, felt, while in pursuit of Helga, the time refused to be sorted out into days in which certain things happened: it remained a blur of a mish-mash. He had spent longer than a week but less than a fortnight trying, it might be said, to juggle with large coloured jellyfish.

However, one central thing, the cause of all, stayed in his memory, refusing to be blotted out by self-censorship. This was the spell, her involuntary sorcery. There were moments during this time, he believed, when he guessed what he knew for certain afterwards — that it was he himself and not Helga who was really responsible for the bewitchment. *Magic for the act kindly supplied by T. Adamson, Esq.* But even if he did guess the truth now and again, it made no difference. Where she was, there the magic was, even if in fact he had brought it with him. There wasn't a glimmer of it when he was away from her and not about to meet her. Indeed — and this was a good reason for spending as much time as possible with her — everything seemed sullen and tedious without her. Away from that entrancing little light in which she seemed to move, London was just one vast grey boredom. While the spell worked, there was no opposition to her worth considering. To feel alive, he had to be with her or on his way to her.

Yet there was one unconquered remote part of him, beyond the spell, that reminded him, increasingly too as one daft day followed another, that when he was with her and her many acquaintances, he was not really himself. There were disconcerting moments when he suddenly heard himself and wondered if he were turning into somebody else. Normally he spoke rather deliberately in a low-pitched voice. So who was this, then, who joined in the excitable chatter with no noticeable break from it in rhythm or pitch? Moreover, when he was with her he accepted without a single snort of disapproval the kind of people — and they existed in Sydney and weren't peculiar to London or indeed, he suspected, any large city — that he'd always avoided before.

Their favourite term — and they worked it to death — was *exciting*. At lunch, at tea, before dinner, during dinner, after dinner until two in the morning, they hurried to meet one another and cry *Exciting!* They seemed to exist not so much on the outer edges of all the arts as on the one far edge of art itself, where painting turned into sculpture and sculpture into some weird form of ballet, which in turn dissolved into electronic music or avant-garde films or drama: all *exciting*. Like Helga herself many of them were as cosmopolitan as a many-starred hotel, exiles from Ruritania or somewhere, able to speak in any country with a foreign accent. And behind this excitement, waiting to be excited it-self sooner or later, was some vague — at least it was vague to Tom — international and very rich jet-set, determined to be trend-setters and switched-on. But the immediate eco-nomics of all this, where any actual money was being earned, who in fact paid the bills, were a complete mystery to Tom, who, though he never associated Helga with prac-tical matters of any sort, couldn't help wondering about her acquaintances. If Helga ever did any business with them, or if they ever did any business with one another, it was never when he was around. To him this whole *It-is-new-experi-mental-very-exciting* life seemed to exist in an economic vacuum.

He knew about some bills, of course, because he paid them himself, for lunches and dinners generally in stagger-ingly expensive restaurants. But it was he who implored Helga to meet him in these places. Even afterwards, when this whole pursuit of her appeared to him so much idiocy, he never accused her to himself of deliberately exploiting his infatuation. She rarely talked about herself, but from one or two casual remarks he gathered she had little or no income; she was one of the mysterious poor who contrive to lead the lives of the rich — and indeed improve upon them by enjoying all the good things without feeling any sense of guilt or dubious responsibility. And he had an idea that she thought him much better off than he actually was. Never-theless, unlike that tireless sponger, Chas, she never once asked him to lend her any money. In fact she never men-tioned money. It was part of her mystery, her golden sor-cery, that she appeared to live in a world beyond economics, like a figure in a myth or fairytale. And it was into some such world, outside history or whatever might be in the newspapers, that she drew him every time he set eyes on

her. A smile, a single glance, enticed him away from all recorded centuries. When they dined alone — and it was
then that the magic worked — they might have been subjects of Agamemnon, King Arthur, or Haroun-al-Raschid.

The trouble was, he could rarely keep her to himself. Afternoon or evening there was nearly always some arrange-
ment, at once curiously vague and yet imperative, that
meant he must either leave her or accompany her to some
gathering, which might be at a publisher's or art dealer's or
a party in a hotel suite or somebody's flat, where more or
less the same people cried *Exciting!* at one another. And as
he didn't want to leave her, with everything grey and flat
after the magic had gone, he had to endure these parties
and conspiring groups, in which she herself never took the
lead but simply smiled and nodded and said what everybody else was saying, though never appearing to be in the
least degree excited herself. But then he was always aware
of her and merely saw the others as so many grotesque figures painted on curtains that shook or rippled behind her.
And sometimes she gave him a special look, touched his
hand, pressed his arm. The Excitings, however, stayed up
until all hours, and by the time he had taken her back to
Ashtree Place, at the end of a long daft blur of a day, she
was beginning to look wan and fragile. Her voice would be
no more than a murmur, in which there were often more
foreign words than English, as if she were now too tired to
remember which country she was in. So it seemed sheer
brutality to demand more than a brief embrace, the ghost
of a kiss.

And then suddenly — and afterwards he remembered
this very moment when he could hardly recall a single word
she'd ever said — he decided this just bloody-well wouldn't
do. He'd had enough of the Excitings and all the arrange-

125

ments that put a glass wall between him and this woman. All right, she was still the golden sorceress, the pale princess, some witch-queen out of a Northern folk-tale, a creature closer to mythology than to the world of passports, hotel registers and bank accounts, but — damn it all — she was a woman too. And while the mythological realm she drew him into might be outside history and economics, it certainly wasn't outside the commerce of the sexes that went a great deal further than hand-touching, arm-pressing, ghostly little kisses. Now he wanted her, magic and all, the lot.

He told her so — and this he remembered quite clearly afterwards — told her urgently, rather bluntly, though not without any cover of tenderness. It was an ultimatum. They would dine together the following night — she wasn't free for lunch — but only if there were no arrangements to go anywhere except straight back to her flat. She knew what he meant, of course, and she protested. It would spoil everything. Rather savage in his new role of the aggressive male, he told her he hadn't heard that one for a long time and had never expected to hear it again. She said sadly that she had spoken only the exact truth. But he hadn't to press her again. Now she suddenly capitulated, and in a weary and melancholy fashion that left him feeling uneasy. If it had been for that night, instead of the next, he might even have abandoned his plan of conquest. As it was, they went to yet another small party, given on the confusing frontier between advanced art and nonsense, and once again heard *Exciting!* exclaimed in a half-dozen different accents — though there was an exception on this occasion, a hairy young genius from Birmingham who cried, "Smashin'! Smashin'!" And Tom sat by himself on a sofa, while the others raved together in the middle of the room, and drank more than his share of a sour white wine. He might have felt happier if he had known then that this was the last of these Excitings parties he would ever attend.

Next night they sat far longer than usual over their coffee. After warning him again that he was about to spoil everything, she was silent, seemingly empty and sad. Nor did he say very much; none of the meaningless bright chat that a man so often spreads over a girl like a cloak when already, in her imagination, she is taking her clothes off and perhaps hastily apologising for some physical defect. He couldn't hear Helga doing this, in spite of her obvious reluctance; he couldn't believe she had any such defect; and he already knew a kind of smouldering lust in which there were sparks of anger. He had never come close to any sort of brutality before in making love; even that tall, too-dignified girl in Sydney, who had submitted to his embraces with an air of faint surprise, as if she were being compelled to try on an obviously ridiculous costume, had never aroused anything brutal in him; but now, even though she was sitting fully dressed by his side in a public place, Helga's suggestion of a weary submissiveness, of something at once inert and yet sacrificial, when accompanied as it was by the sheer physical challenge of her unpossessed beauty, added those sparks of anger that might flame and roar later in brutality.

Without making any further protest or warning him again, she left him in her sitting room with a drink and, after whispering that she would be ready when the light went out, she moved slowly into her bedroom, leaving the door behind her slightly ajar. He waited, feeling already aggrieved, a little angrier still, because, although it was impossible she could be a prude, she was making sure he couldn't even enjoy the sight of her nakedness. Something calculating and grudging here, perhaps paying the smallest possible price he would accept. But wasn't he as bad, even to entertain such thoughts? And then, finishing his drink and looking around the room, he remembered — and it all rose like a fountain — the party here when the mere sight of her had been a wonder and a joy, and how he had tried to catch another glimpse of her while that irritating aggressive girl had been questioning him, and how from those moments onward, until the last twenty-four hours when he felt he had to possess her, all had been magical. This left him feeling uncertain, uneasy; but then a suspicious male in him, bent on avoiding frustration, came trotting and peering out of some primeval forest, and with him came desire heated by anger. And then the light in the bedroom went out.

He entered without a word, stared in the dark and knew rather than saw she was lying naked on the bed, tore off his clothes and took her. And as he did he couldn't prevent himself remembering something he had once read, in an account of fundamentally different human types, to the effect that with some women, no matter how alluring they might seem, a man could feel nothing, through lack of some essential polarity. Because that was what he was feeling now — nothing. It was all nothing, nothing, nothing. Perhaps he may have even said it aloud.

Certainly he never said anything else. What was there to say? While he groped around for his clothes, he thought he heard a faint sound from the bed. By the time he was half-dressed, it was more than a faint sound. So — she was crying, was she? He was about to mutter some apology when sheer surprise compelled him to speak. "Why — you're not crying. By God — you're *laughing*."

"Why not, you fool? And you can't say I didn't warn you." It was the last thing he ever heard Helga say, and the only speech of hers of which he remembered every single syllable.

On the way out he stopped outside the door leading down to the basement, where the shaggy Dr. Firmius lived. He wanted to talk to somebody, and after all at the party the old man had given him an open invitation to call. He rang the bell.

11

"D<small>R</small>. Firmius, I don't suppose you remember me — Tom Adamson —"

"Yes, yes, I do. Come in, come in."

"Do you mind? I mean — it's rather late —"

"Not for me. In you come. I'm just making a fresh pot of coffee. You must have some. Come on, now."

Dr. Firmius looked exactly as he had done at the party except that now he was wearing carpet slippers and an old linen jacket burnt or blackened in several places. He was a troll king at home. The basement room into which he led Tom was really quite large but there was only sufficient space in the middle of it for a desk and its chair, two lopsided and sagging armchairs, and a small stool. All round this central space, in an extraordinary higgledy-piggledy, were books, apparently piled in front of full shelves, all manner of odd objects, and drawings and photographs. It was as if a library and an anthropological museum, threatened by some catastrophe, had been crammed and rammed into this one room. Tom had time to look around him because Dr. Firmius had disappeared between two piles of books, presumably into a kitchen somewhere to attend to the coffee. He returned, carrying a coffeepot and two large cups without saucers.

"It is black. You don't mind?"

"I prefer it, thank you, Dr. Firmius. But you're sure I'm not a nuisance, coming as late as this, when perhaps you want to work?"

"No, no. I have finished my work for today. If you sit in that chair, it is not too bad. That is, so long as you don't argue with too much excitement. Then you fall out of the chair. You would like a cigar with your coffee? I have some somewhere — rather old, too dry perhaps. No?" He disposed of the coffee cups and then relit a large curved pipe, scattering a few sparks, endangering the linen coat again. Tom wondered where he came from; he was certainly not English; he had a kind of generalised foreignness — like Helga — but — no, enough of that.

"No more apologies now, Mr. Adamson. Didn't I say to you that soon you must visit me?"

"Yes. Wisdom in the basement, you said."

"A-ha! You remember?"

Tom looked at him. Somehow it wasn't hard to believe that the old man knew exactly what had happened upstairs and what Tom was feeling. "Did you know I was up there tonight, Dr. Firmius?"

"I guessed you were, Mr. Adamson. Just a guess. No second sight. No sorcery. However, in spite of my age — and I'm eighty — I'm an observant man. And I hear and see and learn a lot down here. So I put two and two together — guess a little — and make them six or eight or ten."

"You won't hear me on my way up there again," Tom told him sombrely. "I've been a dam' fool. And I can't pretend I was never warned. *Nothing*, they said. And — by God! — they were right."

"For you — yes, they were right. There was nothing."

"In the end — no — just nothing." Tom drank some coffee, which was very strong, and brooded for a few moments. "But there was magic while it lasted. Now I'm sensible again, telling myself I've been a bloody fool. Sensible but sad. No magic. Then, who's winning?"

"Nobody wins. We are not fighting a battle or playing a game. As for the magic you speak of, it is not something that has been spent and wasted. It arose from your own depths. As if you had brought up a great searchlight to illuminate and then transform the face of poor Helga, who is neither wicked nor wonderful — rather shallow, rather greedy, rather sly — but with her own good qualities. And now your magic will descend again into those depths. But take care not to fasten a lid over them. There are now so many bored and empty people living on that lid. And when it is blown off then terrible things happen. And after all to run foolishly after Helga — using her as a sheet for your magic lantern — with everything over so quickly, this is no terrible thing."

"Possibly not, Dr. Firmius. No doubt a man loses his sense of proportion when he suddenly falls through the floor —"

"But into the basement, my friend, don't forget —"

"I don't want to explain it all now," Tom went on doggedly, "but I came here to find my father —"

"I know that — yes —" No doubt he was a kind and wise old man, but he cut in a bit too often.

"From the start I knew a mile down that it was essential I must do my damnedest to try to find him. That's why, though I hate making a fool of myself, I didn't hesitate to tell people what I was doing here. It was a kind of test. So what do I do? As soon as I've met Helga, I stop looking for my father, I stop even thinking about him, I hire an old rogue of a private detective to find him and don't even study the reports he sends me. I'm ashamed of myself."

"More coffee? No? Then tell me this. If there had been

no Helga and foolishness, no private detective, would you now have discovered your father?"

"I doubt it. I doubt it very much indeed," Tom added gloomily. "I knew my father had been sent to prison not long after the war. And that was all. I was at a dead end. All I could have done was to appeal for any information about him through advertising. On the other hand, Crike — the detective — had found out by a lucky chance —"

"I don't believe in lucky chances," said Dr. Firmius, at it again. "They are something else. I am sorry — please continue —"

"Crike knew where my father had worked for a time and what name he'd used. And this gave him a starting point, which I hadn't got, because he refused to share this information unless I employed him. And before I began running after Helga, I told him I wouldn't employ him."

Dr. Fermius gave him a bright and crinkly, troll-king look. "Then because you met Helga, the search for your father went on. And now, when there is no more Helga for you, then you can take up the search too, in a way that was impossible before, and you can stop being proud and angry with yourself. Is that not so?"

Tom offered him a grudging nod. "One thing puzzles me, though," he said after a pause. "How did you know about my father? I remember now I never mentioned him to you at Helga's party."

"That is true. But you spoke of him to Miss Judy Marston, who afterwards told me. Miss Marston works for my publishers and comes here to tell me to hurry up with my book —"

"Yes, I heard her say something about your great opus —"

"Quite so. But she comes here also as a friend. When she is tired of the young — who are not so fascinating as they imagine themselves to be — she comes, often late at night like this, to listen to one of the Ancients of Days. We speak about my book too. I believe that men and women in their forties — not all of course, but some — should spend a year at a special kind of university. You understand about the ordinary universities, Mr. Adamson. You teach in one yourself. They offer young people various sorts of knowledge that will enable them to acquire degrees, preparing them for all manner of professions and gainful pursuits."

"I know all about that of course," Tom told him rather grimly. "I ought to by this time. But what about your special kind of university?"

"It will be concerned entirely with culture and wisdom." Dr. Firmius's tone was serious but not solemn, and he twinkled away as usual. "It will try to rescue men and women in their forties — often a desperate age — from emptiness and despair. My book, which already is much too long, I'm afraid, will offer a kind of ground plan for such a university — what it will teach, how it will teach, and who should be its teachers. And so on and so forth — and perhaps too much 'so on' and too much 'so forth.' "

"I'd very much like to read this book, Dr. Firmius. And I'm not just being polite —"

"No, no. I know that, Mr. Adamson. You have too many troubles of your own just now."

"What does Miss Thing — Marston — think about it?"

"Chiefly she thinks it is becoming too long and taking too much time. She brings messages from her employers. Otherwise, as a friend, sometimes she agrees with everything, sometimes she disagrees. She is a young woman who speaks her mind; though, like most young women, she does not bring all her mind to the discussion. Often, most of it is really elsewhere, thinking about other things, some life plan that has not yet matured."

"What made her tell you about me and my father, Dr. Firmius? She told me — suddenly losing her temper, God knows why — I'd never find him and I'd better go back to Australia."

"That is what she believes. She mentioned it again, the other night. She appears to have a special interest in this father-search." Dr. Firmius spoke with a mock-solemnity now, and there was about him an air of mischief that irritated Tom.

"Well, the next time she mentions it, I wish you'd tell her from me to mind her own dam' business," he cried angrily.

The old man shook his head. "It is useless to tell a young woman to mind her own business, because we never know what that business is. Indeed, the phrase is meaningless except in the masculine world. However, it will not be I who will bring you into our next discussion. She doesn't like you, Mr. Adamson."

"And I don't like her." Tom got up. "But it's too late to explain why. And it's been exceedingly kind of you, Dr. Firmius, to let me call here —"

"You feel a little better — ?"

"Twice the man I was when I came down those stairs — blinding and cursing myself and everybody else —"

"Yes, it is better sometimes to try the basement. By the way, what about the top floor? You still see your cousin there?"

"No, I feel I'm through with Chas, who's just no good."

"No good for what?"

"For anything. When we first talked he swore he'd be able to find my father in no time — and of course it was all nonsense. He's been absolutely useless."

"Are you certain of this?"

Tom checked himself, thought for a moment. "No, I'm

not," he said slowly. "In fact, in his own way, he's been far from useless. A lot of things have happened — directly or indirectly — through Chas. Even so, I shall try to keep out of his way."

"But not, I hope, out of mine. Any night when you feel a need to talk — or of course to listen, which of course I would prefer you to do — then you will find me here."

"That's very kind —"

"No, no! Besides, I am curious about this father-seach — like my friend, but not yours, Miss Judy Marston. I wish to know what happens. So promise to come and tell me, Mr. Adamson."

"I look forward to that, Dr. Firmius. Goodnight!"

There was a telegram waiting for him at the hotel:

FATHER FOUND STOP CAN YOU MEET ME FLEECE INN HAYPORT NOON TOMORROW

CRIKE

And he surprised himself as he went up to his room. No joy, no excitement, no impatient longing to start out for Hayport here and now; nor, on the other hand, any definite suspicion of Crike; no, just a vague sad feeling that made no sense at all. But then he was always surprising himself — though not with joy — these days.

12

IT was nearly half past twelve when Tom parked the Allerton-Fawcet, which he had mastered now, outside the pub where Crike would be waiting for him. The Fleece Inn and Hayport together suggested a lingering rusticity, not easy to find in this part of the Midlands. But if Hayport had ever been a charming little market town, it certainly wasn't one now. It wasn't anything to which a decent name could be given. It was a featureless mess of newish concrete and blackened old brick, of small factories and large sheds, of roads going nowhere in particular and streets of houses intended for unambitious dwarfs. The place was unlucky, Tom decided, not to have been bombed to bits. The Fleece was half spoilt-old, half uneasy-new, like so much of England.

Crike was in the saloon bar. He had changed his rusty black for a tweed suit of an unpleasant shade of green, and he looked like an auctioneer waiting to do crooked deals with farmers. He was staring at a racing paper, as if to keep himself in character. For some moments he didn't notice Tom, who kept quiet and regarded him with distaste. This was the man who'd had to find his father for him — while he'd been prancing round Helga like an imbecile!

"Well, here at last, Mr. Adamson! Now what'll you have? On me this time. Must celebrate — um?"

"I'll have a glass of beer, thanks, Mr. Crike."

"Don't recommend it — still, if that's what you want —" And he called for the beer and another whisky for himself, and then suggested they should sit at a little table in the corner where they could talk without being overheard. "Hardly anybody here now but it may fill up about one o'clock. Though they don't do a hot lunch here, just sandwiches and stuff. I'll ask for some presently. Best I can do for you, Mr. Adamson — sorry!"

"That's all right, Mr. Crike. I didn't come here to eat."

Crike decided that this deserved a laugh, but went on to say that although he liked his food, as he'd admitted when they last met, if he was really hot on a case, as he'd been on this one, he hardly knew when or where he ate. This took them to the table, where, after Crike had drunk about half his whisky and had given his moist drooping eye a dab or two, he suddenly burst into speech as if to shatter the odd silence between them.

"With all due respect, Mr. Adamson — and if I may speak frankly to a client — I'm rather disappointed in you. You've come here as soon as you could, of course — drove down, I imagine — and I know that can be tiring, especially in these parts with so much heavy traffic — but I really did expect to find you a bit livelier. After all, your father's here — safe and sound. Unless of course, after all this time, you're rather dreading meeting him." And the good eye gave Tom a sharp look.

"Partly that, probably. Partly feeling tired after the drive down — and it's all so damned ugly round here. Partly — oh — various things! You're sure it's my father?"

"Now, now, Mr. Adamson — really — that won't do! Of

138

course I am — or you and I wouldn't be sitting here. It's not been a long job, as these cases go, but it's been very tricky and I've had to stick at it, as you must know from my reports, Mr. Adamson."

"To tell you the truth, Mr. Crike — and I'm sorry if this comes as a shock — though of course I've had your reports — and have them with me now, in the bag I left in the car — I've not been able so far to consider them carefully —"

"Well, I must say you surprise me —"

"I've had other things on my mind — which incidentally are no longer there — and I didn't read your telegram until late last night. Then I've spent all this morning getting here. So, if you don't mind, let's forget about the reports for the moment. After all, they don't matter if you've actually found my father."

"Not to you, I suppose, Mr. Adamson. But I take a professional pride in my work. By the way, I think we ought to lay our hands on something to eat while we can. More customers coming in."

On the way back from the counter, carrying sandwiches and what were described there as sausage rolls, Crike began again. "It was a tricky trail, going back sixteen years, and I had to keep my nose to it. But I was lucky in one respect. It's all been in one area, roughly between Birmingham and Wolverhampton. If your father had moved right out of this area, it might have taken me weeks and weeks, perhaps months, to find him." They were back at the table now, and Crike, after letting his eye droop dubiously at a sandwich, took a large bite out of it. "Poor stuff, I'm afraid. However, we didn't come to Hayport to eat, as you said. But you must be wondering why I haven't taken you straight to your father."

"It has seemed rather odd — yes. Like this sausage roll."

Crike started a smile, checked it, then let it expand. He had thick cracked lips, now decorated with bits of egg sandwich. This was yet another part, Tom reflected, of the total ugly scene. It was like a seedy nightmare about finding one's father.

"I haven't taken you straight to him," Crike said, "for one simple good reason. He's an old man — he's aged more than he ought to have done, but you'll soon understand why — and he has to sleep till early afternoon. You see, Mr. Adamson, he's a night watchman — has been for the last three years — at a place you may have noticed on your way here. Dawley, Whitehead and Company. They make fittings for car dashboards — or something of that sort. And I thought you'd rather he had his sleep out —"

"Oh — yes — certainly —"

"And it's an ordeal for a man his age and in the shape he's in, y'know, meeting a grown-up son after all these years. He's a lot more excited than you seem to be, Mr. Adamson." There was reproach here.

"No doubt. Probably I'm a cooler type. You were right about the beer," said Tom, rising. "I think I'll try gin-and-ginger-ale to wash this stuff down. You'll have another whisky, won't you? No, I'll do it."

When he came back with the drinks, he said, "You were going to tell me why my father's aged more than he ought to have done."

"It's really all in my reports but of course if you haven't studied them, you haven't." Crike sounded reproachful again. "But here's a man in his fifties coming out of prison and changing his name. With no family, no relatives, willing to help. He's not *in* anywhere. He's on the edge of everything. He'll have to take what he can get. The Welfare State's a featherbed for some people — but not for a man like him. Right?"

"I'm sure you are, but don't forget I'm a stranger here. I wouldn't know."

"Quite so, Mr. Adamson, and that's one thing I keep forgetting, just because you haven't the usual Aussie twang. Now, taking a quick look at the high spots, you might feel he hasn't done too badly. The Sutwick Rep packs up and he gets a job at this pub in Colston through his friend — we'll call her that — Mrs. Jones. But as soon as Mrs. Jones dies and her daughter takes over, he's out. He turns up next travelling for a man called Stane, who's an importer of novelties at a place called Ditterfield, about twenty miles from here. That doesn't sound too bad and he has about two years of it. After a spell out of work or doing any odd job — and I nearly lost track of him there — he turns up working, regular as a Swiss watch at first, for a wine-and-spirits man called Hawkin at another town not far from here, Stenwell. But in the end he loses that job because he's sampling the stock too often. Now he's well into his sixties and dropping fast — no bargain for anybody even if there *is* full employment in the West Midlands — see what I mean?"

"So now he's a night watchman —"

"And older than he ought to be, Mr. Adamson, or would have been if he'd had better luck. And now this is the point. It all sounds better than it really was — except perhaps the pub job at Colston. He had to take what he could get, no picking and choosing. Every time a lot of work and not much money. Bad hours and conditions, and wages below the usual minimum. Take it or leave it, Archer! Like it or lump it! That's what aged him — and would have put years on you or me. See what I mean, Mr. Adamson?"

"You're preparing me for a shock." Tom said it in a level

tone, as if they were talking about a sack of potatoes. Whatever he felt inside he didn't propose to reveal himself to Crike, whom he now sharply disliked.

"Well of course, Mr. Adamson. You remember him as he was when you were a small child — still in his thirties, an actor and painter, handsome no doubt, full of fun. But I've been looking not for that Charles Adamson you remember but for Charles Archer, who'd been inside and came out half-knowing he was already a defeated man who'd have to scratch a living somehow. Let's face it — and don't blame me — he's gone down and down." He shook his head, then looked at his watch. "We'll give him another half-hour. By the way, he's lodging with an elderly couple called Butley. The husband's almost bedridden but Mrs. Butley's fairly spry for her age. All the same — as I'm sure you'll agree — he oughtn't to be there."

Tom nodded, not so much in agreement as to prove he'd been listening, but said nothing. Obviously the silence made Crike feel uneasy. He tried changing the subject.

"Well, Mr. Adamson, how are you finding England so far?"

"You sound as if you're talking about an invalid, Mr. Crike."

"Up to a point — I am. But what do *you* think?"

"I don't know what I think. Strictly speaking, I'm not thinking. That'll have to wait."

Crike couldn't really change the subject. "Nothing to do with me, of course — no right to ask — but had you made any plans what to do after you'd found your father? I don't mean for yourself but for him."

"No, I didn't feel I could until I'd seen him and talked to him. After thirty-three years I didn't know what sort of man he'd turn out to be. From what you've told me, it seems as if he ought to be hurried into an old men's home." But the irony was wasted.

"You might be right, Mr. Adamson. As I said, he's gone down and down."

Twenty minutes later, following Crike's directions, Tom drove down one of those streets of dwarf houses and stopped somewhere about the middle of it. Crike said, "I'll pop in first, just to prepare them, y'know, Mr. Adamson." "You do that, Mr. Crike." Tom got out too, for no particular reason, and stared around, hating everything he saw. Two small children arrived to inspect the Allerton-Fawcet. A window shot up and an angry woman yelled at them. It was a warmish afternoon now; no colour in it, only some queer smells. At the end of the street there was some spare ground where discarded bits of machinery seemed to be rusting away. The angry woman came charging out, glared at Tom as if he might be a potential murderer, and yanked the children away. A man with a purple smudge of a face came along, pushing a handcart apparently filled with broken fenders and fire-irons, and he stopped near the car, cleared his throat and spat, then went on his way to nowhere. Crike reappeared, wearing a peculiarly sickly smile, and held the door open for Tom.

Entering the house was like going into a cave smelling of old stews and warm dirty wool. He just caught a glimpse of Mrs. Butley, who offered him a flash of apprehension and then vanished. An old man wearing a grey cardigan, ravelled and stained, was sitting with his hands on his knees. He looked up slowly.

"Well, here he is, here he is." Crike had all the false heartiness of a master of ceremonies. "Now don't get up, Mr. Archer, don't get up."

The old man smiled as if he had been working at it for

the last day or two, pushing his lips forward to clear a space between his moustache and beard. Tom stared at him, saying nothing. The old man held on to the smile a moment or two longer, and then said, as if they were lines in a play, "Well, Tommy, I don't suppose you recognise your old Dad. Been a long time, hasn't it, a long long time, since we were all together in London? When I used to be doing my painting and acting — eh?"

Still keeping silent, Tom went closer, leaning forward to stare into the old man's eyes. Something was flickering and wavering there. And it wasn't the joy of recognition.

Crike tried a little cough of warning. "Now, Mr. Adamson, I did ask you to be prepared."

"Tommy," the old man said with even less conviction, "aren't you going to tell me how glad you are to see me?"

"No," Tom began angrily, but then, as he stepped back, he checked himself. He couldn't be angry with this abject creature. "You know, you oughtn't to have allowed yourself to be talked into this. So now forget it." The anger returned as he spoke to Crike. "Come on, let's go."

"But — but — I mean, Mr. Adamson —"

"Outside, Crike. Come on." He hurried out himself without waiting to see if Crike were following him. He got straight into the car. Crike arrived, panting and protesting.

"We can't talk here, Crike. Did you keep your room at the Fleece? Then we'll talk there. Get in. And stop that yammering. I don't want to listen to you until I've had my say."

Crike's room was quite large — he'd probably demanded the best they had, Tom reflected grimly — and as well as an enormous brass-knobbed bed it offered its guests competing impossible roses both in the carpet and round the walls. Tom dropped into a chintzy chair and then stared hard at Crike, who was still standing.

"Why? For God's sake — *why?*"

"I warned you — I told you he'd gone down and down — that you wouldn't recognise him —"

"Oh — drop it, Crike! That poor old devil was about as much like my father as you are. Everything was wrong — eyes, ears, voice. And my father never called me Tommy — nobody ever did. I'll admit I had my doubts long before I went into that house. Perhaps I didn't even *want* you to find my father. But I didn't expect anything as raw and impudent as that. What do you take me for — an imbecile? No, no — don't waste time trying to keep it up. Just listen to me now, Crike. If you try to bluff it out, you'll be sorry. I'll go straight back to London and talk to a solicitor. Your only chance now is to be absolutely honest with me. You're no use to me — you're just an impudent bloody old twister — unless you tell me the exact truth. So come on — let's have it."

Crike looked round for a chair, as if he were lost and old and the room quite strange to him, and when he had found a chair he collapsed into it like a balloon with most of its gas gone. His head sank into his shoulders; he stared at the floor; he said nothing.

"Come on, man — the exact plain truth." Tom wasn't so sharp this time. "Nothing else is any use to me. Surely you can understand that?"

Crike nodded and the good eye stopped staring at the floor. He cleared his throat twice and then began slowly, with an effort, as if he were breaking a silence that had lasted for months and not minutes. "I'm rather older than I look and things haven't been going so well lately. I haven't two assistants — haven't even one — and my sister-in-law answers the phone. I'm a good investigator — and I've had a lot of valuable experience — but I'm down to piddling little jobs, cases not worth more than a few pounds. When you agreed to my terms, very stiff for me these days, and advanced me that twenty, I came down here, to follow that lead Bassenthwaite gave me, meaning to do all I could for you."

"I find that hard to believe."

"You asked for the honest truth. That's what you're getting. I half-killed myself the first two or three days. I didn't know then of course you weren't even bothering to read my reports properly. Though when we talked at your hotel, I felt then you'd given me the job because you'd other things to think about."

This wouldn't do. In another minute, Tom felt, their roles would be completely reversed and he'd find himself apologising to this old twister. "Yes, but then you decided to plant that pathetic old fraud on me. And not only to collect a bonus you hadn't earned but probably to work some fifty-fifty racket with the old man —"

"If I could have made a bit, I would have done," Crike admitted. "But the whole truth's a lot more complicated than that, as it generally is, in my experience. To start with, there was more vanity than greed in it. I wanted to show you I could do something you couldn't begin to do yourself, as I'd told you. And I got off to a good start. But then I walked slap into a blank wall. Not a lead, not a clue, not a hope. For all I knew, your father could have changed his name again, could have gone to John o' Groats, Land's End, or the Continent, could have dropped down dead somewhere. I'm not saying that a big organisation, using plenty of men and a hell of a lot of money, couldn't have made some progress. But I knew I couldn't. I'd have been taking your money to sit about biting my nails."

"So you thought you'd invent a father for me?"

"It sounds bad. It's all sounded bad so far. But I'm no

crook, though I know you think I am. Indeed, you'd started thinking that when we were having a drink and a bite downstairs. Right? Right. But now look at it from my point of view. It didn't seem to me you *really* wanted to find your father. You weren't lying awake at night wondering about him. And why should you — at your age and after all that time? You were just trying to keep a promise, that's all. All right, then. I produce a father —"

"And *what* a father!"

"Well, he made a poor showing, I'll admit. Nothing like as good as he ought to have been. But your real father, if he's still alive, which I doubt, mightn't be much better. And that old man I tried to plant on you won't live another year. They're turning him off the job because of his heart. Now let's suppose you hadn't been clever. You'd have kept your promise and found your father. You'd never have wanted to live with him, so you'd have gone back to Australia, arranging to pay a few hundred pounds — which I fancy you could well afford — to have him kept in comfort. You'd have felt satisfied; he'd have enjoyed his last few months; I'd have made a bit and perhaps got on to a few more good cases; and if you ask me, I'd say we'd all have been a bloody sight happier than we are now." And there was defiance in the good eye.

Tom shook his head. "It's an argument on the wrong level. Partly my fault, I admit. Whatever impression I may have given you when we talked at my hotel, I'm not here vaguely trying to keep a promise. I'm here to find my father." He got up and moved about. "I'm convinced — though I couldn't explain why — that he's still alive, and I'm going to find him —"

"Not now you aren't. Too late. Look — I've admitted I'm getting on and doing badly, but I do know how to trace a man — I've had to do it over and over again — just so long as he doesn't vanish, turn himself into a big blank wall."

Tom regarded him thoughtfully. Crike had also got up now, and the two of them had moved closer. "When we came in here," Tom told him, "I'd made up my mind not to give you another penny. Now I've changed my mind. Tell me what I owe you — and if it's not unreasonable, I'll give you a cheque."

"In the circumstances, that's very decent of you, Mr. Adamson, very decent indeed." Crike was humble again.

"I propose to stay in this neighbourhood. Luckily, I packed a bag. And now I'll really study your reports, and then go over the same ground. But of course at some point, you began to fake them. So when and where did the faking begin?"

Crike took several deep breaths and then said rather unsteadily, "I can't tell you that, Mr. Adamson. I'm sorry."

"What? One minute you're thanking me —"

"I know, I know," Crike cut in hurriedly. "And I'm still thanking you. But this involves other people. They asked for promises and I gave them. Wouldn't be fair, wouldn't be right, to go back on those promises."

Tom stared at him. Then suddenly he laughed. "Aren't you a rather peculiar character, Mr. Crike?"

"No, I wouldn't say that," he replied earnestly. "But of course you're new here really, aren't you? Now if you're determined to stay on and do some investigating yourself — and I'll tell you frankly I think you'll be wasting your time — I suggest you stop at the bull in Ditterfield. It's a good little hotel and Ditterfield's fairly central." He felt in his inside pocket. "I'll get back to London. And this is what you owe me, Mr. Adamson. You'll find the expenses very reasonable, considering that it's all daylight robbery these days."

"I'll write you a cheque downstairs, Mr. Crike."

When Tom was ready to move off, Crike came out with him to the car. But Tom didn't get in at once. "Some of these people in your reports actually remembered my father, didn't they?"

"Just a few — yes."

"What did they make of him?"

"It varied of course. Very mixed, I'd say. Didn't give me any definite impression of him."

"When, over the drinks and sandwiches, you wanted me to believe that he must have gone rapidly downhill, were you just preparing me for that messy old dotard here?"

"Not entirely, Mr. Adamson. If you ever do find him, then you'll have to prepare yourself for a shock. A good part of what I told you, I honestly believe. A man of his age and in his circumstances can't help going down and down. It's happened to me, up to a point, and I've never been inside and had to change my name. I don't think you're going to enjoy this investigation of yours."

"Probably not. But in a sense, while I'm listening to people who remember him, I'll be finding him all the time. They may not have liked him, but then I may not like them. Well, I'll take off for Ditterfield — the Bull, isn't it? And remember me to Bassenthwaite. If it hadn't been for him, I wouldn't have known my father's new name. So long, Crike!"

13

THE Bull at Ditterfield wasn't bad, even though determinedly Olde Englyshe and full of horse-brasses and warming pans and painted plaster beams on ceilings that had
been specially lowered about 1955. (The Chas influence
was at work here on Tom, who prided himself now on losing his innocence, which would have told him, before Chas,
that he was booking a room in the world of Henry the
Eighth.) There was nothing Tudor about the girl at the
reception desk, except perhaps her red-gold hair, set off by
her black dress. She smiled and fluttered her eyelashes at
Tom every time she saw him, and not, he concluded, because she regarded him as an attractive lone male but because absent-mindedly he had put his Sydney address in the
hotel register. And indeed, later, she told him she was dying
to get to Australia, to which he replied that many women in
Sydney, Melbourne, Brisbane, were dying to stay at an Old
World inn like the Bull, and added that this was the kind of
world we were living in, a statement that lost her interest at
once.

In a corner of the lounge, crowded with things but not
with people, he sat over a gate-legged table, a pot of very
strong tea and some biscuits, and studied and brooded over
Crike's reports, severely factual, in which his father — his

long-lost, unlucky father — figured as *subject. Barmaid when questioned,* Tom would read, *had not known subject.* Or — *Present proprietor clearly remembered subject when pressed, but suspicious and unwilling to give detailed replies.* And as he considered these reports, Tom found himself sharply divided. One part of him rejoiced in the instinctive excitement, together with the intellectual detective-story interest, of the trail, the hunt, the pursuit. The other part of him, on a deeper and vaguer level, saw his father, a composite figure of the actual man lovingly remembered from long ago and Crike's shabby ageing *subject,* set against, appearing and disappearing in, haunting, a huge huddle and muddle of people and their business, their busyness, meaningless and desperately sad. He felt again what he had first felt after leaving the sheep station for Sydney. To encounter innumerable people, more and more crowding into a maze, without any sense of meaning, of ultimate purpose, was to face despair. And in Australia at least he had known that not far away was the outback, whereas here in England there could be no outback, where people turned into ghost trees among endless leagues of sunlight, but only, as a possible release from despair, what might be called an *in-back,* sunless and dark, hidden and unknown.

When he went upstairs, to have a bath and prepare for a fairly early dinner, he forced himself out of this melancholy brooding by coming to some decisions on practical matters. He would begin, this very evening, exactly where Crike began, where indeed his father had gone after the collapse of the Sutwick Rep had left him out of work. It had been Mrs. Jones's pub in Colston then; but a few years ago, Crike said, it had been turned into a club, owned and managed by Mrs. Jones's daughter, a Mrs. Sedge, and her husband. So he'd start with the Sedges at Colston. His next decision was more important. After much thought he decided that at

Colston and everywhere else he'd no longer admit he was looking for his father; he'd be a legal type who'd come all the way from Australia to find a Mr. Charles Archer. This might cost him some sympathy with a few people, but he suspected only a very few, whereas most people would take him more seriously as a legal searcher, a bloodhound on a good salary and expenses, than as a chump looking for his father after thirty-odd years. Moreover, they would be more likely to be frank with him about this Archer chap. And this was important because he was anxious to discover what kind of man his father was, after prison and that change of name. He wasn't ready yet to accept Crike's pessimistic conclusions, even though he found it hard to dismiss all thought of them.

It was about half-past eight when he arrived at Sutwick, a biggish town with a half-finished Centre and some mysterious gigantic new works but also with plenty of mid-Victorian small factories and tiny houses of blackened brick, so that driving through it was rather like trying to read alternate pages of science fiction and Dickens's *Hard Times*. Colston was a much smaller town, now almost a suburb of Sutwick, and it didn't take him very long to find, at a crossroads and still looking on the outside like Mrs. Jones's pub, the Colston Club — or, as the illuminated sign said — *Vic & Molly's Colston Club*. It had its own car park at the back. One of those oldish and featureless men who invent jobs for themselves by buying a peaked cap did some vague waving and beckoning, and by ignoring him Tom was able to steer the Allerton-Fawcet to a not too inconvenient place among about fifty other cars. When he went round to the entrance and then inside he was directed, probably by peaked-cap's nephew, to an *Office* sign tucked away on the left.

A middle-aged woman was squinting through cigarette

smoke at a typewriter. "I'd say," she remarked, after Tom
had bid her a good-evening, "you're selling something in a
very superior way, and if that's so, then you couldn't have
come at a worse time. First half of the show's begun, and
Vic and Molly are along there as usual, cheering it on." Her
left hand waved the cigarette; her right hand raised a glass
of stout from somewhere; and before drinking she went on:
"They're too busy just now, and I can't buy anything except
paper and stamps, even if you do look rather like Gregory
Peck."

Tom offered her a smile that he hoped was not unlike
Gregory Peck's. "I'm not selling anything. I'm a lawyer, not
a salesman. I'm over here, from Australia, on an important
legal matter, and I believe that Mr. and Mrs. Sedge might
be able to give me some information I need. When will
they stop being busy?" A smile again.

She was now on his side. "After the first half, there's a
forty-five-minute interval — y'know, to get the drinks going
like — and sometimes if they're not talking to the artistes
or some of the posher members, one of 'em — or both of
'em — comes back here to have a quiet drink in peace and
put their feet up. Y'know, they're marvellous the way they
keep it all on the go — specially Vic — but you can do with
a rest from being he's-a-jolly-good-fellow, can't you? Now
I'll tell you what. You go in and see the show — lovely acts,
this week, and it's only just started — and as soon as it's the
interval I'll tell 'em you want to see 'em, all important
y'know. But I'll have to make you a temporary member —
ten bob. What's your name?"

He sat at the back of the big room, where there was a
raised platform, together with some attempt at theatrical
lighting. A waiter lounging against the wall behind him was
just able, by leaning far forward, to hear his order for a double whisky. With the aid of a piano, a bass fiddle, and elec-

tric guitar and various microphones and loudspeakers, three pop-group youths were making a hell of a noise. But so far as Tom could judge, there were very few young people in the audience, and when the lights went up, he saw that almost all the members present were roughly between thirty and fifty years of age. One of those keen dark men with a moustache like an eyebrow — wearing a wide-shouldered midnight-blue dinner jacket — was this Vic? — clutched a stand mike near the platform, and announced the welcome return to the Club of some vocalist whose name Tom didn't catch. She was a large mezzosoprano who'd had a good voice once but was now rubbing away what was left of it. The Club didn't share the keen dark man's enthusiasm and a certain amount of talk and glass-clinking went on, but the singer doggedly concluded her three numbers and took a bow to some halfhearted applause.

Now the keen dark man — it must be Vic — returned to the mike, and it was obvious at once that the act he announced, Dally and Dolly, making their third triumphant appearance at the Club, was the event of the evening. Everybody there except Tom was waiting for Dally and Dolly, ready to be rolled down the aisle. Dally, a fattish middle-aged man with a grotesque wig, was rapturously received when he came on and pretended he was about to recite; and so was Dolly, a kind of battle-cruiser blonde, when she arrived to interrupt his recitation. From then on, all was laughter and glory. This was the stuff for Vic and Molly's patrons. Tom was neither a prude nor a prig but he detested this pair as he had rarely destested any other performers. To begin with, they had no real talent, unless their knowledge of what would please their audience amounted to a talent. They had between them not even a suggestion of genuine wit or humour. Tom couldn't imagine them indulging in the tiniest bit of clowning when they were away from an audi-

ence. They were as far removed from gaiety, high spirits, au-
thentic drollery, as a pair of moneylenders. They had learnt
a lot of gags, some silly, some very dirty, and bashed and
banged away with them to keep the Club roaring, yelling,
screaming, applauding. The world out of which these gags
came, the world it helped to create in that club room, was a
kind of hell of automatic and dreary lechery, of cheating hus-
bands and suspicious wives, of sneering and sniggering and
cheap cynicism, a grey and chilly hell without warmth and
light or any real values of heart or mind. And this apparently was what the people there, the new English who were
certain — foolishly, in Tom's opinion, and he knew more
about it than they did — they had left all insecurity behind,
wanted for their entertainment and delectation. They were
now Dally and Dolly people. And Tom, who'd had enough,
slipped out before the act came to its uproarious conclusion. The big room had been close and thick with smoke —
it was a warm night — and he went outside to get some air.
He tried to think about stars, galaxies, quasars, God knows
what, up there, tried to decide, not for the first time, between the Steady State and Big Bang theories of the uni-
verse, and made no progress whatever.

When he went back inside, the middle-aged secretary
woman found him and took him to the Sedges' private
office. Vic and Molly were sitting at a small table. Vic of
course was the keen dark man, who was now dabbing his
forehead and drinking a whisky-and-soda. Molly looked
about ten years younger than her husband — in her early
forties — and suggested a rather good-looking pinkish par-
rot. She was busy with some long gin drink.

"You're in here, Mr. Adamson," she told him, "because
our Bertha, who does nearly all the work like, has fallen for
you. What will you have — a whisky? Good! Vic?"

"I popped out to the car park just to cool off and take a

look-see — I'm interested in cars — and I wondered about that Allerton-Fawcet. Is it yours? It is? Lovely car if you fancy the sports models," Vic continued, pouring more whisky into the glass for Tom as a mark of his increased respect.

"But Bertha said you'd come from Australia," Molly said, motioning to him to sit between her and Vic.

"I have. But I've a certain amount of running round to do, so I thought I must have a car."

"Quite right, old man," said Vic, passing Tom's glass. "Well — down the hatch! I hear you took in most of the show. Great act — Dally and Dolly — don't you think?"

Tom hated disguising or falsifying his opinions, but candour here might be ruinous. In spite of the elaborate sophistication of his appearance — Hollywood night-club proprietor *circa* 1940 — there was a kind of innocence about Vic, in his enthusiastic acceptance of the role of impresario, still new and exciting to him. Tom suspected that Molly, for all that bursting flesh and her strong local accent, was the harder character. "They certainly know their audience," he told Vic.

"A winner every time. Third engagement here — and now they're asking big money — but they earn it. Now then, Mr. Adamson, I understand you're not trying to sell us anything but making some legal enquiries, Bertha says. What can we do for you?"

"I'm trying to trace a man called Charles Archer —"

"Oh — *him!*" cried Molly, clearly disappointed. "We had a chap with a funny eye asking about him —"

"Yes, Crike. He was enquiring on our behalf, of course." Tom was immensely solemn; a legal type. "We thought we'd employ a private investigator — and we were wrong. That's why I'm here."

"And y'know you'll do a lot better than he did," cried Molly. "I didn't like the look of that chap."

"Neither did I," Vic said. "In fact there were things I could have told him — and I didn't." And he looked very cunning. Vic tended to overdo everything.

Even so, this confession was important. Tom took charge now, a tremendous legal type. "This enquiry is concerned with a possible inheritance in Australia. There's a morals clause," he added gravely, looking from one to the other of the Sedges, who were loving this. "So not only have I to try to trace this man Archer, I've also to try as I go along to discover what kind of man he is — or was. I may add that any information you care to give me I shall regard as being entirely confidential."

"Quite right, old man. Only way. You start, Molly."

"Well, I'll tell you right off, Mr. Adamson, I never took to Charlie Archer like."

"And I can tell him why —"

"Shut up, Vic. Y'know, Mr. Adamson, my mother owned this place when it was a pub. And every Monday she went to the first house of the Sutwick Rep. She'd a free pass for showing their bills like. Well —"

"Sorry to interrupt you, Mrs. Sedge, but I must explain that I know already that Archer joined that company, came out here on Sundays whenever he could, and that when the company packed up, your mother, Mrs. Jones, gave him a job here —"

"I'll say she did!"

"Stop that, Vic," said Molly sharply. "Yes, Mum took pity on him — she was very soft-hearted like — and gave him a job, living in, half manager, half superior barman. Y'know I wasn't here then. I'd already married Vic and we were living at Ditterfield, where he'd a business. Of course I was always coming over. And y'know I'd been with Mum a few times to the Sutwick Rep and seen Charlie Archer acting — just small parts but I must say he was very good and Mum told me once he used to act in the West End before the war — under some other name. Y'know that's why she was sorry for him — and then he'd real nice manners like. But I must say it shook me a bit when I found him settled in here, giving orders. Mind you, I'll never believe there was anything between him and Mum —"

"Don't make me laugh," Vic said, giving Tom a wink.

"And don't you be *disgusting* —"

"Now look — he was a man, she was a woman —"

"I know, I know. But she wasn't your mother. And he wasn't young, and she was years older than him, too old for that like, and I think you're *disgusting*."

She was leaning forward, talking across Tom, and for the last moments he had felt the pressure of her leg against his, but imagined it to be accidental. But on the second *disgusting* the pressure increased. Fortunately Vic spoke up now and Tom could naturally turn towards him, moving his leg away.

"Don't let's waste everybody's time, Molly," Vic said crisply. "They were sleeping together — and you know it when you stop kidding yourself. The old girl didn't tell you too much. She thought you'd come back at her. She was easier with me, specially when we'd both had a few. So now I'll tell you something you don't know. Once he was installed here, she wanted to marry him, and he said it was no go because although he'd been separated from his wife a long time, there'd never been a divorce. Any use to you, Mr. Adamson?"

"It's no use to me," Molly said, getting up in a temper. "I don't believe it. Just one of your Vic Sedge big tales. I'm not going to listen to any more. And all I need tell you, Mr.

Adamson, is that I didn't like him 'cos of the way he got round my mother and battened on her, all the time trying to be so bloody grand and snooty. And after Mum passed on and this place belonged to me, first thing I did was to tell Mr. Charles Archer he'd had it. Out!" And out she went too, banging the door behind her.

"You'll do better without her." Vic had been lighting a cigar during his wife's speech, very much in his Hollywood night-club role, and now talked through puffs at it. "She's not going to admit her Mum was being rogered. Disgusting! Matter of fact I always thought the old girl was a lively randy character. Mark you, though Molly told him to clear out the first day she was here, it's a fact that once I'd decided to get rid of my business and make something out of this place, there wasn't room here for both Charlie Archer and me. But I didn't like the way Molly did it, between ourselves. And I did quite like Charlie Archer. I was sorry for him too."

Sharply concerned now, Tom asked him why.

"A man needs a bit of money of his own, don't you agree, old man? Now Charlie Archer had been getting barely enough to live on at the Rep. The old girl told me that. Well, he was comfortable enough here of course — plenty to eat, plenty to drink — *she* saw to that — keeping his strength up, you know the way they are — but she wasn't going to give him anything but a quid or two as pocket-money. She didn't like parting with money, and anyhow if he'd had enough to save, he might easily have buggered off. He always seemed a bit restless to me, Charlie did."

"If he was half-managing a big pub, and if he was kept so short of money, he must have been tempted to help himself —"

"Quite right, old man. See what you're getting at. Character stuff, eh? Well, he didn't, I'm sure of that. He drank a

lot, often with customers — you know how the silly sods
are? — but he never dipped a finger into the till. Charlie
Archer was an honest man. That's another reason why I
liked him and did what I could to help him."

Tom found himself warming towards this Vic, in spite of
his Club, Dally and Dolly, fourth-rate impresario style.
"Mrs. Sedge mentioned his being 'so bloody grand and
snooty.' Was this just her prejudice?"

Vic grinned. "Plenty of that of course. But she had a
point. Archer, especially when he'd had a few, could suddenly come West End over you. He'd been an officer in the
war and that came into it as well, when he was in that
mood. But that wasn't often. My guess is that between the
end of the war and the time he worked with the Sutwick
Rep, he'd taken a caning somehow, somewhere. And when
the old girl, Molly's Mum, suddenly went out like a light —
bad heart it was — poor Charlie Archer knew he was for it,
old man. And I doubt if he'd ten quid in the world. So I felt
I had to give him a hand. After all he'd been popular here
and I was coming into the business. And Molly — you
know how bloody ruthless they can be — didn't care if he
starved."

"It was you then who sent him to that novelty merchant
in Ditterfield — what's his name — Stane?"

"In the end, yes. Joe Stane and me had been partners.
But it wasn't my first idea. I knew Joe too well — he's a
hard case. I tried something else first —"

"But you didn't tell Crike this — I mean the private detective with the queer eye —"

"No, I didn't bother. But if you want the lot —"

"Yes, please —"

"Then here it is. We were buying some furnishings and
odds and sods of stuff from a shop in Sutwick run by a peculiar pair called Neckerson. It's quite a business. They sell

furniture, antiques, fabrics, anything to tart up the joint. I talked them into taking Charlie Archer on, partly to serve in the shop, partly to knock off a lot of paintings for 'em they'd sell for about eight hundred per cent profit —"

Molly came in, flushed and excited but no longer out of temper. "Now where've you got to like?"

"Neckersons," Vic told her, without removing his cigar.

"I can tell him about Charlie Archer and the Neckersons. Y'know it's time you went along, Vic, and told 'em to settle down for the second half."

"Okay, okay! Do I see you later, Mr. Adamson?"

"I'm afraid not, Mr. Sedge. I've had rather a long day. Drove down from London this morning." Tom had not sat down since Molly's entrance, and now held out his hand. "I'm deeply obliged to you, Mr. Sedge. You've been most useful. Thank you." They shook hands, then Vic hurried out.

Molly, also standing, reached up to put a hand on Tom's shoulder, to force him down. "You don't have to go this very minute like. Have a drink with me while I tell you about Charlie Archer and the Neckersons. Yours is whisky, isn't it?" Tom sat down, and while she was pouring out their drinks, she went on talking. "Y'know Vic's not usually very soft like. He's smart and he can be hard, that's why he's so good in this club business. Also he loves wearing his fancy dinner jackets, smoking a big cigar, doing his M.C. act at the mike. And he's just right for 'em round here. They come and spend about a quid, y'know, and he makes 'em think they're nearly in the West End. It was the West End touch that made him so soft about Charlie Archer. Cheers, dears!"

"Cheers!" Then, after he'd taken a sip of the whisky he didn't really want, he said, "I didn't gather that from him, Mrs. Sedge —"

"Molly — Molly — for God's sake! Though I do like your nice manners, specially after some of 'em along there — common loud-mouthed bastards!"

"Well, Molly, he told me he was sorry for Archer because the poor devil never had any money of his own. And it's what I've begun to feel about Archer, that for some reason or other he was condemned to stand outside any decent hours-and-wages system. Yes?" For she was looking at him darkly and obviously wanting to speak.

"Y'know he liked to talk about himself in the war. But I never remember him saying a word about what happened after he left the army. That made me suspicious. If he was so West End why didn't he go back to it? 'Cos he couldn't, I say. He'd got into trouble like somehow. And y'know I wouldn't be surprised if he'd landed himself in prison."

Except his father himself, nobody was more sharply aware of that prison sentence than Tom, yet when this rather silly woman guessed at it his immediate reaction was one of shocked surprise. He had to work hard to keep his detached legal character going. "It's just possible, I suppose, but I'll have to make some enquiries. But tell me about the Neckersons, Molly."

She put a hand on his arm and squeezed it gently. "As it's you, I will. Y'know we did a lot of business with Herbert and Hilda Neckerson when we were turning this place into a club like. Had lots of talk with both of 'em. And Charlie Archer came into it a few times though this was long after Herbert Neckerson gave him the push. Y'know it was just the opposite there to what it was here. I didn't like him and Vic did. Well there, Herbert didn't like him and Hilda did — yes, and if you ask me, it wasn't just a matter of liking with her. I've always thought she fell for him, good and hard, though I don't say anything much happened between them like — Herbert'ud see to that. She'd be about fifty then, very smart and attractive though — but of course at a funny age, as I expect you know. D'you know about women?" She smiled and did some more arm work on him, rather to his dismay because he found her slightly repulsive, certainly far from attractive. "Where are you staying, big boy?"

There was a cue here. He eased himself out of the arm pressure and got up. "I'm at the Bull in Ditterfield."

"Not a bad little house," Molly said, not without a touch of professional patronage. "Vic and I used to go there a lot when we were in Ditterfield. But they haven't moved with the times the way we have. Here — you're not going, are you?"

"I must, Molly. I really have had a long day."

"Well, when am I going to see you again?"

"I'll look in as soon as I can —"

"Any time. I'll fix it with Bertha —"

"But I must push on with these enquiries as fast as I can, Molly. The Neckersons in the morning —"

"Their shop's at the corner of High Street and Market Street — you can't miss it —"

"Good! Then this man Stane in Ditterfield —"

"You won't like *him*, I can tell you that now. Biggest bloody liar between here and Birmingham. Don't believe a word he tells you. And keep your hand on your wallet. I always say he swindled Vic when they were partners. And Vic's no fool. Y'know I'd say sharper than you. Well, I must get back to the show. You might say a word to Bertha on your way out. Keep her happy."

Bertha still had a cigarette and a glass of stout but seemed to be entering up a ledger. "O-ho — you again!" she cried. "Did she make you?"

"Make me do what?"

"Now then, now then, it'll get really dirty if you put it

that way. But I'll bet anything she fancied you. How did you get on with 'em?"

"They were very useful, Bertha. Especially Vic. I didn't think at first I'd take to him — but I did."

"Same here but a long time since. Where are you going next?"

"The Neckersons in Sutwick — tomorrow morning —"

"She's all right but I can't stand him. And you'll be lucky if you get to her. He's the boss — the great *I am*. Oh — how did you like the show?"

"Bertha," he whispered with mock-solemnity, "I think Dally and Dolly ought to be locked up and then cleaned up."

"So do I," she whispered back. "But they love 'em here. Silly twerps! But just for saying that, I'll save you some time and trouble in the morning. Go straight to the back on the first floor at Neckerson's. Mr. and Mrs. have two connecting offices up there. And come and see us again, handsome."

14

Iᴛ was nearly eleven next morning when Tom watched Herbert Neckerson come out of an inner office, leaving the door behind him ajar. Tom wondered if Mrs. Neckerson were in there. He used the same story and the same legal manner that had worked so well with Vic and Molly. Neckerson was a tall man in his sixties who had the ratty features usually found on small men. He was also one of those disagreeable men who stare hard and listen in complete silence, never offering a word, not even a friendly noise, to the people who have to talk to them. Before Tom had even finished his opening speech he had taken a sharp dislike to Herbert Neckerson.

"This is a waste of time for both of us," Neckerson said. "It's true I remember this man Archer, though it's years ago and he was employed here, on a part-time basis, only for two or three months. The picture scheme was a complete failure — I'd never believed in it myself — and he wasn't the kind of man to make a useful shop assistant. Too big for his boots. Never really reliable. I was glad to get rid of him. That's all I can tell you."

The woman who came out of the inner office now said hastily, "If you want to be off, Herbert, perhaps I could answer a few questions about Charles Archer —"

"I dare say you could, my dear, but I can't see any reason why you should. Come along, Mr. — er — Adamson —"

Mrs. Neckerson hesitated, so Tom did too. It seemed to him that the appeal, directed only by her fine dark eyes, swept from her husband, who turned away, to him, the man who wanted to know more about Charles Archer. So he gave her a quick nod, then followed Neckerson, who was apparently leaving the shop on some business. As soon as Tom was outside and alone, he went in search of a public telephone.

"Mrs. Neckerson, this is Adamson. You heard me asking about Charles Archer. Where can we meet so that you can tell me what you wanted to tell me?"

"Oh, I don't know — perhaps my husband was right — I mean, I'd hate to be brought into anything legal —"

Tom came to an instant decision. "That was all nonsense, Mrs. Neckerson. I'm not a lawyer, I'm a university lecturer. And I'm Charles Archer's son, desperately trying to find him."

She was even shorter of breath now. "There's a café — the Flamingo — halfway along Market Street — there's a room upstairs — we can meet there — about quarter-past —"

He wasn't surprised to find he was there before she was. There were only three women taking coffee together in the upstairs room. He claimed a table as far as possible from them, and, to save time, ordered a pot of coffee for two. The café looked new; it had a mural of stylised flamingoes running round the room; everything there seemed to be made of plastics; it had the dauntingly homeless air of a café in an airport, so that Tom felt that at any moment a voice would come from a loudspeaker — *British Overseas Airways announce the departure of Flight 539 to Honolulu, Greenland and Teheran.* It was part of that new world in which wherever you are isn't too bad but anywhere else would be better.

Hilda Neckerson was old enough to be his mother — and perhaps she might have been in some other better-organised existence — but he couldn't help feeling a little in love with her as she hurried across the room, with light nervous steps much younger than herself, to join him. And he was sure now that this fragile-looking woman, whose life was in her eyes, had once loved his father.

"You really *are* his son, are you? I mean, it wasn't a trick to get me here to talk —"

He gave her some coffee. "Certainly not. I'm going round talking all kinds of nonsense. But not to you, Mrs. Neckerson. You're in quite a different category. We must tell each other the truth."

"That's never as easy as people seem to think. If you're his son, why do you call yourself Adamson?"

"Because that's my name. His name too. He was Charles Adamson."

"Oh — and he never told me. Yet he told me he'd been in prison —"

"It was after that he called himself Archer. And I can understand why he didn't tell you his real name was Adamson. He didn't want to begin confusing himself. Prison was the big dark secret, and he told you about that."

"But he never said anything about you. Tell me."

He told her as briefly and quickly as he could — there probably wasn't much time — how he came to be in England. She listened as if every word were the gift of a diamond. "By the way," he ended, "my name's Tom. And yours I know is Hilda. Can we use them?"

"Of course, Tom. And of course I'll tell you anything that might be of the least help, though I'm afraid you're going to be disappointed. But you must promise me one

167

thing — please. If and when you do find him, will you please write and tell me?"

"I will, Hilda. It's a promise. Mind you, I've no evidence he's still alive, but I can't help feeling that he is."

She was alight at that. "I feel that too, Tom. I believe I'd know if he wasn't, though I don't pretend to be the least bit psychic, you'll be glad to know. But I've always felt that below the obvious outward pattern — what people who are so sure about everything call the *facts* — there's an underlying hidden pattern, no real facts anywhere, that we occasionally catch a glimpse of — and say it's a feeling we have. I'm not being silly, am I, Tom?"

"No, you're not, Hilda. I deal in facts — I'm an economic historian, so I have to — but I'm more and more certain that underlying hidden pattern is there." He waited a moment. "Can you tell me what happened between you and my father?"

"I fell in love with him. Then, though it was all so short, I loved him. We never had a so-called affair. I'd have risked it. I'd have run away with him if he'd asked me to. But he wouldn't hear of it. He said he had to keep his bad luck to himself. We met whenever we could — and it was never easy — just to look at each other and talk and talk — real talk, not the usual rubbish. We turned out our minds for each other. And that can be wonderful for a woman, Tom — at least to a woman married to the wrong man. You've met Herbert —"

"Very briefly. And I must admit I took an instant sharp dislike to him, Hilda."

"I noticed that. Poor Herbert!"

"Why not poor me? *He* was being so damned rude. *I* wasn't."

"I know. But as soon as you mentioned Charles Archer, he began to feel jealous all over again. And they disliked

each other almost at sight. It was Vic Sedge — really a
rather nice man pretending not to be — you've met
him? —"

"Last night. And I know exactly what you mean."

"Well, it was Vic who suggested we should try to find a
place in the shop for your father. And the idea of setting
him to work to paint a lot of cheap bad pictures, as part of
the new lines in furnishing, wasn't mine, it was Herbert's.
So were the terms. We supplied the materials, paid him a
pound for each picture and another two pounds if we sold
it. Our price was between fifteen and twenty guineas. I
don't think we sold more than half a dozen. The few people
who cared about pictures didn't want them. And most of
the others, who imagined they were good pictures, hadn't
the least desire to buy any pictures. I don't suppose you
know very much about Charles as a painter, Tom."

"Not much, no. I believe that in the thirties, when he
must have done most of his painting, he wasn't bad and not
very good — middling. I've seen one picture of his — a figure in a garden in summer — that I really did like, but I
think it was exceptional. How was he as a bad painter —
bashing out highland cattle, rose-covered cottages, pretty
sandy bays — um?"

She laughed, surprising him. He'd seen her up to then as
friendly and intelligent but rather solemn and soulful,
probably born to suffer. "He really *was* bad — and in the
wrong way. If he'd been even worse, we might have sold
him as a primitive, a folk painter — they were just coming
into fashion then — but he missed it either way. Then he
spent his afternoons in the shop — four pounds a week and
a tiny commission. He wasn't any good there, except now
and again perhaps with an exceptional type of customer,
but that wasn't because he was careless and didn't try.
Goodness — how he tried — poor Charles! And of course

Herbert and the floor manager were complaining all the time. So he had to go. And, as you probably know, Vic Sedge got him a job, travelling and selling on commission, with his former partner in Ditterfield."

"Did that mean you stopped seeing each other?"

"No, not entirely. But it became difficult in more ways than one." She looked as if she had a good deal more to say, but then she drank what remained of her coffee and kept silent. All she had to offer was a rather apologetic little smile, which seemed to drain courage and strength out of her face, out of her whole personality. It was as if the woman who'd told him she would have run away with his father was no longer sitting there, looking at him. Another woman was offering him this apologetic little smile, timid but also perhaps a trifle sly. As if he were not Charles's son but another Herbert Neckerson! Had this transformation, suddenly identifying her with some flaw in her character, arrived with a recollection of a change in her relationship with Charles? *It became difficult in more ways than one,* she had said. He had to know. And it was significant that now she looked at her watch.

"I know you haven't much time, Hilda," he began gently. "But there are two things I have to know. Now, first, I'm trying to piece together, like a jigsaw, some sort of picture of my father. It's part of finding him, I feel. Tell me how you saw him. And please don't leave out anything unpleasant. The whole man, warts and all, please."

No smile this time. She nodded, then thought for a moment or two. "He was the exact opposite of Herbert, of course. Herbert, as you can imagine, is dominating, hard, narrow, rigidly honest in his own way but really quite ruthless. I'm none of those things, though he could never have built up the business without me. And of course neither was Charles. He couldn't be dominating or hard. His world was

ten times the size of Herbert's and infinitely richer, but he
didn't really move in it — never had done, I think — he
simply drifted, like a balloon, or was blown about like a kite
without its string. He was anything but ruthless, of course,
but he wasn't scrupulously honest either. Any woman
would know she couldn't completely *depend* on him. He
was really more actor than painter and he was very easily
influenced by people and surroundings. I think he was at his
best here, even though both parts of his job flopped, because he was leading a quiet life, after that pub at Colston,
not drinking very much, and needing and then enjoying the
kind of relationship we had, talking ourselves out and not
racketing round and then stumbling into bed half-tight.
When he went to Ditterfield and travelled about, trying to
sell that silly trash, he began to drink hard again and
coarsen, and when we did meet — and that became increasingly difficult — it wasn't the same. But he never blamed
me, always himself. People never seem to talk about 'weak
men' now — all out of fashion — but I suppose we could
call him one. Everything that happened to him may have
been his own fault, as men like Herbert always believe, or
he may have always run into bad luck whenever there was
any around, as I think most women would believe, just because there was in spite of everything an essential sweetness
in him, which anybody except a hard selfish bitch would
recognise. You loved him as a child, didn't you, Tom?"

"Indeed I did, Hilda. That I can remember very clearly."

"He'll be nearly seventy now, won't he? Not much left
perhaps," she sighed. Then she looked hard at him. "But
something. I think you're stronger in every way than he ever
was. Find him, Tom."

"If he's somewhere to be found, I will. And that's the
second thing I must know. What became of him after he
stopped working for Stane at Ditterfield? Did you ever learn

that he went after that to a place not too far away called Stenwell, working in a wines-and-spirits shop, Hawkin's?"

She shook her head slowly and sadly. "No, he simply vanished from Ditterfield. Why — I never knew."

"I'll try to find out. So — you never heard from him again?"

"Oh yes, I did."

"*You did?*" Tom almost shouted at her in his excitement.

"Yes. A letter came — oh, about ten years ago — suddenly out of the blue. You might say literally out of the blue, because it came from the West Indies — Trinidad."

"Oh — my God — if he left the country —"

"No, he was working on a ship. As what I couldn't make out. The letter's an awful scrawl — I'm afraid he was rather tight when he wrote it. Even so, I've kept it, but hidden away in a secret place. The best thing I can do, Tom, is to send you a copy of it as soon as I get a chance of copying it — not so easy as you might think. So don't give me any temporary local address."

"No, I'll be back in London in a day or two." He found an envelope addressed to him at the hotel and gave her that. "Send the copy of his letter there. And I don't need to tell you how important to me it is, Hilda."

"No, you don't, Tom. Now I really must go. No, please don't get up, I'd much rather you didn't. Or see me out." She looked down at him, one hand going out to touch him and then being shakily halted. "Tom, you'll keep your promise to write and tell me when you've found him, won't you? Bless you!" She bent and kissed him lightly and quickly. He watched her go out, back into the Neckerson world, and felt he was about to descend into some abyss of melancholy. He rescued himself by doing some brisk planning.

15

HE paid his first call on Stane's Novelties at half-past two, only to be told that Mr. Stane was lunching in Birmingham. The secretary, bold and busty, might have been a younger version of Molly Sedge. "And he never gets back like till about four," she added. "So I'd try then if I was you. Sometimes he's in a good mood, sometimes he's anything but, y'know. You selling or buying?"

"Neither."

"What's the idea then, Mr. — er — ?"

"Adamson. I'm making enquiries about a man who used to work for Mr. Stane — a man called Archer. But he'd be long before your time."

"Last Christmas was before my time," she said, pulling a face. "And next Christmas'll be after my time. I like to keep changing, I do. Y'know as soon as they think I'm good and settled and think they can keep me on the trot, I push off. You always get more consideration like when you're new. So I keep on being new all the time. If we've got Full Employment, I say, then let's make the best of it. What do you say?"

There were many things Tom could have said, beginning with office efficiency and ending with Britain's balance of payments, but he merely gave her a grin. "I'll be back just before four. If Mr. Stane happens to come back earlier than that, you might please tell him about me — Adamson, remember?"

"I'd got it. And there's something you'd better remember. Mr. Stane can be quite nice sometimes. And at other times he's just downright bloody rude." They exchanged grins.

She followed him out and stared hard at the Allerton-Fawcet. "Smashing car! Y'know if you offered me a nice long ride in that tonight, I don't think I'd say no."

"Good idea — but I think I'll have to get back to London. Sorry!"

There was nothing in Ditterfield he wanted to see so he returned to the Bull, where he began packing his bag in an idle sort of way. He found that in fact he was eager now to get back to London, once he'd done with Stane, and was puzzled to know why he should be feeling this sudden urge. Helga was out, definitely. So was Chas. He might enjoy telling Dr. Firmius what had happened, but the thought of that old troll king oughtn't to be generating so much excitement. Nevertheless, that was the best he could do, and he decided then and there he would call on Firmius if he did get back to London that night. And not only did he pack his bag but he also paid his bill, the red-gold and eyelash-fluttering girl, still dreaming of Australia, kindly allowing him to cancel his room for that night without paying for it.

"Just got back," Stane's secretary whispered. "Not in a good mood, but I've seen him worse. Didn't want to see you, but I said you looked important and came here in an Allerton-Fawcet. It worked like. Come on."

Stane was a shortish, fattish, frog-faced chap, probably in his early fifties. His room appeared to be crammed with the novelties he imported and sold, all the ingenious rubbish that no sensible man ever wanted to buy — glasses with clothed girls painted on the outside and naked girls on the inside, dipping and pecking birds, plastic animals, dolls that did tricks, apparatus for practical jokes, all manner of elaborate imbecilities direct from Western Germany and Japan, which had lost the last war but were obviously winning this one.

Stane might be an importer and distributor by trade but in his private life he was essentially a consumer. He looked as if he had consumed an enormous lunch in Birmingham; he seemed to be consuming rather than smoking the cigar in his mouth, and when he took it out he consumed by the handful mysterious coloured sweets from a tin box on his desk. Even his speech was a kind of gobbling as if he were tempted all the time to eat his tongue. But he was not a Central European Jew, as Tom had rather expected him to be. He was just as much a Midlands man as Vic Sedge or Herbert Neckerson. He was one of the new men in the old country.

"Half a sec!" he cried before Tom could explain why he was there. "You must look at this. Just arrived — lovely novelty — Japanese! Now watch! Keep your eye on it. Off she goes!"

He set in motion on his desk a doll about six inches high, sketchily representing some old peasant woman, and it moved forward, stopped hesitatingly, and then peed. "Marvellous, isn't it? Give me a month — or, say, six weeks — and I'll have these old trouts peeing on half the bar counters in the West Midlands. Can't miss. Best novelty I've had this year. A winner! Well, what can I do for you, Mr. — er — Adamson, isn't it?"

Tom wasn't going to tell this chap he was looking for his father. He assumed his legal character again. And he ended, "I realise, Mr. Stane, you've already answered some questions by a private enquiry agent we employed — a man called Crike."

"Certainly I have. Told him all I knew. Don't see why you have to start all over again. Beats me, frankly. Y'know — busy man and all that. And it's years since Archer worked for me."

Tom was still standing up. He hadn't been asked to sit down, and anyhow both armchairs were filled with novelties. So now he moved closer and gave Stane a long hard look. It was returned boldly, and Tom had had sufficient experience, especially with students, to know that this opaque stare usually didn't mean that the truth was about to be told.

"Just two things, Mr. Stane, and then I won't waste any more of your time. First, did you tell Crike that after Archer left you he went to work for a wines-and-spirits merchant, Hawkin, in Stenwell?"

"Well, I did and I didn't." There was still nothing shifty about Stane's answering look, but Tom felt there was some uneasiness in his tone. "If it was wrong, don't blame me. I told him I wasn't sure. But I'd once done a bit of business with Hawkin. He gave some of my novelties away one Christmas. Nice idea, but he was too bloody mean to keep on with it. That's what's wrong with half these shopkeepers. No real enterprise! Not 'with it'! I'll tell you frankly —"

"You're the busy man, Mr. Stane. What did you tell Crike about Archer?"

"All right, all right, all right! Don't push me. Don't crowd me. You're not doing me a favour. I'm doing *you* one. All I told Crike was I'd heard Archer'd gone to work for Hawkin's. I never saw him there. Never been near the place myself. Just a rumour I heard." His hand moved towards the peeing doll. "No good. She has to be filled up again. A snag there. But you can't have everything. And

176

they'll be working her with beer. Unless it clogs her up. Nothing said about that by the manufacturers. Lovely novelty though."

"Crike showed me an old man," Tom said doggedly, "and told me he was the man I was looking for. And he most certainly wasn't. Do you know anything about that?"

"Of course I don't. Think I've nothing else to do? Don't be ridic. I run a good business here, a growing business. I'm making nice money. Why the hell should I bother about a traveller I sacked years ago — and a shabby-arsed old enquiry agent — or, for that matter, *you*?"

"I don't know. But even so, I don't believe you."

"I'm lying, am I?" And he didn't sound at all indignant.

"I think you could be," Tom told him.

"Right, I could. Always a possibility. But before you turn on the How-dare-you bit, let me tell you something. I *might* be lying. But I *know* you are. You're not a lawyer, looking for somebody for a client. You're an Aussie professor or something, trying to find your father. Crike told me, over a drink or two."

"What else did he tell you?" Tom was trying hard to control his anger.

"Nothing worth repeating. Now look — let's turn this up. I've things to do. Crike couldn't pass off his old man, so that's that. If you ask me, he didn't think you were all that serious about it —"

"Well, I am. And I'm not only trying to find my father, I'm also trying to discover everything I can about him. He worked for you. What did you think of him? Why did you fire him?"

"Oh dear, oh dear, oh dear!" Stane squashed the messy remnant of his cigar into an ashtray shaped like a woman lying on her back. Then he began to consume another handful of sweets. And though his words were offensive, his tone was quite amiable. "Why don't you just piss off? You're only asking for misery. And anyhow I could just start lying again, couldn't I? So where are you?"

"I'm here," Tom told him angrily. Unable now to control his temper, he swept an armful of assorted novelties out of the nearer chair, sat down and glared. "And I'm not pissing off as you call it until you've given me a few answers."

"Now wait a minute, wait a minute, wait a minute!" Stane looked and sounded alarmed.

"I *am* waiting."

"Okay — okay — anything for a quiet life, as the actress said to the bishop. I'll tell you the truth, but you won't like it. Vic Sedge, who used to be my partner, recommended Charlie Archer to me. Travelling, mostly on commission. I needed a new traveller and Archer seemed just right. He'd a bit of class. And having been on the stage, he could tell a good story. We'd a few nights out together at first. But it didn't last, neither on the personal side nor the business side. Not on the personal side because after he'd had a few he'd get snooty, both with me *and* my girl friends. And that didn't help when the business side started to go wrong. He was drinking hard, always a dam' silly thing to do on the road, except with a few old customers. I had complaints about him. And he wasn't selling as he'd done at first." He stopped for a moment, took out a cigar but then decided not to light it. "Now look — this is the honest truth you're hearing —"

"Yes, yes, I believe you. Go on."

"Right. Now you've got to understand we need good salesmen in this business. I needed Archer, when he was doing the job properly, just as much as he needed me. I was ready to make allowances. I did make allowances, even after the complaints kept coming in from some of my best customers. I wrote letters, sent apologies, all that. Now I'm not a suspicious man. Ask anybody. I'm tolerant, I am. Have to be, in the novelty business. Have to be free-and-easy. But there's a limit. Always is. So I begin to get suspicious. His business and commissions drop and drop. I warn him. Then all of a sudden, he's sending some big orders in again. He's back in the money. But then one of my best customers says there's been a mistake, we're trying to send him four or five times as much as he ordered. And at the same time — within a few days anyhow — I'm told by an old pal in Birmingham, man I hadn't seen for some time, that my Charlie Archer's real name was Adamson and he'd done time for passing dud cheques. That was enough, more than enough. I'm tolerant, free-and-easy — ask anybody — but I'm not exactly a mug. I called him in, told him to clear off and think himself lucky he wasn't in the dock again. And that's the lot — and all the honest truth."

Tom waited a moment. "When you had it out with my father, what did he say? Did he admit he'd been faking the orders?"

"Well — no — he didn't. He admitted he'd been inside and had changed his name. He also admitted he'd gone round half-stoned some days. Said he'd come to hate the bloody novelties. But wouldn't admit he'd deliberately faked the orders. Said they were honest mistakes. But what the hell?"

"*What the hell* is right. By the way, did you lose any customers because of those wrong orders?"

"No, I didn't. Chiefly because I rushed round myself as soon as Archer had gone and — y'know — turned on the charm."

"What charm? No, don't bother with it." Tom shot out of his chair, and Stane's eyes widened in alarm. "I'm sorry my father stopped doing his job properly. But a few months of your novelties would drive any sensitive man to despair and drink. And I think you're as cheap and nasty as they are, Stane."

"Now, look here —"

"Shut up. Because he'd been in prison, you wouldn't give him the benefit of the doubt. And I'm quite sure now you were up to your neck in Crike's silly little swindle —"

"Bugger off!"

"Certainly." Tom swept up all the novelties from the other chair and threw them at him. "Good afternoon!"

Tom drove back to the Bull, giving himself half an hour in which to cool off, if only because an angry man in an Allerton-Fawcet, on a main road to London too, could easily be roaring towards murder. As it was he drove coolly and carefully, and after a bath and a change of clothes he was still just in time to take any odds and ends that had been left in the kitchen. "Oi've kept a few very special portions just in case you came back, Mr. Adamson sorr," whispered Michael the headwaiter, who then described the odds and ends as if he'd had a message about them, in code, from the Wine and Food Society.

16

I⊤ was ten o'clock when he left to call on Dr. Firmius, who, rather to Tom's relief, had no telephone and therefore couldn't be asked if he was free to receive a visitor. It was a fine night and Tom might easily have walked there, but for some obscure reason, a sudden whim perhaps, an extension of that mysterious excitement he'd felt during the afternoon, he preferred to use the Allerton-Fawcet.

When Dr. Firmius opened the door at the top of his basement stairs, he was wearing the same carpet slippers and burnt linen jacket and smoking the same large pipe. "Yes? Oh — it is you, Mr. Adamson. Come in, come in."

But Tom had caught some vague sound from downstairs. "You've somebody with you, haven't you? Perhaps I'd better —"

"No, no, no — I insist." The old man dropped into a mock-solemn whisper. "Indeed, perhaps it is very important you come in now." He turned and began going downstairs as if he were quite sure that Tom would follow him. And he was right.

In the small central clearing in the higgledy-piggledy below, a girl was sitting on the low stool. Though she was dressed differently, Tom saw at once that she was the girl who had scowled and jeered at him at Helga's party, Firmius's young publisher-pal, Judy Marston. She scowled again when she first looked up and saw him, but then, to his surprise, welcomed him with a grin.

"You remember each other, of course," said Dr. Firmius. "Excuse me — but I will make more coffee." And as before, he disappeared between two piles of books.

Miss Marston's grin had vanished now. She was scowling again. "Dr. Firmius thinks you've been really trying to find your father. But I told him," she added aggressively, "you were probably still trailing after that silly woman with your tongue hanging out."

"You did, did you?" His tone was rather sharp. "Well, he was right and you were wrong. You can be wrong of course?"

"Half the time. And I'll admit I was damned rude to you at that party."

"Yes, you were. But now I think I deserved it, Miss Marston."

"Cut out the Miss Marston. It makes you sound pompous. Make it either Judy or just Marston. What's your name?"

"Tom," he muttered, feeling rather foolish.

"Oh — Tom." She repeated it as if tasting it. "Tom Adamson. Yes, I can see it might work. Well, Tom, if you've been looking for your father, where have you been?"

"In the West Midlands. The only wild goose chase the West Midlands have seen for some time."

"Are you going to be funny about it?"

"No — although there are some funny bits. But if you're really asking me if I took it seriously, Judy, the answer is that I did. And do. Very much so. By the way, Dr. Firmius suggested you were very curious about this search of mine. Why are you?"

"Oh — well — it's all odd, very unusual — what you call

this search of yours, Tom. It may have happened to lots of people — to start looking for a parent after years and years — but I've never met one before. And probably most of 'em couldn't write. And don't forget — and I *did* tell you — that part of my job is to scout round for possible books." She waited a moment. "Satisfied?"

He looked hard at her. She didn't look away but he seemed to catch a flicker of embarrassment in her eyes — greyish with thick dark lashes — and she tossed her hair back, as if out of patience with it but really, he thought, to cover her embarrassment. "If I'm not satisfied, still rather puzzled, that's probably because I don't know anything about publishing in London — all this 'scouting' as you call it. Quite new to me. Almost everything here is new to me."

"Well, never mind about that," she said impatiently. "What happened?"

"You want the whole story?"

"Most certainly we want the whole story," said Dr. Firmius, bringing in his coffee tray. "But not before we have all taken some coffee. Then you must give us everything — what was done, what was said, what you thought and felt — a true picture of one part of father-search. Now — some coffee."

When they had taken their coffee and the other two had settled down, Dr. Firmius buried in his old armchair, Judy somehow curled like a cat on her stool, and were regarding him expectantly, Tom felt something he never remembered feeling before, as if it came out of another existence, a kind of completeness that wasn't new but very old, part of some ancient long-forgotten pattern that suddenly revealed itself. It was this feeling, which he didn't want to lose, and not any doubt about what he should tell them — they could have the lot — that made him hesitate.

"Come on, Adamson," Judy growled. It was really a

mock-growl, essentially feminine, rather as if she was suddenly wearing boys' clothes. It didn't annoy Tom; it pleased him. So he gave her an amused glance before turning to Dr. Firmius.

"When I went back to my hotel the other night, Dr. Firmius," he began, "I found a telegram from the private detective, Crike, telling me he'd succeeded in finding my father and asking me to meet him at Hayport. It's a smallish town in the West Midlands. So next morning I drove down there." He stopped to drink some coffee.

"Don't be maddening," Judy said severely.

"Sorry! I didn't mean to be dramatic and tantalising. I suddenly felt that before I tell you all that happened I ought to explain one or two things. I wanted — and still want — to find my father in two different ways. If he's still alive — and I can't help feeling that he is — then of course I have to find him in the ordinary physical sense. He might be ill and helpless somewhere, for example, and of course I must make myself responsible for him. And if he isn't, then so much the better — we can get to know each other, perhaps help each other. In the other sense, I wanted to discover for myself what kind of man he was — or is. That was the other part of the search. When I went to Hayport, I'd already found out certain things. I knew that not long after the war he'd been sent to prison —"

He stopped there because Judy had cried out, "Oh — no!" and was staring at him out of eyes that seemed much darker.

"What's the matter?" He was staring too.

"Oh, I don't know. I suddenly felt sorry for him and you — and everybody. You know the way one sometimes does. Just as if a black huge bird suddenly came through the ceiling. Not sensible. Sorry! Go on, Tom."

"And tell us everything, please," said Dr. Firmius, smiling. "Omit nothing. You will not bore us."

So he did tell them everything, at least everything that concerned his father, from the moment that he met Crike in Hayport to the final flash of anger when he threw the novelties at Stane.

"And jolly good for you!" cried Judy, who had listened with close but wide-eyed attention.

"No book in it, you know," he told her.

"Oh — shut up!" She sounded quite cross. Obviously a girl who moved like lightning from one mood to another. Now she was looking away, scowling.

"You have formed now some picture of your father?" Dr. Firmius asked, twinkling away again.

"Not really. Not yet. It's a jigsaw puzzle with pieces missing."

"No, it isn't," said Judy rather sulkily. "It's a *man*. It's a *person*."

He turned on her sharply. "I ought to tell *you* to shut up. What do you think I am? My God — this man's *my father*. I may not have seen him for thirty-three years. But I still remember him from my childhood. I remember *loving* him. And I don't know where he is — what's happened to him — what he's doing. Don't forget there's a lot of the story even so far that you don't know —"

"All right, tell me."

He ignored this and looked at Dr. Firmius. "All I've left now is the letter Hilda Neckerson had from him, after he'd gone to sea, that she promised to copy out and send me. And it's years old. All I can do is to go to the shipping company, if it's mentioned in his letter, and try to find out if anybody there remembers him and knows where he went, because he couldn't have stayed at sea. I'll do everything possible," he ended, rather miserably, "but I can't help feeling it's going to be just another dead end."

"There will be an end that is not dead," said Dr. Firmius. "Yes, Judy? You have a question?"

She nodded, then looked at Tom. "This Hilda Who's-it? Do you think she's still in love with him?"

"Not really. She was — but not now."

"Are you one of those men who think they know all about women?"

"No, I'm not. But I'm also not one of those men who think they're a complete mystery. Do you mind?"

"Don't be silly. Why won't you tell me what happened before you went dashing down to the Midlands?"

"Well, for one thing I don't think there's time —"

"Time? What time is it? After twelve? I must fly." She glanced at Tom. "I live miles away — Hampstead, if you know where that is —"

"I don't, but I'll take you there. I've a car outside."

"Oh — good for you!" They were all standing now, and she had moved a pace or two nearer the stairs. However, she turned to look at Dr. Firmius. "Isn't it all rather peculiar about this father-search thing? I mean, we're getting along all right, but Tom doesn't understand why I'm interested, and I don't understand why you're interested. What don't *you* understand?"

"Nothing," Dr. Firmius told her, smiling. "Or everything. But I hope you have enjoyed this evening."

"I have," Tom said emphatically. "I used to think I was fairly self-sufficient, but just *telling* somebody what's been happening makes it all seem different, removes the Kafka-nightmare suggestion."

"We must go, Dr. Firmius," cried Judy. "And as you know everything, you know I've loved it." She led the way upstairs.

186

The Allerton-Fawcet surprised her. "I didn't think you were the sort of man who'd have this sort of car."

"I'm not." He waited then until he was sitting by her side. "My cousin Charles — or Chas — Adamson hypnotised me into buying this car from a friend of his. It was in fact a great bargain, though I always have an uneasy feeling that it doesn't belong to me and didn't really belong to the man who sold it to me, and that the police may confiscate it at any moment. Well now — you'll have to show me the best way from here to where you live in Hampstead."

"That's something I'm not really good at. However, if I go wrong this car can easily whizz round and charge about. You know how to get to Knightsbridge and then Piccadilly, don't you?"

Though sometimes he had to concentrate on his driving and she had to remember the way, they contrived to exchange a fair amount of information about themselves during the journey. In return for a rapid sketch of his life in Australia, she told him she had lost both her parents in a plane crash when she was twelve, had then been adopted by her aunt, a painter, had won a scholarship to Oxford, had spent three unhappy years in an advertising agency (chiefly to make sure she wouldn't have to sponge on her aunt, not as well off as she had been), and had now been with these publishers, not miserable but not particularly happy, for just over two years. Which made her, Tom calculated, twenty-six or twenty-seven, rather older than he had taken her to be. On the street where she shared an upper maisonette with two other girls ("And you can have that," she had added), she made him stop the car.

"This isn't a signal for necking —"

"I know it isn't. We've passed so many much better places. I wouldn't insult your intelligence —"

"None of that lecture-room stuff. There's enough light

here and I want you to get out your pocketbook or an old envelope and write down my address and telephone number both here and at the office."

"I was going to suggest that myself," he began but was interrupted.

"The reason is," she continued firmly, "I want to know what happens if and when you get that letter from Hilda Who's-it and go looking for your father again. And don't say anything about a dam' book or I'll be angry again. I'm just curious, that's all. I'm bungful of female curiosity. Nothing exciting is happening to me at the moment, so other people have to lend me some. Now you will, won't you — I mean, tell me?" She put a hand on his arm.

Tom promised he would and then carefully recorded the two telephone numbers and addresses.

"Good! I'll get out here. I'm sure it's an insult to this car to ask it to move about fifty yards. Oh — but just a minute! What's the name of your hotel? I think I ought to know — just in case I have an idea that might help you — or you rat on your promise —"

"I don't rat on my promises, Judy. Still, I'd like you to know where to find me." And he told her where he was staying. "It's very Catholic and Irish — which incidentally I'm not — and full of priests and pious old ladies. You feel that at any moment an Abbey Theatre play might get going in the writing room."

"No time now for witty comments, Adamson —"

"Why not, Marston? You're not living in a hostel. You're on your own —"

"I'm not. I'm living with two other girls. And if you think I'm curious, you should try them. Never stop asking questions, they don't. And I'm not going to serve up you and your father, and they already believe that Dr. Firmius is really a young television actor with long hair and insatiable lust. So goodnight, Tom. You're quite different from what I thought you were. Much nicer. 'Bye!"

And so was she, he told himself on the way back to the neon lighting, which hinted, just before going out, that he was an empty melancholy fellow, not leading much of a life. As for the girl, she was by no means unattractive — indeed when she'd been listening eagerly he'd found himself drawn to her — but, even so, her particular combination of flippancy and brashness and intense curiosity, which was really damned cheek, didn't appeal to him.

There was no letter from Hilda Neckerson next morning, and he passed the day in spiritless sightseeing. He wasn't really *with* London and he knew he wouldn't be, couldn't be, until this search was over. He thought once or twice of ringing up Judy Marston to ask her if she was free for dinner. But probably she wouldn't be free and anyhow she might get the idea, which would have been all wrong, that he was chasing her, a conclusion most girls arrived at much too soon. So he had an early dinner and then went to a highly commended "off beat" film, for which he'd had to book a seat, that seemed to him mostly idiotic. He left the cinema feeling it was time our society found a beat worth staying with and then firmly got *on* it.

17

HE was down early the following morning, but the post was late and he'd had his breakfast before the letter arrived. But of course it was really two letters, Hilda Neckerson's to him and the copy she'd made of his father's letter to her. In the remotest armchair in the lounge, he considered first his father's letter, realising with mounting excitement that this was the closest he had come so far to his father. It had evidently been written on the ship's writing paper for Hilda had conscientiously copied the heading: *Blue Caribbean Line — R.M.S. Coralla.* And this at least told him what he chiefly wanted to know, knocking a hole in the blank wall he'd been facing. And indeed the heading turned out to be far more informative and useful than the letter itself:

My dear Hilda,

  Thought you might like to hear from me. I'm writing this in a (something) bar in Port of Spain, Trinidad, and must admit I'm a bit (something). This is a cruise ship and I was taken on as a steward at the last minute because they were suddenly short-handed. Don't envy me — it's (something). After a 12-hr. day we sleep fourteen in a hole among the steam pipes and fellows half my age find it hard to take. My first long

*voyage — and my last! However, after I'm paid off at
Avonmouth I should have a few pennies in hand giving
me time to look for another job, possibly in the West
Country. Perhaps by this time you couldn't care less —
and I wouldn't blame you, my dear — but the way I'm
feeling tonight I must write to somebody and you can
always throw this in the nearest fire. And after all I
can't help remembering —*

And that was all.

Disappointed at first, chiefly by the lack of any promising
information, he read it again, a son now and not a detective,
and found himself shaken almost to tears. After giving himself time to recover — and there had been a rush of memories of a laughing acting-and-painting Daddy of 1933 — he
read Hilda's letter.

Dear Tom,

*Here is the copy I promised you. It stops after "re-
membering" because the rest is strictly private. I put in
the "somethings" for words I still can't quite make out,
but I think the first is probably "crummy," the second
"pickled," and the third, I'm afraid, "murderous." He
didn't date the letter — he wouldn't! — but I know
this is important to you and I remember from the post-
mark it was sometime in February 1956.*

*By the end of our talk the other day, Tom, I liked
you very much. And I mean for yourself and not because you are Charles's son. (You and he aren't very
much alike, neither in appearance nor I think in tem-
perament and character.) So I must tell you that I've
been worrying about you ever since that morning. (A
woman with no children has to worry about somebody.) Of course you must find Charles if he can be*

found. But now you must also find yourself and your own life. You are 35 or 36 and still unmarried. I doubt if you enjoy very much the work you are doing, otherwise you wouldn't have dismissed it so quickly. And — I'm sorry, but I must say this — you gave me the impression that in your own real life you are at a standstill, like a fine large railway engine in a siding. And that I feel is completely wrong — not for some people — but for you. And please don't forget your promise to tell me about Charles as soon as you know something definite — whether it's good or bad news. And — I mean this — Bless you!

He read this letter again, reread his father's, told himself there would be plenty of time later to think about them, and now tried to plan some action. The only address for the Blue Caribbean Line on the *Coralla* writing paper was Avonmouth. Did this mean he must take off at once for Avonmouth, which he seemed to remember was somewhere beyond Bristol? But wouldn't a shipping line have some kind of office in London? The telephone directory told him it had, at an address in the City. It was now nearly ten o'clock, time to start the Allerton-Fawcet on its way to the City.

But when he reached the City, it gave him a shock; it was almost like a ghost town. And why? Because of course — and how could he have forgotten? — this was Saturday. And tomorrow would be Sunday. Two whole days of sitting about, cursing the luck! Nevertheless, he didn't reverse the Allerton-Fawcet; he kept on moving rather slowly along streets that he had last seen, on an early exploration, choked with traffic; and very soon he was asking a policeman to direct him to the rather obscure address he'd found in the telephone book. After all, the Blue Caribbean, although on no Cunard scale, was a shipping line and might have *some-body* still on watch even though today was Saturday. And — the luck not having all run out — *it had.* In a side street, up two dusty wooden flights of stairs, behind a door that didn't seem to have been painted since the Boer War, it had.

The youth who grinned at him across the *Enquiries* desk was a type familiar enough to him in Australia and now easily recognised in England, which had far more specimens of it than he had first imagined. This youth had longish hair, no coat, and a green sports shirt well open at the neck. Ten to one he was lazy, rather unscrupulous, open to bribery, impudent, not giving a damn for the shipping business — his soul remaining with the drums waiting for him in some distant suburb — but ready to be cheerfully obliging on a personal basis. Tom felt his luck was in again. He would probably have got nowhere with some fussy and pedantic middle-aged clerk, out of Old England.

"Good morning," he cried cheerfully, after returning the grin.

"Not for me it isn't," the youth said. "As you can see. Comes round once a month this Saturday bit. And I was up till all hours last night. With a combo — and everybody else but me lying in this morning. Now look, chum, if you've come about anything serious, you can forget it. You want to send four bulldozers to Kingston, Jamaica — or twelve old women to Barbados next December — push off till Monday. Get me?" All this was said with great good humour.

"No, this is something quite different. I'm here to ask you to do me a favour. I've come specially from Australia to find a man called Charles Archer — an elderly man too — and the last thing I've been able to find out about him is that he was working as a steward on one of your ships, the *Coralla,* which was on a cruise to the West Indies —"

"The old *Coralla,* eh? When was this?"

"The only date I have is February 1956 —"

"Christ — ancient history! Though she's still on the run. It's all that white paint that keeps 'em from falling apart. Though we're not as bad as the wogs who'll be running her — fabulously, mind you, every bloody thing fabulous — years after we think she's had it. But what have you got in mind, Aussie?"

"I want to get in touch with the chief steward or the purser who might remember my man from that trip and might know what happened to him afterwards. It's the last thing I know about him, remember, and frankly I'm getting desperate. Help me if you can."

"Okay — do my best if only to pass the time. But the crew records aren't here, chum, they're in the main office at Avonmouth."

"Well, if I have to go to Avonmouth, I will —"

"Hold it, hold it! Had a week there once and died of misery. I can get 'em on the blower. Charles Archer, wasn't it? Well, if you don't object to paying for a call or two — know what I mean?"

Tom knew what he meant and put a couple of pound notes on the counter. They vanished, and then the youth vanished — through a door at the back. After about five minutes the youth returned, his grin wider than ever.

"You're lucky, Aussie. The bloke at the other end is one of their older blokes who thinks 1956 was last week. He'll call me back. And I'm ready to bet you ten bob he gets you what you want. How d'you like the Old Country — Land of Hope and Glory?"

"I've been too busy trying to find this man so far. But I get the impression, for what it's worth, that England's trying to move and to stand still all at the same time, which takes a bit of doing."

"And you're not far out, man. If you ask me, we're all living in different bloody centuries. My Dad doesn't understand me, and his Dad — he lives with us, if you can call it living — doesn't understand *him*. Even Sis and me's miles apart — what she wants, I don't — and what I want makes her ready to throw up. Talk about sixes and sevens, we're all at twos and threes, eights and nines. Half the people I know think the spades — y'know, the coloureds — ought to be thrown out, and the other half think they're all bloody marvellous. So where are you?" And he elaborated this theme of division and confusion until the telephone called him to the other room.

There was no sense in it, no possible explanation of it, but while Tom waited in this dingy little outer office and glanced round at the boring photographs of steamers on the walls and occasionally heard the voice of the youth in the other room, he was suddenly held and entranced by one of those spells of happiness, undeserved and unaccountable, that seem to belong to some other level of being: he might have been sharing the sunlight on the window with a demigod. There was a moment when he seemed to be contemplating infinite possibilities, a hundred, a thousand lives, an incredible breadth and depth and richness of being; just a moment; and then of course the spell weakened, the happiness thinned out, and he was a chap waiting rather impatiently for another chap on the telephone next door. No thought of his father, no thought of anybody or anything, had come into it at all; it was a visit out of the blue, probably lasting not more than a minute or so; but he never forgot it.

The youth came back in triumph. "Dad at the other end had it all sorted out. Now then. Charles Archer, steward, only made that one trip. So even Dad's lost him. And the bloke who was chief steward in the *Coralla* then is dead

now." He stopped to give Tom a grin. "Now wait — wait!
You haven't thrown your money away, chum. Dad says that
the purser — bloke called Jimmy Fetch, famous character
according to Dad — *isn't* dead but's retired. He lives in a
place called Pontisford, this side of Bristol. Moreover —
Dad knows it all — this Jimmy Fetch helps to run Bingo at
the Pontisford Palace. So if you can get there tonight —
Saturday remember and nothing else to do, the poor old
sods — you can ask this Jimmy Fetch about your Charlie
Archer, can't you?"

"I can and I will — and I'm much obliged — though it's
heavy odds against his remembering a steward who made
one voyage with him ten years ago —"

"Hold it, hold it! Dad wouldn't agree with you there. He
says Fetch might easily remember this Archer 'cos there was
something special about him or he did something special
for Fetch. Dad's forgotten what exactly it was — y'know
there's a limit, and I'd say up to this that old sausage in
Avonmouth's been a bloody marvel — but he swears there's
something. You go and catch this Fetch at his Pally de
Bingo, after he's done his last *Legs Eleven* and *Clickety-
click* — and what a way to spend an evening! — he must be
crackers after forty years of it — anyhow, you ask him about
this Archer. By the way, what d'you want him for? What's
this Archer done?"

"Nothing. But there may be some money coming to him.
So you may have done him — as well as me — a good
turn —"

"Lovely, lovely! Passing the morning too, thanks very
much!"

"There's just one more thing. Can I use your phone? I
have to talk to a girl —"

"Certainly, certainly. Come through. This way. That's
the trouble with birds. Have to keep talking to 'em — day

and night — any bloody subject, they don't care — not interested half the time — just so long as you're talking to
'em, then you can't be talking to some other bird. London
call? Okay, leave you to it."

Tom rang the Hampstead number. One of the other two
girls answered him, and then he could hear her shrieking for
Judy because a "heavenly man" was asking for her.

"Tom Adamson here, Judy," he began. "I thought
you'd like to know that I've heard from Hilda Neckerson —
you remember? I've been making enquiries at the shipping
company — he went as a steward on one of their cruises,
ten years ago — and I've been put on to a retired purser
who might easily remember him. Apparently there's a special reason why he might. So I'm driving down to a place
called Pontisford, somewhere near Bristol."

"You're pretending not to be excited, but you are really,
aren't you, Tom?" Her voice, low-toned, a trifle hoarse, was
nearer than ever to a feminine growl over the telephone.

"I'd be a wooden-headed mutt if I wasn't feeling excited.
Don't forget I've been on the trail, arriving at dead ends
and then starting again, ever since I arrived here. If you
were in my place —"

But she cut in, speaking rapidly. "I just don't want you
to expect too much, that's all, Tom —"

"I'll try not to, Judy. And this is what I'll do. If I'm given
any sort of clue to where my father might be now, then of
course I'll stay down there. But if it's another blank wall,
I'll drive back late tonight. And if I do, will you have lunch
or dinner with me tomorrow?"

"Oh — no, I couldn't. I mean, I can't —"

"I see!" But his tone suggested he didn't.

"No, you don't. And I can't explain — blast it! Now listen, Tom — please. If there isn't any clue, if it *is* a blank
wall again, and you drive back late tonight and don't know

what to do with yourself tomorrow and feel miserable or furious, will you please — *please* — not do anything silly but just sit around quietly and wait for something to happen. You haven't to do anything but wait — to let something happen."

"Is this you or Dr. Firmius?"

Her short laugh sounded like relief, as if she' expected a different reaction from him. "Perhaps both of us. I must run now. I've got the bathroom."

"Well, thanks for listening to me," he said dryly.

"Oh — damn! I wish now —" but she checked herself, said a hasty goodbye, and put down the receiver.

"How did it go?" the youth asked as Tom rejoined him in the outer office. "Not so hot, I'd say, by the look of you."

"I still don't know what she was talking about," Tom muttered.

"Birds! That's what's wrong with talking to 'em on the blower. Half the time, come back at you as if they're already up the wall. You've got to have 'em there in front of you, looking 'em deep in the eye, doing the whisper bit, with the old hand creeping out to clinch it. Well, Aussie boy, if you're going to what's-it — Pontisford — you want to get moving. Fine Saturday — and all the poor sods who've bought cars for family outings will be grinding along the roads. What kind of bus you got?"

"Allerton-Fawcet." He turned at the door to say that.

"Christ! — you'll be taking a razor to chop a tree down, man. Well, thanks for paying for the call. So long!"

It was quite as bad as the youth had said it would be — England was choking itself to death with cars — and he seemed to spend half his time just waiting to move. But this gave him many chances, which he accepted, of going back over that talk with Judy Marston on the telephone. He decided, not once but several times and never quite satisfying himself, that all that enigmatic stuff really came from Dr. Firmius, an old master now in the enigma gallery; though even so, that didn't explain why, when he asked her to a meal, she had said, "Oh — no, I couldn't. I mean, I can't —" That suggested, if it meant anything, not Dr. Firmius but a jealous boy friend. Well, she ought to be made to understand that Tom Adamson wasn't competing. Only of course, to make her understand this, he'd have to see her again pretty soon.

He had some sandwiches in a pub somewhere along the road, and after some brief explorations off the main route he reached Bath in the late afternoon. He had never seen this noble city before, and after parking the car and wasting precious time and temper, he walked around and opened himself to its golden enchantment. His training and the bent of his mind had checked any temptation to be a worshipper of the past and a despiser of the present, the huge, struggling, tragi-comic present; he knew too much about the eighteenth century to wish he'd lived in it; but Bath, like the Cotswolds, shook him and made him wonder if it wouldn't be idiotic even to think of returning to Australia. He did most of his wondering over an early dinner — and he had to be early to secure a place even for one — down in a cellar called the Hole in the Wall, a glorious mixture of wilful eccentricity and really magnificent food, which it was a shame to eat alone. A man — as he had concluded several times before — needs a woman to enjoy things with, not perhaps in Australia but certainly here in the old country. On the other hand, he reminded himself he was here to find his father, not a woman.

It was about quarter to nine when he arrived at the Palace in Pontisford, still looking like a cinema but now proclaiming itself to be a Bingo Hall. Impressed by the Allerton-Fawcet, his appearance, and half a crown, the commissionaire was helpful at once. Mr. Fetch was still on the stage, in charge, having kept things going in full swing since seven-thirty, putting his heart and soul into it, but after all Mr. Fetch wasn't as young as he was and might decide to knock off very soon and leave it to young Mr. Bird, assistant manager. If the gentleman liked, he could take a peep at Mr. Fetch, keeping it all going, and then wait for him in a little office, where Mr. Fetch, when he'd done, went for a drink and a cool-off, in evening dress as he was and often sweating like a bull. So Tom did take a peep — and there on the stage, rather hoarse by now, hot under the lights, wearing a dinner jacket that seemed rather too small for him, was Jimmy Fetch, ex-purser of the *Coralla* and a big fat chap, probably well into his sixties and looking not unlike a senior American senator. The place seemed to be full, with middle-aged women in the majority, all laughing at short intervals in a mechanical sort of way and really concentrating on the numbered boards in front of them. Tom was glad to leave them and wait in the little office, though it was musty and seemed to smell of glue and old paper.

Jimmy Fetch came in mopping himself with an enormous handkerchief. "Soaked through," he announced. "One of these nights it'll be pneumonia. You wanted to see me, Old Joe said."

"Yes, if you don't mind, Mr. Fetch. It's about a man who sailed with you once, ten years ago, and it's important to me — urgently so, in fact —"

"Let's have a drink first, if it's all the same to you, Mr. — er —"

"Adamson."

"Don't want to hold you up, but I need this, Mr. Adamson. Soda or water? Right!"

Watching him pour out the drinks, Tom saw that his large ruddy face was permanently creased with lines of good-fellowship and jollity, but that behind or showing through this professional mask was the face of another man who, though decent enough, was not at all a jolly-good-fellow-and-so-say-all-of-us. The eyes above and between all the smiling wrinkles were cool and shrewd and might easily be narrowed by contempt. Tom decided then to be completely frank with him.

"Ready if you are now, Mr. Adamson," Fetch said briskly as soon as they had swallowed some of their whisky.

Tom explained what had happened during the morning at the Blue Caribbean office, and then added a brief account of his search for his father. "By the time you knew him, Mr. Fetch, he'd changed his name to Archer —"

"Charlie Archer? Well, I'll be damned! Yes — yes — yes — Charlie Archer. And you're his son, eh? His only son. Oh — he told me he had one — yes. Now look, Mr. Adamson, we can't talk here, can we? Let's go to my place and talk in comfort, eh? Quite close. If you've a car, we can be there in five minutes. Drink up and let's go."

In the car he told Tom he had the ground floor of a house owned by an elderly couple, that he was a widower with a married daughter now living in New Zealand, and that one reason why he ran the bingo sessions, to augment his pension, was that he was saving up to visit his daughter and to see his grandchildren. "Fact is, I'm a lonely man. Everybody thinks the opposite, but what the hell do they know about it? Here we are — third house on the left."

His sitting room was smallish for such a bulky chap, but it was comfortable enough. A substantial old bookcase had all its shelves filled; photographs almost covered one wall; the other wall, beyond the bookcase, had two shelves above a long low cupboard that he was using to display various spoils and souvenirs of travel. From the cupboard he brought out whisky, syphon, glasses, but before he offered

Tom a drink he went rummaging in the other half of the cupboard, and finally brought out and unrolled a poster.

"This is what I wanted to show you, Mr. Adamson." It was a lively sketch of people wearing comic paper hats: *R. M.S. Coralla, Feb. 22nd 1956, Captain's Dinner.* And Fetch let him stare at it for a minute or so.

Tom cleared his throat. "So my father did that for you — um?"

"He did, Mr. Adamson. And three more, different occasions of course, before he did that. You must have been wondering how I came to remember a steward who only did one cruise with us, ten years ago at that. Here's your answer. It gave me an excuse to ask him into my cabin, give him a drink or two, have a talk. Once inside my cabin we were friends, you know what I mean?"

"I do — and I'm glad, Mr. Fetch. I've seen a letter he wrote to a woman friend when you were in Port of Spain, Trinidad, and he seemed to feel he was having a rough time."

"Can't blame him. We were jam-packed and short-handed — that's how he got taken on. He wasn't used to the work or the conditions, which were rotten bad. He was nearly sixty, as he had to admit when he knew I was friendly. Also — and here he was very unlucky — our chief steward then — dead now — was a bit of a bastard and didn't like him. Poor Charlie Archer hadn't a hope of signing on again, even if he'd wanted to. And of course he didn't. He'd had it."

"That's what I thought. Now, Mr. Fetch, this is the great question. What became of him after he was paid off at Avonmouth?"

"I wish to God I could tell you. But I just don't know. Here, let's have a drink."

"A very weak one, please. I'll have to drive back to London soon." Tom sounded as he felt — defeated.

"You're disappointed, aren't you? I'm sorry. I've often wondered about him myself. Fact is, we were doing a very quick turn-round that time, and as soon as we docked I'd to work full speed till all hours. Archer got lost in the shuffle. And he'd never told me where he was thinking of going or what he wanted to do. All I know is that he'd had enough of the Midlands, didn't want to go further north, and rather fancied staying on down here in the South-West. And that empties the basket, Mr. Adamson. And I'm sorry — dam' sorry. If he's still alive, then wherever he is he could do with a son like you. You could try advertising of course — Somerset, Devon, Cornwall — local papers."

"It may come to that now," Tom said gloomily, "even though there's no real proof he stayed in this part of the country. I'm staring at a blank wall again. Though God knows it's nothing to the walls he must have stared at!" He stopped to take a sip of his whisky-and-soda. "Did he tell you much about himself?"

"Plenty. A man wants to open up after a drink or two late at night at sea. Told me how he'd ended up as a captain in the war — home service of course, his age — and after trying to stay in the army as long as he could, he'd tried to live the same sort of life in Civvy Street and passed out a lot of cheques that bounced —"

"Landing himself in prison —"

"Right. They were very hard on him, chiefly, I fancy, because he tried to take a high line with 'em in court. He was bloody foolish, let's face it. But he was no crook — just one of those chaps who are too optimistic, spend half their time in dreamland. He imagined sooner or later he'd clear those cheques. He told me he'd a niece who'd married money.

There was another woman he'd lived with once who'd never miss a few hundreds. And so on. He'd borrow enough to meet the cheques — he'd made a careful note of 'em all — then pay back later. He'd schemes — I remember a touring company was one of 'em — another was a new sort of art school — but his idea of costs was all prewar. *And* dreamland. And of course the police and the lawyers didn't believe him. He was just the sort they wouldn't believe. So they made an example of him. Too much of this kind of thing — must put a stop to it. Never been in trouble myself, but I've had to give evidence a few times, and I hate these cold-hearted, narrow-minded, conceited buggers. I'm supposed to be Good Old Jimmy Fetch — everybody's pal — the jolly Bingo Man — but I don't mind telling you, Mr. Adamson, that after years of it at sea, especially with the twerps who used to come on cruises, and then more of it still, five nights a week shouting stale old jokes at half-wits, there's a hell of a lot of people I don't like and very few I do."

"But you liked my father?"

"I did, yes. He was good company. He could talk — and not just yap. He'd seen a lot, done a lot, even though he reckoned himself a dead failure. I think some of his so-called bad luck was his own fault. He'd imagine that things would work out all right for him without making sure they did. When they didn't he'd start drinking to keep in dreamland. Then he'd have to begin, worse off, all over again. But if he was a bit too eager to be dreamy and happy himself, he wanted other people to be happy, which is a dam' sight more than I can say about most of the passengers and bingoers I've known. For nearly forty years now I've been listening to people cackling at silly gags my elder brother told me he heard in 1915 in France, when they used to play housey-housey in *estaminets* back of the front line. And I'll tell you what I like to do, when I can get away from all these twerps. I like to sit in this chair, fill a pipe and a glass, and read one of the old travel books — y'know, Waterton in South America, Burton or Park in Africa — that bookcase is full of 'em. That's what Good Old Jimmy Fetch, everybody's pal, likes to do. I was at sea forty years, but I did no real travelling. But I'll do some when I go to visit my daughter in New Zealand. Another whisky?"

"No, thank you. I must be off in a minute. But two things please, Mr. Fetch. You've no idea at all where my father might have gone after he left the *Coralla?*"

"I'm sorry — no. And I tried to find out myself."

"That almost answers my other question. You'd have liked to have seen more of my father — um? It wasn't just a matter of having somebody to talk to, late at night, out at sea."

"Well, that came into it, of course," said Fetch carefully. "But I'd have enjoyed seeing him again, and I wondered many a time what had become of him." He waited a moment, looking at Tom but not really seeing him. "I think it was touch-and-go with Archer at the end of that voyage. He'd have to go one way or the other. If he gave a bit of thought to what he could do and made an effort, he might have found something worth doing, and might be doing it still. If he went the other way, told himself he'd never had any luck, then I think he'd have sunk fast. And that means he'd be dead now — and better dead. You know what I mean? No offence intended."

"I'm much obliged to you, Mr. Fetch." Tom had got up and was now holding out his hand. "Altogether you've given me more than anybody else. If it hasn't ended very cheerfully, that's not your fault."

It was a dark night, not a star visible. Watching that curious sharply illuminated stage set that cars seem to move through late at night, Tom thought in a dreary and unrewarding way about his father. There seemed to be nothing left now but advertising, not only troublesome and expensive but somehow fatuous. Even if it worked, it wouldn't be finding his father as he'd imagined himself doing. Then he had to remind himself, very sharply too, that it was not Tom Adamson and his attitudes and moods that mattered now; it was Charles Adamson, nearly seventy and God only knew where. Nearer London he stopped thinking about anything except driving and the road, for now he was challenged and overtaken by cars apparently filled with noisy lunatics, the daftest of them at the wheel, men who could hardly have been more dangerous if they had been given machine guns and hand grenades. They were all half-stoned and had probably been celebrating the end of another meaningless week in a meaningless society. Perhaps in another twenty years, machine guns and hand grenades would be allowed on Saturday nights, just to add a once-a-week spice to the lives of London's twenty million citizens.

18

SATURDAY night's thick cloud had turned into a drizzle by the time Tom looked out on Sunday morning. Lashing rain would have been better. This Sunday drizzle looked as if it might go on and on until everything worth having had been drizzled away. Not that Tom felt he had much to lose. Afterwards he regarded this Sunday morning as the low point, the Dead Sea, of his father-search. The blank wall seemed wider and higher and even blanker than ever before. He couldn't begin to think about advertising for his father, not on this Sunday of defeat and stagnation, and there was nothing else he could usefully think about. There was nobody to look forward to, thanks to Judy Marston's jealous boy friend or whatever else was the matter with her; nobody who might raise his spirits simply by listening to his account of how low they were; not even Mrs. O'Shea, for when he enquired about her, not long after breakfast, he was told she was off for the day. He wandered rather listlessly through a couple of Sunday papers, and then, about eleven o'clock, tried a walk, but it was all a damp misery. He had spent little time up to now in the bar of his hotel, a gloomy place, rather like an enlarged priest's hole, but just to pass the time he went in as soon as it had opened, ordered a gin-and-

Campari, and brooded over it in a corner. The only other people there were two men standing at the counter arguing about beef cattle, as if they were a hundred miles away from London and outside was some bright market day. Tom played with this fancy, imagining tricks with time and space, but it didn't help much.

Then, as it so often does, the totally unexpected happened. A man rushed in, spotted him in his corner, checked his rush long enough to shout, "A double pink gin, George — sharp!" and then joined him. It was Chas.

"The luck's in," Chas cried triumphantly. "I offered myself four to one against I wouldn't find you. But here you are, my dear old cobber. Now listen — this is serious. I know you decided you didn't like me. Fair enough! I've kept out of your way, haven't I? I put you on to Helga and she was a dead loss — though you can't say I didn't warn you —"

"I can't, no, Chas. But then we never like the people who've warned us, after they turn out to be right. But what's the matter? Money?"

"Yes, and this time I'm not touching you for the odd fiver, though I could do with one. As I said, this is bloody serious. Tom, I'm for it tomorrow unless I can find two hundred and fifty pounds. And that wouldn't break you, would it? No, of course it wouldn't. But they're going to break me tomorrow if I haven't got it." The barman brought the gin he had ordered. Chas drank half of it, then gave Tom a long appealing look. "This isn't just another touch, Tom. It's an honest-to-God S.O.S."

"I'm sorry, Chas. Nothing doing."

"You don't believe me?"

"It's worse than that. I'm not even bothering to ask myself if I believe you or not. I just don't want to give you any money, Chas."

"Now just a minute, before you freeze on to that. Did my sister Leonora tell you how your father appealed to her for a few hundreds and how her dear Dudley turned him down flat? Did she? All right, I see she did. Then what happened? I think you know a lot more about your old man now than I do. How did he get along as an ex-gaolbird? You needn't tell me, it's written all over your face. And don't think I'm going to get off with a warning. There are too many people who'd like to see me safely inside. But then perhaps you're *one* of them. Are you? Why, for God's sake? After all I've done to help you find your father!"

"What?" Even from Chas, this was an astounding piece of impudence. "Come off it, Chas. Why — after boasting when we first met you'd find him for me in a few days — you've never done a dam' thing!"

Chas had just swallowed the rest of his gin and now he stared in apparent amazement. "You're not working things out, old boy," he said reproachfully. "Look — I'll just go across and fetch another of these and leave you to work things out."

And no sooner was Chas standing at the bar counter than Tom realised, to his surprise, that Chas had in fact been responsible, directly or indirectly, for much that he had discovered about his father. It was through Chas that he had met his cousin Leonora and been told that his father had been in prison; through Chas he had gone to Lady Ellowstone's and there met Bassenthwaite and Crike and subsequently learnt that his father had changed his name to Archer, with all the rest that followed, by way of Crike, in the Midlands; and indeed it was through Chas he had gone to Helga's party, with all that followed *that*, including of course his knowing Judy Marston and Dr. Firmius, who, though they had contributed nothing to his father-search, somehow mysteriously appeared to be part of it. No, now that he had "worked things out," it seemed that in a rum sort of way Chas had helped enormously, and he'd been wrong and Chas had been right.

"See what I meant?" said Chas, returning with his glass. He didn't sit down but took a sip, still staring at Tom.

"Yes. But what am I to believe about tomorrow? Are you really in danger of being charged or are you just touching me for two hundred and fifty to play more games with?"

"Now listen. Remember my telling you about a nice little deal with a pair of nits in Manchester? I started shouting too early. They have an uncle in the City called Julius Morgen, a hard old sod. He's the one who has to have two hundred and fifty — or else. And I don't even want you to make the cheque out to me. Make it out to Julius Morgen — M-o-r-g-e-n — and then I can forget him and you can forget me. My God — Tom — if I hadn't found you in or if you'd turned me down, I was going to try my dear sister Leonora and her Dudley — and that'll tell you how serious this is."

"All right, Chas. My cheque book's up in my room. Julius Morgen with an *e* — um? And don't forget — this is the last time. I mean it. You'll have to find a job."

"Been thinking about one all morning, old boy. Meet you at the front entrance. By the way, I told the barman the drinks are on you."

"You surprise me," Tom said, though he knew all irony was wasted on Chas. A few minutes later, cheque in hand, he joined Chas below. They went outside together, still sheltered from the drizzle by the canopy. A car was waiting, a few yards to the left, and Tom was astonished to discover that the woman sitting behind its steering wheel was Helga.

"I thought you didn't like Helga," he told Chas.

"Quite right, cobber. But somebody lent her a car, and I need one."

"What's she doing now?"

"Getting ready to move on. If she told me where to, then I've forgotten. But I do know that wherever it is the men'll see her as the glamorous foreigner — you remember, old boy, and don't pretend you don't — and the women'll see straight through her. You wouldn't like to stand us a dam' good Sunday lunch at the Savoy or the Ritz, would you?"

"Certainly not, Chas."

"Up to her, then. Thanks for the cheque, cobber." And he made a dash for the car.

The hotel had looked almost empty all morning, but when Tom went in to lunch he found more people than he had ever seen before in the dining room. "It's because so many restaurants are closed today, sorr," said Michael the headwaiter. "And with your gracious permission, sorr, I'm putting an elderly gentleman at your table with you this once. He's a decent old gentleman, sorr, and some kind of a general."

"And I'm obliged to you, sir," said the General, after Michael had shown him to his place. "Know what it is to have one's table invaded, privacy broken, having to talk and so forth." He must have been at least in his late seventies — the brown spots on the back of his hands could be seen across the table — but years of self-discipline had kept him looking erect, trim, alert. He had one of those long narrow heads and long obstinate faces, with a lot of chin and not much upper lip, that suggest uncommon bravery and all too common stupidity, and that have in fact thrown away British lives in too many parts of the world.

"I've no strong objection to talking over a meal," said Tom, smiling. "We do a lot of talking everywhere in Australia, where I come from. My name's Adamson, by the way."

"Dantmore. Major-General. Retired, of course. Years ago."

In between ordering their food and trying the mulliga-tawny soup, a speciality of Michael's *maison*, they exchanged a few random remarks, and it was not until Sunday's roast beef had been set in front of them that they really began talking. By this time the General had ordered and received a half-bottle of one of Michael's dubious burgundies and had insisted upon Tom's taking a glass of it. The meat and the wine, such as they were, eased and opened out the old man.

"Don't like London, Mr. Adamson. Used to, of course — soldier on leave — but not now. Partly age. Not altogether, though. Place begins to look like Constantinople or Calcutta. Packed with riff-raff, seems to me. Can't taste this horseradish. Can't taste half the stuff I eat these days. Not entirely age, I think. Food's losing its flavour, isn't it?"

Tom said he thought it was, murmuring something about tins and refrigerators and deep freezes. But this was just to keep the old man talking, in the hope that he would soon explain how he came to be in London. And it worked.

"Live part of the time with my only daughter — widow. Begged me to come up — damnably early train too — to talk to her son — only son — my only grandson. Fine child he was. Played with him for hours. Devoted to him. Now he's twenty. Lives in London. Tells his mother nothing. Only asks for money. Not much, give him his due. No expensive women, cards, bookies, moneylenders, that sort of thing. All different. Called to see my grandson half-past eleven. Three young men living in a pigsty. Couple of dirty little trollops pigging it with 'em. Never saw such a place. Had to hold my nose. Stank of beer, stale tobacco smoke, vomit and filthy underwear. No exaggeration, I assure you, Mr. Adamson." The General tasted his wine, thought about it for a moment, then looked enquiringly at Tom out of faded blue eyes. "Having the cheese, aren't you? So am I. Safest — and helps the wine." Tom nodded and smiled and let him brood in silence until their plates were cleared. "I'm out of date, of course. Realise that. Just an old has-been. But you're a young man, Mr. Adamson. Older than my grandson, of course. Really a different generation. But still a young man. Profession — business — what? Mind telling me?"

"Not at all. I teach colonial economic history at the University of Sydney."

"Do you now? Clever fella, I've no doubt. All the better. Tell me what the devil's happening. Take this grandson of mine. Looks like a down-and-out fiddler. Lives off his mother. Doesn't do a stroke of work. No intention of doing any. Might as well be what we used to call a tramp. By God — we got rid of the tramps at one end and now they turn up at the other end — our own grandsons. And when I was his age, Mr. Adamson, I was getting ready to serve a great empire, the greatest, the British Empire — eh?"

"I know," said Tom easily. "After all, I teach some of its history. But these youngsters can't serve it if it isn't there —"

"Quite true. Aware of that, of course. All different now. See some of these puffed-up darkies on the television. Telling us what to do and what not to do!"

"They overdo it sometimes, certainly —"

"Down with colonialism! And if it hadn't been for colonialism, instead of riding in big cars and strutting in and out of jet planes, they'd have been still squatting on their arses waiting for the witch doctor to point a finger at 'em." This long sentence robbed the old man of any further speech for some moments. "Talking too much, dare say. Care for a glass of port, Mr. Adamson?"

"No, thank you. I never drink it but I'd very much like to ask Michael — he's the headwaiter — to bring you the best he's got. I've an idea that without a special request, it might be poor stuff." He signalled to Michael.

After he had tasted the port and pronounced it excellent, the General said, "Suppose there must be some of these weird lads — like my grandson — in Australia, eh? Come in contact with 'em?"

"Yes, lots. We get 'em slopping around in the University for a year or two. And of course they're damned irritating. They look awful, they're both cocky and ignorant, they're lazy, won't make an effort —"

"My grandson all over. Won't look ahead. Refuses to accept any responsibility. Why? Any idea?" He caught Tom's fleeting grin. "Not really funny, is it?"

"Not really, no. But I understand what they feel. They think that kind of responsibility pushed their grandfathers — your generation — into the First World War. Then pushed their fathers into the Second World War. And now it's been assembling sufficient nuclear bombs and missiles to finish us all off. So they want no part in it. They don't like our society. For that matter, neither do I."

"Can't say I do. All this advertising and spending, pushing and shoving for money. Nasty. Cads on the make. But all these lads do is loll about, booze and copulate. Why not pull themselves together? Improve the world if they don't like it."

"Chiefly because they don't know how. It's all too big and complicated. And there's no longer a simple programme for world-changing. So they just attend in their own way to their own little bit of life."

"Just sit about and let their hair grow."

The old man sounded so contemptuous that Tom, who

really hadn't wanted to talk, accepted this as a challenge. "No, General, I won't take that. As I told you, they aren't my style. And I mistrust the way in which they shuffle out of any sustained effort. But even so, if I had to choose, I'd prefer them to the students I've had at the other extreme — those who attend every lecture, fill all their notebooks, pass all examinations neatly and nicely on their way to the right degrees, are very careful and tactful, have no real opinions of their own, and you know will always say yes to anybody in authority for the rest of their lives. Those are the people I'm really afraid of, not the 'beat' lads and girls — like your grandson. Don't imagine these kids have done nothing but avoid work and responsibility. In their own little corners, they've already done a hell of a lot."

"Don't see it. What?"

"Well, for instance, among themselves they've done more in ten years to destroy the power of social position and money than the rest of us have done in the last hundred years. They've really made a new kind of revolution —"

"That can't keep anything going. Children letting the adults do the work. If it wasn't for his mother, my grandson wouldn't have a clean shirt or a whole pair of shoes."

"I know, I know. They'll have to see that. But in the end — it's possible — just possible — they might stumble on some better way of providing shirts and shoes than the one we have now. And please don't imagine that youngsters like your grandson are simply a British phenomenon —"

"Wondered about that. Things just going rotten here. Decay of Empire — all that."

"As far as I can gather," Tom continued, "they're turning up in every advanced industrial society. Even the Communists — except perhaps in China — can't really check this new and very odd revolution-in-small-corners." He stopped there. The General had glanced at his watch. "Sorry! It's the lecturing habit."

"Not at all, Mr. Adamson. Food for thought. Have to talk to the lad's mother later today. Poor girl — no husband — fussing and fretting away. Try to explain — lad's not a dead loss. Plenty of time anyhow — I mean for him, not for me in any sense. Later than I thought. Train to catch." Not without an effort he got up and glared around, finally raising high an imperative forefinger. "Always the same with the dam' bill. Think they didn't want you to pay. Hey — you there!" He was now scarlet with impatience.

"Look — I live here, General. You go — and let this be my lunch. Please!"

"It's extremely civil of you, Mr. Adamson — but —"

"No, please! I'd hate to think I helped you to miss your train. And I enjoyed our talk."

"Well, if you insist. Many thanks. Here's my card. Give me a chance to return your hospitality, Mr. Adamson. Don't forget."

Michael was about to intercept the General's brisk progress but Tom was able to catch his eye and wag a finger at him. "Got the signal at once, sorr," whispered Michael a little later. "All on your bill, isn't it? Will you be with us for dinner, sorr?"

Tom hadn't given dinner a thought, but now he decided he'd go out. "I'd like to be — but I can't," he replied mysteriously. "You know how things are, Michael — these days — um?"

"I do that, sorr." And Michael gave him a nod and a wink, as if they'd just agreed to dynamite a reservoir.

Leaving the Allerton-Fawcet undisturbed for the day, Tom went by Underground to the National Gallery. He'd been twice before — he enjoyed looking at magnificent painting so long as he could be quiet with it — but on both occasions on weekday mornings. But now he arrived at three o'clock on a wet Sunday. It might have been Derby Day in there. To catch more than a brief glimpse of any major painting took some doing, and the idea of standing quietly in front of one of them was obviously ridiculous. It was a time and place not for Art Appreciation but for Mass Observation, to which Tom didn't propose to devote himself — at least, not there and then. However, he saw enough to start off a melancholy train of thought.

There were of course a lot of youngsters, jostling and guffawing or giggling, who'd come in out of the wet and never mind the pictures, boys on the lookout for likely girls, and girls pretending to be interested only in one another but with eyes and minds working faster than those of the boys: the same old story. But after he'd worked his way through half a dozen packed rooms, some minutes before he finally fled, Tom concluded that most of the people there, people of various ages and probably coming from very varied social backgrounds, wanted just what he had wanted — to spend a rewarding hour or so in the quiet contemplation of noble works of art. And of course they couldn't, just as he couldn't. Their sheer numbers were self-defeating. So many people — nice, sensible people, who deserved whatever was offered them — were now reaching out for all the real prizes of life and then immediately destroying them, crushing or withering them by the sheer weight or heat of the crowd. What a hundred and fifty people could enjoy, a hundred and fifty thousand could only ruin. He remembered sourly the week-end beaches near Sydney and certain favourite rambles in the Blue Mountains. And that quaint fishing village, with its Spanish mission, to which a Californian friend had taken him one Sunday, when thousands and thousands of other people had had the same idea, so that the village had been almost submerged in a sluggish river of hot and hooting automobiles. And now all these people — himself included, of course — eagerly frustrating themselves, because there were too many of them. They were as hungry in their way as the world's undernourished masses were in theirs, and like them could no longer be fed. And he asked himself on his way back to the Underground — what next? Would a meritocracy insist upon some very definite privileges? Or would all, from a day's mountain-climbing to an hour in a picture gallery, have to be strictly rationed?

After tea he wrote a longish letter to Hilda Neckerson, telling her about Jimmy Fetch and the absence of any further clues, and a newsy note, funnier than he felt, to Andrew and Madge Wentworth. He even began a letter to the Marston girl, elaborate and from a lofty height, but tore it up. Just before seven, the drizzle finished, leaving a heavy, steamy kind of evening, through which he set out to walk to nowhere in particular, apparently quite a popular destination on Sundays in West London. Bored, rather tired and sweaty, and beginning to feel depressed, he ended up in a little Italian restaurant in a basement that was uncomfortably full but brought him some surprisingly good food. Two girls who shared his table offered to take him with them to hear some folk-singing, but he told them he had to go along to another basement, to see a friend. At which, assuming at once that this friend must be a girl and the basement all bed and cushions and dim lights, they exchanged those merry but meaningful glances that flash out of so many girls at the very thought of somebody making love. So he added, "My friend's an eccentric but amiable old scholar who's writing an enormous book." At which again, the saucier of the two, perhaps a typical young citizeness of the new London-Venusburg, gave him a look and cried, "My God — what a waste!" and off they went to their folk-singing.

In fact, until they spoke he'd had no intention of calling on
Dr. Firmius, but now he felt that he must.

The old man seemed pleased to see him, but this time —
and Tom was surprised to find how sharply the disappointment struck at him — he was alone. (And where in London-
Venusburg was Judy Marston slipping hastily out of her
clothes now?) "And this evening, my friend," said Dr. Firmius, beaming at him, "I have the coffee ready for you. So?
Not too strong for you? Good! Tonight I have been imagining very carefully, in all parts, what you might call a Forest
Lodge. It is on the edge of the forest, this small one-storey
house, on the ridge of a hill, with a long view of the valley
in front of it and the tall trees, old trees, indeed the whole
forest, behind it but not too close. I have always wanted to
live in such a lodge, among other houses of course, sometime but not all the time. And now I shall."

"You will? When?"

"Now we should be discussing the father-search," said
Dr. Firmius, smiling, "but I will answer your question first.
In the Third Time we must live with what we have imagined. Which of course can be very good or very bad, Heaven
or Hell, but our own Heaven, our own Hell. God has other
things to attend to — galaxies, perhaps whole universes.
We mustn't get out of scale. An ant in Central Africa must
not ask the Annual Meeting of the British Association to
hold up all proceedings, to decide whether it has been be-
having well or badly recently. More coffee?"

"Thank you, Dr. Firmius. I can see I may need it. But if
that's the Third, what's the Second Time?"

"Where we recompose our lives, with some help from
others who have shared them, out of our memories of this,
the First — and generally thought to be the only — Time.
Our conveyor-belt to the grave and oblivion. All we have

apparently, if you are foolish enough to believe such a thing. But all this you will find in my book — when of course it is published. Now for the father-search. What news have you for me?"

Tom gave an account of everything that had happened since they last met. "All I can do now is to advertise — a miserable business," he ended rather miserably, "and a wretched sort of anti-climax."

Dr. Firmius was twinkling at him from those shaggy caverns of his. "I advise you to do nothing for the time being. Wait now and allow things to happen."

Tom nodded at him, unsmiling. "Dr. Firmius, you know something. I've suspected this before. Now I'm certain."

"If I denied this, I would be a liar. If I pretended that this knowledge came from wisdom and a deeper insight, so that a pattern of events hidden from you had been revealed to me, I would be a charlatan. Though often I appear to be a charlatan — it is an old accusation — I am not a charlatan. My position is a difficult one, my friend, because of the character of this age. What I am concerned with cannot be proved or disproved in laboratories. It begins where the sciences end. Now most people may know little about physics, chemistry, biology, but it is true to say that their idea of life, how we live, why we exist, the scope and character of our existence, has been imposed upon them by these sciences. But not — and here is irony for you, my friend — as these sciences are now, in the minds of their leaders, but as they were a whole lifetime ago. Ordinary people today may be said to be out-of-date scientists. This explains their great respect for the nearest doctor, who is likely to be also out-of-date. But soon, though I may not live to see it, there will come a big breakthrough — in nuclear physics or in astrophysics and cosmology — that will revolutionize our thinking. And when the advanced leaders rush through the gap, I promise you they will find me — or at least my book — waiting for them. If this sounds conceited to you — and after all, father-search or no father-search, you are still an academic, Tom —"

"I doubt it. But go on."

"I say if this sounds conceited, then I must remind you that a man of my age cannot live here as I do — alone, almost unknown, like a mouse in a library — without some help from conceit. But though much of my book has come from the far unmapped edge of our existence, where all solid tested evidence is lacking, where I deal in what some will call guesswork though I know it belongs to intuition and insight, which we can achieve when we strike the chains off our minds, I am no charlatan."

"I never said you were, you know, Dr. Firmius," Tom told him, smiling. Why was the old man being so half-defiantly eloquent tonight? Did he realise that Tom was feeling depressed, sliding towards an admission of defeat?

"No," said Dr. Firmius, with an answering smile. "I am talking — just talking. And perhaps I am remembering Sunday nights long ago — with many friends, much talk and music, much happiness. However, I know it has not all gone, that it is still there. Perhaps you are still too young to care, but later I hope you will discover for yourself the profound difference between efforts of memory and the sense of living time, of everything still happening in its own place. I have almost convinced our friend, Miss Judy Marston, of this. She should be with us."

"If you ask me, she's out somewhere with a jealous boy friend." Tom tossed it lightly.

"Then I don't ask you, friend Tom. You are quite wrong. She tells me everything — I am her grandfather-confessor

— and though she has many friends, she has no lover. And if she had, he would not be a jealous one. She is not that kind of woman and he would not be that kind of man."

"No? Then I'm being stupid. But she turned down my invitation in such a curiously confused way, quite out of character, I thought —"

"She spoke to me of going away on a short holiday. She may have seemed confused because she did not know exactly when she was going and did not wish to explain. I explain too much. She explains too little. Perhaps you, Mr. Tom Adamson, are just right — not too much, not too little."

"I wish I felt just right about anything. At the moment I feel profoundly dissatisfied with myself. Rather as if I'd made a lot of mistakes that I can't put right because I don't really know what they are."

"That can be anything — too much dinner, lack of sleep, absence of good news — and does not matter so long as you do not go on and end by taking a great dislike to yourself. It is the people who dislike themselves who are the enemies of a good life. We must like ourselves a little — not too much, but a little. Now I am sorry I have no telephone, but if you go away on your father-search, perhaps you will write me a little note when you have found him?"

"Gladly," said Tom, rising. "Though I don't see it all happening for some time. By the way, I forgot to tell you I saw your two neighbours this morning." And he explained about Chas and Helga. Dr. Firmius listened carefully, though still with a twinkle. Then he took Tom by the arm as they were about to move out.

"My friend Tom, while you are feeling sad because nothing appears to be happening for you, everything is changing. Except for the one that is too old and deep in the basement, the pieces are being removed and then shaken together. A new pattern will appear." He gave one of his troll-king laughs. "My last prophecy tonight. Very easy, very safe! Charlatanism!"

The drizzle had come back. No empty taxis to be seen. It wasn't really far from Ashtree Place back to his hotel but far enough, quite far enough, after some fast walking, for the drizzle seeping through his shower-proof coat to meet and mingle with the sweat oozing through his shirt and suit. And when and how would any new pattern appear?

19

MONDAY morning, and fine if rather steamy. Expecting nothing, in spite of Dr. Firmius, he came down later than usual for breakfast and the letter was waiting for him. It was the last and most important of all those morning letters that now seemed like mileposts along the road to his father. It was signed Alison Oliver and was dated from Two Cottages, Stonebridge, S. Devon. In a handwriting that was at once small, feminine, decisive, its message ran:

If my niece, Judy, had not chosen to be obstinate and self-willed, you could have been saved much trouble and anxiety. Your father is alive and reasonably well and lives and works only a mile from here. Because I know him I feel that you and I should have a talk before you meet him. I have a pleasant spare room — two, in fact — and I hope you will stay here because this is now the holiday season and I imagine there is not a hotel or boarding-house in all S. Devon that could offer you a bedroom. If you do not mind being looked after, rather sketchily perhaps, by a widow in her sixties who also happens to be a painter, then do please come — today if possible. Judy tells me you have some dash-

*ing kind of car so if you are free you could probably be
here by early evening, however bad the roads may
be. And now — for housekeeping reasons — will you
please telephone me at once to say if you are coming
or not?*

And of course he did, to say that he was.

The day stayed steamy and close. He was hot after packing —he was nearly always hot after packing — and he was
never able to cool off. The temperature might have been
comparatively low — and this was cool weather by Australian standards — but Tom could hardly remember a day
that had seemed more oppressive. Nowhere from London
to South Devon was there any bright clear air and real sunlight. He felt as if he were driving through a jungle, and it
was a jungle largely composed of hot steel car bodies and
even hotter engines. When he stuck his head out of the
window to get some air, all he got were thicker petrol and
diesel fumes. But unlike most of his fellow-drivers, he was
sensible enough, in spite of his anxiety to question this Mrs.
Oliver, to realise that it was idiotic and dangerous to hurry
inside yourself, cursing every obstacle, if you couldn't hurry
outside yourself. If the overloaded groaning truck or lorry,
maliciously hogging the centre of the road, couldn't be
overtaken, then it couldn't be overtaken, and he reduced his
speed and jogged along thinking about something else,
often asking and answering certain questions. How, for example, could Judy Marston have told her aunt that he had
"some dashing kind of car"? Answer: only by talking to her
on the telephone either late on Friday or early on Saturday.
Again, if the irritating and mystery-mongering Judy had
been "obstinate and self-willed" about keeping his father
from him, did this mean she thought he was not good

enough for his father or — equally detestable — his father was not good enough for him? No answer. Again, and far more important, what was his father like now and what was he doing? No answer.

The way to the South-West more than hinted that the people of England and their government were at cross-purposes. Clearly the people wanted to go there — about half of them seemed to be on the road — and the government, judged by its transport arrangements, wanted them to go somewhere else or stay at home. So for hours and hours he crawled and stopped and crawled. And when at last he arrived at South Devon, three times he lost the way, wandering along deep lanes that were almost like tunnels, coming to villages of old churches and thatched cottages, no doubt delightfully picturesque, that had never heard of Stonebridge. Baffled, sweating away, in need of oxygen, he began to feel he might soon be smothered in lushness and thick cream. Was this to the taste of Mrs. Oliver, painter too? Would he soon be in the company of a large gushing female, ready to show him acres of bad pictures? But she hadn't written or sounded like that on the telephone. And it was with more than one sort of relief that at last he climbed to a small village, with a long white building, probably a hotel, just outside, that really *was* Stonebridge. He was directed to Two Cottages further up the hill, which had a rugged dark skyline behind it. And the cottages weren't thatched and determinedly picturesque but plainly built of stone, probably granite. They had been separate originally but were joined now by a passageway. Both front doors had been painted a brilliant orange, but the first of them — the first as he turned in from the lane — had a sign that said *No — the other,* so it was outside the other that he drew up and then rang the bell. He also took in a deep breath of the

first real air offered to his lungs for many hours. The long
oppression of the day lifted at last.

"Mrs. Oliver? I'm Tom Adamson."

"You are? Ah — well — now I see."

He didn't like to ask her what she saw, so early in their
acquaintance. He picked up his bag and followed her indoors, where they had a good look at each other, standing in
a tiny entrance hall. She was wearing a painter's smock, and
seemed to be a small wiry woman, with white hair cut
rather short and a dark snapping-eyed face: a mixture of a
widowed aunt, a painter, and perhaps a gypsy fortune-teller.

"You look hot and weary."

He admitted that he was.

"A drink? A bath? Which first?"

"A bath, please."

"Sensible. And the drinks are in there — sitting room —
and help yourself when you come down. I'm going to clean
up and then do some cooking. I'm not a bad cook when I
give my mind to it. But it's no fun cooking for oneself. So
half the time I live on cold scraps, like a hen. Come on, I'll
show you your room. And explain as we go along." She led
the way, still talking. "In this half there's that sitting room,
the kitchen, the dining room — and three fill it and four
crowd it out — and then upstairs are my bedroom and
bathroom. In the other half — along this passageway I built
— there's my studio, hogging the whole ground floor, and
above it the two spare rooms and their bathroom. One of
them really belongs to my niece, Judy, and is still full of her
things. I'm putting you in the other one. Up we go."

This end had a mixed healthy smell of turpentine and
whitewash. The bedroom she ushered him into was small
and very simply furnished, but it had a shelf of books and a
bedside lamp, and several unframed red-chalk drawings had

227

been tacked onto its off-white walls. The window looked out onto the back, framing the rugged dark skyline he had noticed earlier. "Dartmoor?"

"The start of it. And I love it but never paint it. Nothing but still life now for me. Well now, do you think you've everything you want? Speak up if you haven't because soon I'll be over there in the kitchen, miles away, though you could always stick your head out of the window and try a shout."

Like his room and probably its bed, the bath was rather small for him, but after he had done with it and had put on some clean dry clothes he felt curiously at home in this strange place, feminine but almost austere and quite unlike any other house he had known. Yet it was as if another part of himself, hitherto detached, had been there waiting for him to join it. He went downstairs and along the passage-way to the sitting room as if this was not the first but the hundredth time he had done so. He mixed himself a short gin drink, sipped it in the depths of the largest chair, stared rather vaguely at some pictures on the opposite wall, dozed off.

A noise at the drink tray woke him up. Mrs. Oliver was there, dressed for dinner in a brilliant green coat and a black skirt. "Have another drink? Sure? No wine, only whisky or beer. And I like wine better, but I forgot. I'm pretty dim at times. However, there's lamb casserole," she announced, "onion tart, cheese, fruit, which may seem a scratch job after the London fleshpots but round here, I assure you, looks like a banquet. And I'll back it against whatever they're serving tonight at Abbey Lodge, the hotel down the road — you must have noticed it coming up here. Incidentally, it's where your father works." She threw this at him just a little too casually.

"What does he do there?" He tried to keep his own tone light and casual.

"Kind of odd-man waiting. But we'll come to that later. Let's go and squeeze ourselves into my dining room. Everything's on the table. Bring the whisky if you'd like some."

Over dinner she insisted upon his telling his story first, right from the beginning. "Your father and I are friends — Judy too of course — but he hasn't a lot of time to reminisce and never seems inclined to go further back than the last few years. So naturally I'm curious. And if you can tell Judy and her old Dr. Firmius, you can tell me. And more, if anything. The whole story, please, beginning to end."

There were interruptions for clearing away and then coffee in the sitting room, and it was well after nine before he had done. "After all that, Mrs. Oliver, you'll understand that I'm not flattering you when I say that your letter this morning gave me the biggest and best surprise I've had since I came to England. I'm tremendously grateful." He smiled at her. "But now I've told you all, I think you've some explaining to do."

"Where do I start?"

"Well — let me see —"

"Just a minute — Tom! I can call you Tom, can't I? Don't ask me any questions that really involve Judy and not me. Young women like Judy are furious if anybody else tries to explain what they're up to. They believe they're so complicated, and anyhow they like explaining themselves. So when I think you're trespassing on Judy's ground, I'll warn you. But perhaps I ought to tell you a little about me first. I promise to keep it short."

"I'd like that — do I say Alison?"

"You do, Tom. I lost my husband six years ago. He was a history don — first, Exeter — he was a Devon man — then

Manchester, then Cambridge. That's one reason why I was glad to ask you to stay. You're a history don too, aren't you? We took charge of Judy after her parents were killed, fourteen years ago. Her father was my brother. I'm a professional painter. Nothing grand, but I've had several one-man shows in London and sold work to half a dozen public galleries. I'll show you the kind of thing I do sometime tomorrow. Mostly still life, supposed to be very feminine, all very delicate and fastidious, which is a dam' sight more than I am. But I keep flirting with abstract because — no, not because — if I start talking about painting you'll never hear a word about your father."

"I've been wondering if you knew he'd been a painter of sorts —"

"Oh — yes, indeed. Abbey Lodge, his hotel, is open most of the year and once the main holiday season's over it's fairly quiet. Then, when Judy's here, we sometimes go down for a drink. Charles — everybody calls your father Charles or Charlie — is kept on when most of the summer staff have gone. Not because they're fond of him but because he doesn't cost much. However, I don't want to go into that now. We'll leave the hotel out until you've seen it for yourself. But Judy and I got to know him. He overheard us talking about painting. Finally, he came up here sometimes on his afternoons off, and I'd lend him some gear, let him have a piece of hardboard or some old canvas to paint over, and we'd work away in opposite corners of the studio. He wasn't much good, and knew it, but he'd worked out a theory, a new approach, while he'd been moving round for hours with martinis and potato crisps, and he was happy trying it out. And now I must tell you — it's rather important — I have absolutely no romantic or sentimental sexual interest in him myself, so don't imagine for a moment I have

— or ever have had, as Judy can tell you — any intention whatever of marrying him or asking him to live with me. I'm deeply interested in him, I'm sorry for him, I've been curious about him — but that's all."

"How did Judy spot the connection with me so quickly?"

"Because we knew certain things, even if we didn't know the whole story. We knew his real name was Adamson. We knew he'd a family — a son, too — who'd gone to Australia years ago. We even knew your name was Tom. Now if a Tom Adamson comes from Australia —"

"Yes, yes, Alison, fair enough!"

"Suddenly he has a son looking for him. And this son finds him, an old man just hanging on, stretched nearly to breaking point. And the son's all wrong. He's contemptuous, behaves as you did to that bogus father you described. Then what? You see, Tom?"

"Yes, and as you won't trespass on Judy's territory, I'll do it for you. She met me at that party and didn't like me — and I don't blame her. I wasn't myself just then, anyhow. So she tells you at once, over the phone that night probably, that there's this fool of a son looking for poor old Charles. Then it turns out I'm not so bad after all, so I can be told where he is but not before you've had a chance to take a look at me and talk to me. That's why you didn't tell me in your letter exactly where he was — um?"

"Of course. And there's something else. Wait." She had switched on the lights some time ago, and now she got up to adjust the shade of the standard lamp by her chair. "I think you ought to go down there tomorrow morning and see for yourself. But I also think you oughtn't to tell him who you are — and don't imagine for a moment he'll recognise you — before we've had some more talk. Or is that asking too much?"

"No, no, I agree to that."

"After all, you haven't made any plans for him, have you?"

"How could I?" He was rather impatient. "I didn't know where and how I'd find him. I didn't know what shape he'd be in. Have a heart!"

"I've got one. And you're not going to steal it away, Tom, if you speak to me as sharply as that —"

"I'm sorry, Alison. I never meant —"

"It's the don in you, my boy. Robert — my husband — was just the same. He was impatient and rather cross immediately if I asked what he thought was a silly question. But I hope you're not too donnish, Tom."

"I'm hardly donnish at all. And I don't even much like what I've been doing. I've not been thinking about the future, but I have an idea that when I do, and take a good look at myself, I'll find I no longer want to go back to Sydney University."

She began to question him then, and he sketched his life in Sydney for her. No special girl. Only a few friends. Rather a flat sort of existence, partly explained no doubt by the fact that he'd had his mother living with him. "But don't get any wrong ideas about that, Alison," he went on. "I've known some mothers' boys but I've never been one. I'm not the type at all. But she'd had a long spell down at my uncle's place, miles from anywhere, and he was rather a grim character, so she wanted to try living in Sydney. And if I could help, I felt I ought to. Though she made some friends and a life of her own, she'd have been miserable living alone there. She was always hoping I'd bring home some blushing young thing — a really nice *good* girl — and leave them together to talk about the wedding, and of course I never did. One odd thing, though. The last year before she was taken ill — and of course long before she learnt my father mightn't have been entirely to blame — she changed. She'd always been puritanical, like all her family, a great disapprover of all goings on, pulling her mouth down at the very mention of them — but then she changed. Not dramatically, just gradually. If I'd been to anything a bit raffish, I had to tell her about it. Sometimes I had to pile it on a little. She pretended still to disapprove but she made me feel she didn't really. It was as if she was coming closer to my father. Almost as if she *knew* months and months before that letter arrived. Judy's friend, Dr. Firmius, would say she did." He waited a moment. "By the way, you said something mysterious, in the Firmius style, when you answered the door and I told you I was Tom Adamson. Remember? You said *Ah — well — now I see.* What *did* you see? What did you mean? That I was like my father?"

She laughed and looked mischievous. "Not at all. You aren't. I meant something quite different and I wouldn't dream of telling you what it was — not at this moment, anyhow. You'll have to go to bed still curious." She got up and then he did too. "Not that you *have* to go to bed. But I must. I like to work early in the morning, this time of year. Now about the morning. I'll leave a note for Mrs. Honeydew — that really is her name, though don't expect anything honeydewish — telling her to give you some breakfast about nine. It'll have to be tea; her coffee's horrible. Then I suggest you have a look at the moor and go down to Abbey Lodge about twelve or so, try the cocktail bar or the terrace just outside, where your father generally helps to serve drinks — and observe him carefully. But don't for goodness' sake get tight and then blurt out you're his long-lost son — no, no, I'm only teasing you. I know you won't. Sensible programme, do you think?"

"Couldn't be better." He took her hand. "And I feel miles deep in your debt, Alison. Thank you."

"I'm beginning to suspect you're that rare and dangerous creature — the don charmer. There are some books in your room and if they don't appeal to you, you can go next door and look at Judy's. Being in the trade, she has masses — but an awful lot of them are rubbish, I tell her. Goodnight, Tom. Sleep well!"

20

He spent nearly two hours up on the moor, walking briskly whenever the way was clear before him, moving cautiously through the occasional patches of mist. And his thinking was not unlike his walking, except that it had more and larger patches of mist to deal with, far fewer clear ways. His thought was divided between his father and himself. What could he do that would be best for his father? And what did he want to do with himself? Go back to Australia? Stay in England? What? He didn't know, and he began to feel that he wouldn't know until he was compelled to answer some fairly tough questions. We can't really interrogate ourselves, he decided; either we let ourselves off too easily or we press so hard we fall into despair; so he would have to wait until somebody interested, honest, and rather ruthless, put him to the question. Then, just before noon, compelled to walk quickly by a mounting excitement, he went down to explore the hotel and to take his first look, as a man, at his father.

Though Abbey Lodge was considerably larger than the Bull at Ditterfield, Tom had imagined that it would be equally Olde Englyshe, with even more horse-brasses and warming pans and cosy nooks gleaming with copper. He saw at once that he'd been wrong. There were some old things about, but there was no antique-shop effect. It suggested something between a sporting country house and a country club. The entrance hall — and you couldn't call it anything else — was large and rather austere, and though it had the usual reception and porter's desks, they were unobtrusive, almost apologetic, as if the owner of the place had installed them as an after-thought.

Just to see what would happen, Tom tried the reception desk. A young woman in black, wearing those decorated and oblique spectacles that always look sinister, was busy with some sort of ledger or register, filling in entries, rubbing out other entries. He stood there looking at her but she went on with her work, and not for the first time he wondered why receptionists are so curiously unwilling to receive, to offer the tiniest hint of welcome. But finally, as if he'd been invisible for the last few minutes but was now taking on solid form, she asked if she could help him.

"I know you're full up just now," he told her apologetically, "but I thought I might just look round, with the idea of staying sometime later."

"Nothing until the middle of September."

"I see. But you are open, I'm told, until after Christmas —"

"Here you are, Miss Parker." This was a man, to whom Tom was apparently still invisible, and he tossed several letters on to Miss Parker's ledger or register. "Came this morning. See if you can cope."

"Yes of course, Major Hewson-Smart." And she actually smiled.

Tom was now visible even to Major Hewson-Smart. "Tell you myself when we're open and when we're not, my dear sir." He spoke in a kind of high bark, as if he might turn at any moment into Field-Marshal Montgomery. "Quite simple. Open until end of first week in January.

Closed then until end of February. Go to a little place we have in Majorca — just for six weeks, all we have. Yes, my dear?" But this was not to Tom or Miss Parker but to a rather tall, angular woman who'd come rushing across to him.

"Darling, it's about the Trents. *Can* we or *can't* we?"

"*Can't*, I'd say, my dear. Look into it, though, if you're really keen."

"Well, darling, in a *way* I am — but not madly, you know. Let's talk about it, darling. And I *must* have a cigarette."

And off they went, Major and Mrs. Hewson-Smart, proprietors of Abbey Lodge (and a little place in Majorca) and the employers for some time now of one Charles Archer. Tom disliked both the look and the sound of them, and if he hadn't wanted to hang around, to watch his father, he'd have asked Major Hewson-Smart why the hell he'd been so rudely interrupted by him. They were both very tweedy, perhaps to prove they were really country gentlefolk with no sober-suited hotel-keeping nonsense about them. Mrs. Hewson-Smart wore green tweeds, not a wise choice, if only because she was one of those middle-aged women who put on too much make-up too hastily so that they always look either feverish or angry. The Major's tweeds were brown and hairier than he was; he was bald in front, and had a great reddish beak of nose, curving over a narrow grey moustache; and he looked as if he drank too much, was livery and bad-tempered. And Tom decided there and then that, whatever his plans for his father might be, they would certainly include getting him away from Major Hewson-Smart at the earliest possible moment. Meanwhile he was still lingering by the reception desk. Miss Parker was now filling in and rubbing out again. Tom too had been rubbed out. "Thank you, Miss Parker," he said with ironical precision. And if she looked up it must have been after he'd wandered away.

He went into a bar that had french windows opening on to a terrace. There were only four people in there, two middle-aged couples, dressed elaborately for casual living and looking ridiculous, and all shouting at one another and laughing like extras in a bad film.

Tom looked at the barman, young, trim, keen, like a barman in the same film, and then glanced at the terrace, where he could see people sitting at small tables. "I'd like a drink," he said vaguely, "but perhaps I might have it out there —"

"Why not?" said the barman. "You go out there; Old Charlie'll serve you."

"Poor Old Charlie!" cried one of the women in the quartette, the one in yellow pants and the shirt with horizontal blue-and-white stripes. "Arnold, you've deserted him, coming in here."

Slowly, carefully, his heart banging away, Tom went out to the terrace. Apart from a group of youngsters, who were probably not staying in the hotel, the people round the tables looked like the four inside the bar, even if they weren't quite so noisy. Leaning with his tray on an empty table on the far right was an elderly man wearing a white jacket and black trousers. Tom moved away to his left, where there were several vacant tables, sat down, and tried to stare across at his father without appearing anxious to be served.

Then a curious thing happened. He seemed to be aware all at once of the whole progress of what Dr. Firmius called his father-search, from his first talking about it to Andrew and Madge Wentworth after dinner, then through every twist and turn, right down to this very moment; and all of it, he felt, just for one flash of perception, was there and *still going on.*

"Yes, sir?" His father, carrying his tray, had come across and was now standing in front of him.

"Oh — yes — of course," he heard himself stammering. "Er — oh I think a gin-and-tonic — large gin, please —"

"Slice of lemon?"

"No, I don't think so — thanks —"

The top of his father's head shone in a peculiar fashion as he walked away. He had left the hair above his ears its natural greyish white but the rest had been recently dyed a horribly unconvincing dead black. Thin, rather pale, almost hollow-cheeked, he looked not unlike the photographs Tom had seen of the old tragedians, Irving and Edwin Booth and their imitators. At first he seemed more grotesque than pathetic, but then this fact itself suddenly touched him with pathos. Tom felt ashamed of him and then immediately felt ashamed of himself. There was no doubt whatever that this was his father at last. The eyes, though faded, were the eyes he remembered. He couldn't swear to the voice, which after all had so far spoken only five words — *Yes, sir?* and *Slice of lemon?*, all in an impersonal tone; he would have to hear a good deal more of it for any memory to be awakened. And of course the elderly, slightly stooping figure told him nothing. But he was as certain that this man was Charles Adamson, his father, as he had been that Crike's old fraud wasn't.

"One large gin-and-tonic. *And* a few potato crisps." His father put them down, slowly and perhaps a bit shakily, together with a folded bill.

"I'll have my usual, Charlie."

"Yes, Mr. Riseburn." And as his father turned to go back into the bar, a man shouted from a group further along,

"Come on, Charlie, buck up!" And Tom saw his father hesitate, then move towards the shouter.

The Mr. Riseburn who wanted his usual was sitting alone at the next table. He had an enormous round face decorated ineffectually by a moustache about the size of a decent eyebrow. And, as Tom realised at once, he was one of those super-extraverts who cannot endure sitting in silence and must talk to somebody.

"My fourth time here, counting Christmas before last," he began. "Old Charlie knows me as well as I know him. Only have to say *The usual, Charlie.* He knows."

"A good memory, has he?" Tom's tone was encouraging. This man might be useful.

"No, in a general way I wouldn't say he had. In fact he hasn't. Getting on, y'know. Almost past it, you might say. But Old Charlie understands *me*, and I understand him. And he knows I'm not afraid of putting my hand down, giving him a bit more than I would any of the others — cheeky young sods, some of 'em. Nothing like that about Old Charlie. Seen better days, I'd say. Now and again we get a rise out of him — kid him along — for instance, the way he keeps dyeing his hair — terrible, did you notice? —"

"He looks like an old actor to me," Tom ventured.

"Now it's funny you should say that. My wife — she'll be here in a minute — swears she once heard him say he'd been on the stage, but I tell her she dreamt it. Some of us who've been here a few times try to draw him out — *Now come on, Charlie, tell us what else you've done* — y'know the sort of thing — but the old boy's not having any. Mind you, he's a favourite here, Charlie is. The Major, who's very sharp, dam' good businessman even if he does pretend not to be, wouldn't part with him. Whoever else has to go when the season's over, Old Charlie stays. Last November I stayed just a couple of nights — I'd some business in Plymouth — and Old Charlie was still on the job, bringing me the usual. Ah — here's my wife now."

Tom, who said his name was Macpherson, had to be introduced to Mrs. Riseburn, a plump and pouting woman, more genteel than her husband and apparently intensely aware of obscure class divisions. It was her opinion, brought out almost at once, that although Abbey Lodge was still one of the better hotels, perhaps because Mrs. Hewson-Smart was definitely *County*, not all its guests now were *quite you know*, a certain class of people were pushing their way in. Didn't Mr. Macpherson agree? At which Mr. Macpherson smiled amiably, but explained that he knew nothing about the hotel and had lately arrived from Western Canada, where they all tended to be rather vague about classes of people. As soon as he had said this he saw his father coming out of the bar very slowly indeed, carrying a heavily loaded tray.

"What d'you want, my dear?" Riseburn enquired. "Old Charlie'll be here in a minute, bringing me my usual. And somebody in that lot ought to get his hand down for a good fat tip. Poor Old Charlie's properly weighed down. What about you having the other half, Mr. Macpherson?"

Tom thanked him, but said he would nurse the half he already had. Mrs. Riseburn wondered aloud what she ought to drink, perhaps to prove that she didn't belong to the class of people now pushing their way into Abbey Lodge. Good Old, Dear Old, Poor Old Charlie finally arrived with Riseburn's usual, and Tom noticed that his hands were shaking, not having yet recovered from that heavy tray. "Good morning, Mrs. Riseburn! Can I bring you a drink?"

"Well, yes, Charlie, but I'm going to leave it to you this morning. Make it a nice surprise."

He nodded, smiled, went away. Tom, watching him, no longer felt simply indignant but confused, already divided in his mind.

"This is something for you, my dear," Riseburn began. "Just before you joined us, Mr. Macpherson said he thought Charlie looked like an old actor."

"What did I tell you?" Mrs. Riseburn was triumphant. "My husband won't have it, Mr. Macpherson, but I'm ready to swear that Charlie dropped a hint to me once that he'd been on the stage. And I believe that's one reason he's such a favourite — at least with all the better class of people who come here. There's a certain *manner* — you know what I mean, Mr. Macpherson? Or perhaps you don't, coming straight from Canada."

Major Hewson-Smart and Mrs. Hewson-Smart were now moving around among their guests, contriving to give the impression that the folded little bills on each table were really an illusion, that everybody on the terrace was enjoying the hospitality of the Hewson-Smarts. The Major, grinning and barking away, finally came up to the Riseburn table. "Any complaints? Everybody happy this fine day?"

"Couldn't be better, Major," said Riseburn. "But you might settle a little argument we're having here. Has Old Charlie ever been on the stage?"

"Ah — Dear Old Charlie! Can't tell you for certain. Might have done some acting. Might not. Mystery man. Came here out of the blue. Looked like a lost old dog. We happened to be short-handed. He'd had some catering experience. Claimed to have had a wartime commission in the army too. Couldn't prove it — or didn't care to — but stood up to pretty stiff cross-examination. Told you all this before probably. Anyhow, he's still here —"

"And we're all very fond of him, Major," cried Mrs. Riseburn. "I mean those of us who understand what proper service is —"

"Couldn't agree with you more, Mrs. Riseburn. And of course, between ourselves, Old Charlie makes a dam' good thing out of it during this high season."

Tom had had enough, and anyhow it was now after one. Picking up his bill and muttering to the Riseburns something about having to go, he now made a move that very soon afterwards he sharply regretted. His father was at the bar counter waiting for his tray to be loaded. There was nobody drinking in there. His bill was five-and-six, and he gave his father three half-crowns and waved away any thought of the two shillings change.

"Thank you, sir."

"By the way, Mr. Archer," Tom enquired softly, "do you like this job?"

His father gave him an unfriendly look. "It's a living."

Tom couldn't resist it. "I've just heard Major Hewson-Smart say you make a dam' good thing out of it."

Another look. Then — "I don't think you're staying here, are you?"

"No, I'm not." Tom tried a smile.

It wasn't returned. "Well, I think you've had enough for your gin-and-tonic." He showed Tom his back. "Right, Phil — is this the lot?"

"Every bloody drop, Charlie. And quite a load — take it easy."

Tom walked slowly up the hill, hardly noticing it was there, his mind so thickly clouded with uneasy bewilderment and doubts about his father, himself, and everybody and everything else. It was as if he'd just been fighting two or three different kinds of battles and had been defeated in each. And though of course his father hadn't known who he was, the fact remained that after exchanging stares and words, his father hadn't liked him — and he wasn't even sure, now that he'd seen and talked to him, he liked his father. And the prospect of eating a solitary lunch, then poking around dismally in this mess of thoughts, half-thoughts, impressions, wasn't pleasing.

There was something of a clatter coming from the little dining room, so he looked in. A girl in a green linen dress with a dark red collar and belt was hastily laying the table for two.

"Hello!"

"Oh — hello!" Judy Marston smiled, then scowled, no doubt ready to be aggressive.

"How did you get here, Judy?"

"Not interesting. I stayed with a girl I know in Dorset on Sunday night and then last night. She has a car and brought me here but wouldn't stay for lunch. There's only corned beef and salad, cheese and fruit."

"Sounds fine."

"Aunt Alison likes garlic in salad. Do you?"

"Not much, no."

"Neither do I. And as she won't be here — she stays in the studio and has beer and sandwiches, staring at what she's done during the morning — then you and I don't have to fool around with gracious living garlic. I mean, it's gracious living here, not over there of course. Have you ever been in a bus in the South of France? Crikey!" Then she gave him a quick shy look. "Did you see your father down there — talk to him?"

"Yes, but only as a customer. I promised your aunt —"

"I know. Alison told me. It was my idea too you shouldn't tell him who you were. So I'm very glad you didn't. Though I must say I don't think I could have resisted the temptation. I'd have flown at him on sight. Look

2 44

— Tom — let me finish this and you go and have a wash or a drink or something. Then we can eat — I feel half-starved; my Dorset girl friend's rather mingy about food — and talk properly. It'll be all ready in five minutes. So till then — get lost, man."

He stared at something that wasn't quite a smile, wasn't quite a grin, and because he was staring, taking her in, it vanished, and she kept still, looking serious, almost solemn, as if offering herself for some very important inspection. And for the first time he saw that she was in fact a very attractive girl. He said lightly, "Now that you're in the country, you look wonderful, Judy."

"I'm really a country girl. Now buzz off, Adamson, till you hear me shout."

Over lunch, as if by some unspoken agreement, they postponed any talk about his father. She asked him how he'd got along with her aunt. "She likes you," she added. "I could tell that although we only talked for about a minute. She hates interruptions when she's working."

"I decided last night that if I ever saw you again I'd tell you I'd fallen for your aunt. Now I'm telling you."

"Quite right. But what was all that about ever seeing me again? You didn't think I was going to leave myself out of this father thing, did you? After being up to the neck in it — phoning Alison at all hours? What's the matter with you?"

"Well, you see, you turned down my invitation to lunch or dine with me on Sunday, and did it too in a curious confused way. It sounded to me as if you had a very jealous boy friend. I called on Dr. Firmius, late on Sunday night, and offered him the jealous-boy-friend theory. But he rejected it at once, said you hadn't a jealous boy friend —"

"He did, did he? A fat lot he knows about me and boy friends!" She was genuinely indignant. "Hasn't a clue. I've at least four jealous boy friends. Five, perhaps. No — *six*, counting you." Then she began to laugh. "What a pair of idiots you must have looked, huddled down there, trying to sort out my private life and neither of you knowing anything about it! What else did he say about me?"

"Not much. Men of our intellectual calibre have other subjects to discuss —"

"Oh — shut up! But if you're still interested, I'll tell you why I seemed confused, perhaps rather unfriendly, when you rang up on Saturday morning and asked me out for Sunday. First, I wasn't certain about staying with the Dorset girl. Secondly — more important — I didn't want to be alone with you on Sunday because I knew then, on Saturday, you were rushing off only to find another dead end. And I'd promised Alison over the phone not to tell you about your father — she had to talk to you first — and I knew that if you were feeling miserable I'd blurt it all out. Now do you see?"

"Of course I do, Judy."

"I pretend to be a tough girl-about-town but I'm really a sympathetic character, soft as mush, and weep in the theatre — at least when they stop making dirty cracks or blasting off at each other — and at sad films all the time — even at some of those awful television plays. I'm really a softie pretending to be a toughie. In London, not in the country."

"I see. But it's another pretence of yours that puzzles me, Judy."

"Oh? What? And I'd like an apple, please."

Handing her the apple gave him the pause he needed. "I'll put it like this. I'm thirty-six, you're twenty-six. Not much of a difference between a man and a woman. And I need a woman, badly, right now at this moment. I'm not talking about bed work — at least I don't think I am — but what a real woman represents and brings to a man — and it has to be a woman far nearer his own age than your aunt is. All right so far?"

She said it was, though in rather a muffled tone. The apple perhaps.

"But it can't work if you talk as if I were fifty-six and you about sixteen, not twenty-six. That's the pretence I meant. And I'm not getting at you, Judy. I'm honestly puzzled. And I don't want to be, not with you. This father-puzzle's quite enough to be going on with, just now. Before I came here — I mean, to England — I see now I was too self-sufficient, too complacent, and you may have forced me back into that attitude, sheer masculine vanity probably. But now I tell you frankly — I need some help — a woman's."

He gave her a long steady look and she returned it steadily too, twenty-six now and not sixteen. He was looking at her as if he'd never really seen her before. And when at last they both glanced away, he felt that never before had he known such intimacy with another person. Compared with this meeting of eyes, all that he could remember — and it was surprising how little a man *did* remember — of skin against skin, thrustings and heavings, moans and gasps, on or around beds, had merely been intimacy in the newspaper sense, not one person being intensely aware of another.

They had finished eating. "If you can listen," she said, "I can talk while we're clearing and washing up."

"Now we met at a cocktail party. I have to go to a lot of cocktail parties, loathing most of them. So I take a line — a sort of rather brutal, blurting-out line. It's not really sixteen — about fourteen, I'd say. Now if we'd talked longer — and I'm going to admit I was attracted to you, as I afterwards told Alison — I'd have soon departed from the cocktail-party line. But then of course I saw you weren't interested in me but were ready to start drooling over that idiotic Countess woman. By the way, are you going to tell me about her?"

"Yes, but not now. And anyhow I think Guru Firmius told you something."

"He did. Well, I'd thought you were a fool and then found out you weren't. That made me feel very self-conscious when we met at Firmius's and you afterwards drove me home. I fell back to some extent on the party line, really hadn't time to change into Judy Marston aged twenty-six — and a fairly ripe and experienced twenty-six at that. And don't forget that because you were shy and away from your own background, you often sounded more like fifty-six than thirty-six. I don't say you were pompous and condescending — that would be a bit much — but you weren't quite a man dealing with a woman his own age. And you're quite right, of course, when you tell me now we really *are* the same age. Here — you've skimped a bit, haven't you, with this salad bowl? No — I'll do it. As a matter of fact it's up to my standard but not Alison's. She's a perfectionist both in the studio and the kitchen. I'm not one anywhere — just a rough-and-ready type."

She put down the salad bowl, took off the apron she'd been wearing, and swept some hair off her forehead. It was very fine soft hair, he noticed, of a dusty brown shade that set off her darker eyebrows and the grey eyes that in this light seemed to have a touch of green in them. He noticed all this — and other things — while, standing close, she looked enquiringly at him.

"Well, did you accept that? Will I do — for help, I mean?"

"Of course. That was settled as soon as you'd spoken, Judy. Just now I've not been considering you but admiring you." He bent forward, laid a hand on the top of each arm, and kissed her quickly and lightly on the mouth. Releasing her at once, he said, "Now what's the programme, Judy?"

She drew a long breath and then spoke rapidly. "I've been thinking about that, Tom. A walk on the moor — unless you've had too much of it already. No? Good! But no father talk until dinner and after, so that Alison can hear it when I do and you're not trotting it all out twice."

"All right. I'll try to keep my father bottled up. So what do we talk about then?"

"That's easy. We'll talk about ourselves," she said firmly. "And now I'll get into slacks and find my walking shoes. You'll do, I suppose, but it'll be fairly rough going up there where I shall take you."

The mists had vanished from the moor. There were cars and people on the road and some walkers on the broader tracks, but Judy, leading the way along paths that were hardly visible, soon left them all behind or far below. They climbed through the heather towards a tor that looked like some ancient monument. They were in another world that they had to themselves.

"Heavenly up here, isn't it?" She had stopped and was looking round at him, her eyes alight.

"Glorious!" He waited a moment and hoped she wouldn't notice he was out of breath. "But we aren't doing much talking, are we?"

"Just wait. There's a favourite place of mine up here. I've spent hours and hours alone there. Now, with somebody to listen to me, I'll probably talk my head off. Come on — one last push and you'll make it, you Allerton-Fawcet pampered weakling!"

They climbed through the heather again and finally reached a patch of smooth moorland grass that went in a gentle slope into the shadow of an overhanging rock. "This is it," she announced, and threw herself down. He stood for a moment, chiefly to prove he was no pampered weakling, then sat down beside her. There was no wide scene below to stare at; they were in a little green-carpeted hollow; so he leant back and peered up at the sky, which now seemed to have a depth and intensity in its blue that he hadn't seen anywhere since he left Australia. Up here they might have been clean out of England.

She turned to face him, resting a cheek on her bent arm. "Who first?"

"Ladies. You."

"Really aged twenty-six — and, as I said before, a fairly ripe and experienced twenty-six at that. Two affairs. I'm getting this stuff out of the way first. Not stinkers — none of that. Rather sweet attractive men — one my age, the other older than you — and for a time I enjoyed the frantic notes and telephoning, the early and late eating and drinking that seem part of affairs, and bed and all that. But then I knew I couldn't make a life, a real life, with either of them. I couldn't *live* with them, and that's what matters. The second one ended just over a year ago. Nothing since. Too serious — me, I mean."

"Glad we've done with those two fellows," Tom murmured. "Taken a great dislike to them. No more love life. Go on about you."

"I've tried to write. I *can* write — up to a point. I could produce, without tearing my hair, the sort of novels by girls that we publish regularly. Chunks of autobiography — the last affair but one — with a few names changed and a different background. But why should I? I don't really care. What I really care about now — well, first, a personal life that means something all the time — and secondly, at the opposite extreme, about the condition, the health, the meaning, of our whole society, Tom." She laughed. "I think

I put in the *Tom* in the hope you wouldn't feel I was sounding too grand."

"That's very English of you, Judy. What the hell does it matter if we sound too grand? The state of our society's a life-and-death concern. Incidentally — and I'm not trying to hog my turn — I think it's rotten."

She put out her free hand and pressed it against his cheek. "So do I. And I'm a fraud now as a publisher's reader and scout. I'm no longer interested in ever-so-contemporary literature and drama, though I have to pretend I am. Most of it is messes coming out of a general mess. Reading it is like standing just outside a hospital ward and listening to the patients screaming their symptoms at one another. These writers don't tell us how to get out of the mess. They simply describe what it's like further in and lower down, where every wall has *fuck* and *shit* painted in large letters. I want books that show me a way out. Literature and drama can wait until we *are* out — or at least on the move. This is why I've taken so much trouble with Dr. Firmius and his monster manuscript, though now of course he's a friend, I'm really fond of him. However maddening he can be at times, he's sweet."

"I like the old man. And I want to read his opus. What's it about — I mean, apart from universities for people in their forties, which incidentally, I think is a dam' good idea?"

"Dear God — it's about *everything*. There are eighty thousand words before he even mentions his universities. He starts with Unamuno and Otto Rank and other people who've believed that the question of death or immortality is absolutely central in humanity, and then begins building his pagoda. I don't know how he'll strike a man like you, but he's liable to drive most educated women half-barmy."

"Why would he do that? Why women and not men?"

"Because so many of the things he says correspond exactly to what most women *feel* about life. The kind of things women take for granted when they're talking intimately to other women. They aren't part of an intellectual system, an ideology, just a lot of feelings and vague convictions that women don't argue about but are always prepared to *act upon*. But of course he formulates and systematizes them, builds his whacking great pagoda that the education in an educated woman has to reject. I never read him without shuddering to think what the linguistic philosophers we had at Oxford would do to him. Yet they themselves never say anything that a woman wants, that she *feels* to be true. And he does, all the time. So where are you? See what I mean, Tom?"

"I do, Judy. Sooner or later we'll have a big Firmius session."

"Oh? But when? How? Not airmail Sydney-London, London-Sydney, we won't."

"Not possible — no."

"When do you plan to go back, Tom?"

"What a question! I haven't even planned when to tell my father his son's here. Or even if I do it at all, after I stupidly accosted him in the bar — but we're saving all that. Sorry!"

"Well, tell me about you."

"I don't think I can at this moment. It'll come out sounding so dam' dull. I'll answer questions, of course."

"It'll be like an interview — God help us! I had to interview two of our authors — one an American, one an Indian. The American on sound radio. The Indian on the telly, no less. Both interviews sounded completely idiotic to me. The only response from the public was a nasty letter from a woman in Carlisle who said she didn't switch on her telly to see my legs and I'd better remember next time. Whatever happens to your father, you'll have to go back to Sydney fairly soon, won't you? Term starting and all that."

He shook his head. "There's no hurry." He waited a moment. Then he added, slowly, "I have an idea I'm not going back. Just an idea so far."

She changed her position, folding her hands on the grass, resting her chin on them, then looking up at him. Her eyes seemed enormous, and perhaps a little more green had crept into them. "You mean you're thinking of staying on here?"

"No, I don't." He was definite, almost sharp.

"Oh!" And now she was looking down, not up at him.

Tom didn't want to explain himself, not at this moment, but now he felt he had to say something, if only to make her look up again. "If I were thirty years older and had an income or a pension, I could live in England — choosing the right place very carefully. But I couldn't work here. If I were a real Englishman — and just remember, please, that I'm not — perhaps I'd feel I ought to live and work here. There must be some people, though I haven't met any of them, who are trying to bring back something the English had in the war and then lost. A jigsaw was nicely fitted together on a table. Then somebody booted the table. The pieces are still there but now they aren't joined up, any of 'em. That's England now to me, Judy, but if you tell me I've only been here a few weeks, mostly spent looking for a father I hardly remember and who certainly doesn't remember me, and that I don't know what I'm talking about, I've no reply ready for you."

"I've a reply. Don't move." And she pushed herself up and then forward, put her arms round him, kissed him long and hard on the lips. But as his arms moved, his lips too, she pushed herself away. "No, no, not now." She recovered some breath. "Don't think I'm not all for it. But not now. If we really start, we'll never stop. And this is talking time. If you don't want to go back to Australia and you don't want to stay here, then what *do* you want? Not a desert island, I hope."

"Just the opposite, I'd say. But while I've been looking for my father, I seem to have been finding myself —"

"Dr. Firmius said that —"

"I know he did but not first, so let's leave the old troll king out of this, girl. Somehow I've discovered I don't want to live and work for this country or that — for beer, tennis and picnics in Australia — for football, bingo and the telly, or country house gardens and cocktails with really nice people, here in England. If they'd let me, I think I'd like to live and work for the world, for the whole bedevilled human race, for a global civilization. What's the matter?"

She was sitting back on her heels now, and so was able to clap her hands. "I'm applauding you, that's all."

"You mean — I asked for it, so I'm getting it — um?"

"Partly. At the end you were addressing a meeting, not talking to me. But I meant it too. You said what I've wanted to hear a man say. You with your civilization, me with my worry about our society, we're really thinking about the same thing but looking at different ends of it. But what would you do? Where would you go?"

"I'd have to go — certainly at first — where I was sent. Probably some dam' awful place. But I'd rather be in a dam' awful place with a sensible purpose than in some pleasant place, not knowing what I was supposed to be doing there. As for what I'd do, it would mean joining a U.N. special agency or one of the big international organizations. It mightn't be easy. I'm not grand enough to go in on a high level, not young enough to start near the bottom. But I know several men who might be useful and my qualifications aren't bad — training in history, economics, teach-

ing; passable French and German, and some Spanish I
picked up in California; I'm no writer but I can draft a lecture or a report that's reasonably lucid. And though I
mightn't look it, I can get along with people, especially the
young."

"You *do* look it, Adamson," she told him, with mock-
solemnity. "And you're hired. You report on Wednesday
week to Ghana, Cambodia or Ecuador. By the way, we
ought to be moving soon. I want to catch Alison in the
studio after she's stopped working but before she's finished
cleaning up. It's the best time for her to show you some of
her paintings."

"And I want to see them. Up — girl!" He gave her a
hand to pull her up, then for a moment or two they stayed
close. The late afternoon was burning all round them. They
stared at each other in tender amazement.

On the way down, first moving across the heather in single file, they hardly spoke for some time. Then, catching up
with her, he said, "There's something I've just remembered, Judy. And we have to discuss it — even though it
brings in my father — before your aunt joins us and hears
everything that's said. Last night she declared most emphatically that she had no romantic or sentimental interest in
him. She meant, of course —"

"I know. She was telling you that you mustn't think
she'd ever dream of marrying him. And it's true. So any neat
little plans in that direction are out. Neat little plans generally are. I'd say that if he can afford to invite a woman to
live with him —"

"And I can fix that —"

"Then he'd better try your friend Hilda Thing, who
probably still adores him —"

"No, that's all over —"

"I doubt it, from what you told me," Judy said firmly.

255

"Besides, though he's older, he's probably in much better trim than he was towards the end of their affair, when he was trying to sell those ghastly novelties and hitting the bot. However, I mustn't break my promise to Alison. But I can talk about her. She likes seeing people, but she also likes living alone, working as hard as she can. The point is — she's struck a good seam — as you'll see."

And he did see. When they got back to Two Cottages, Judy did some quick peeping through the studio window, waited for the right moment, then took him in. It was quite a large studio and Alison, still wearing her painting smock and now cleaning her brushes, looked small in it, a kind of handsome insect, almost buzzing and humming with energy and purpose.

"Hello, Tom! Doesn't it seem a long time since we last met? However, I've been thinking about you and Charles at odd times. Incidentally, you two look as if you've been necking a bit. No, I don't want to know. I must explain about these pictures. Only one — that one, is just about finished. The others are somewhere along the way, not too far off. I keep about six canvasses going, and spend a lot of my time staring at them and brooding. All still life, as you see. I don't want to do anything else now — not ever. Anyhow, take a look while I finish these brushes."

What she painted was quite simple — some flowers in a jug, a decanter and a couple of glasses, some fruit and a plate or two. But all these things seemed to glimmer in the dusk or shine in the sunlight of another world. They existed, these simple and familiar objects, in a household at the end of time, in the home we are promised in our childhood but never appear to reach, the one that entices us round every corner unless we sullenly abandon all hope. This was the shifting Helga magic, with all its false promises, now caught and secured and brought home to stay, with simply so much paint and canvas. It was a long time since he had felt so strongly the enchantment of art.

"You like them, Tom?" he found her enquiring, suddenly at his elbow.

"No, Alison, I *love* them." And, hardly knowing what he was doing, he hugged her and kissed her cheek. Then he tried to tell her what he felt. "And unless they're promised elsewhere," he ended, "I must have that one — and that. I don't care what you charge, I *must have them*."

"Oh darling!" cried Judy, forgetting herself.

Alison gave them both a sharp look. "Thank you very much, Tom. You've said just what I love to hear — I don't mean the buying part of it. We'll talk about that later. Now I'll clean up and then do something very fancy with a chicken for dinner."

"Alison, suppose Tom and I go down to Abbey Lodge and see what happens when Charles has to serve us both — um?"

"You could — but I'm not sure you ought." Alison sounded very dubious.

"Neither am I," Tom told them. "I did something rather stupid when I was leaving this morning." And he explained what had happened after he had asked his father if he liked what he was doing. "My fault, I suppose," he concluded. "But it was obvious he didn't like the look and sound of me and so risked being rather offensive. I blame myself, not him. But it left me wondering what the hell I do next."

"Oh dear — oh dear — oh dear!" This was Judy, pulling a face too.

"You two pop off and serve each other drinks," said Alison briskly. "We'll thrash this out during and after dinner. Now — scoot!"

21

Once the chicken, which had been stuffed in some Roman fashion, had been safely served, Tom began by describing what he had seen and repeating what he had heard at Abbey Lodge. Then he added, "I want to make two points, even though they may be already obvious to you both. First, I couldn't stand that hotel and Major Hewson-Smart and all his guests. They add up to about half the things I most dislike about England and the English. So all the time I was there I felt irritable —"

"I know," said Judy. "Like hay fever."

"And this could have disturbed my judgment. Then again — point number two — I realise now how much my pride was involved and offended. These clots talked about my father — *my father* — as if he were an old pet dog. That Riseburn man actually said that the Major *wouldn't part with him*. For God's sake! Don't tell me I was thinking more about myself than about him. I know I was. But this wounded pride didn't help me to see anything down there very clearly. So I don't know what the next move ought to be." He looked at Judy, all fine and clear in a dark yellow dress; then at Alison, dusky and wrinkled and wise in her brilliant green coat; then back to Judy, who passed some raspberries and cream and raised her eyebrows at him, perhaps as a change from scowling.

"You surprise me, Tom," she told him. "If you can afford to do it, the next move's very simple. You yank him out of there. But first giving him a chance to throw something at Major Hewson-Smart."

"*Can* you afford it?" her aunt asked. "Or ought I to mind my own business?"

"Come off it, Alison," said Tom rather impatiently. "We're all in this together. Well, with what my mother left me and the little I've been able to save, I suppose I must have — let me think — oh! — about the equivalent of sixteen or seventeen thousand pounds sterling. So let's say I give him half of it —"

"Not in one great lump, I hope," said Alison quickly. "I know *that* wouldn't work."

"So do I. Now let's see. If I invested his half for him, he'd probably have about four-fifty a year — say about nine pounds a week. And that's not very good. By the way, can't he draw a pension soon?"

Alison shook her head. "He told me once he couldn't. Hadn't obeyed all the rules, he said. Outside the Welfare State, just peeping in."

"I'll bet Major Hewson-Smart or that great horse of a wife of his," said Judy, scowling, "has never bought a single national insurance stamp for him. He's down there on an old dog basis, poor Charles."

"I'll have to see about that. But if I let the capital go and bought him an annuity — say, for about eight thousand or so — he might have something like a thousand a year, with little or no income tax to pay."

"You talk just like a solicitor or an accountant," cried Judy, not accusingly but almost in wonder and admiration.

But he took it badly. "After all, I *am* an economist —"

"Don't be stuffy now. And no more points one, two, three. Your next move's quite simple. You march straight down there, tell him who you are, and say he hasn't to put up with those ghastly Hewson-Smarts and their idiot guests a day longer. Then you take him to London and buy him an annuity or something. That's two moves, really. Next move — you ring up Hilda Thing — you know the one I mean —"

"Hilda Neckerson."

"Hilda Neckerson — and you tell her he still adores her, so what about her leaving Husband Neckerson at once and then living happily in sin, with Charles now painting like mad. I know this sounds all very slapdash, but it's because you seem to me to be woffling, Dr. Adamson. *Direct action*, I say."

"But it's not quite as simple as that, darling," Alison told her. "Even though Tom may be complicating it a little —"

"I don't think I am. And anyhow I haven't explained yet what I feel. Now remember, I've been following him round, so to speak, learning how he popped up here, arrived there, then faded out, flopped. A dismal record. But this time, at last, he's held on to a job, God knows how, making a hell of an effort, just holding on, holding on. Now up comes the long-lost son — the very chap he didn't take to in the bar this morning. And just bear in mind *my father doesn't have to like me —*"

"Why not?" cried Judy indignantly. "You aren't *my* son, and you haven't been running all round the country trying to find me, and you're not going to set *me* up with an annuity, but *I like you —*"

"I'm very glad, but it's not the same thing. He's held on, then I suddenly turn up. And I have money, more than he's seen in all his life, and I say in effect, *You've had enough of*

this Good Old Charlie caper, Dad. You may think he'll fall
on my neck, probably bursting into tears. But I think he
might equally well blow up in my face and tell me to go to
hell. I've already mentioned my wounded pride. What
about his?"

"But it's all so silly," Judy protested. "Why — any
woman —"

"We're not talking about women now, dear," Alison put
in smartly. "Men, y'know. Quite different."

Tom ignored these remarks. "Now suppose he reacts in
this way — and he very easily might — then what? I've
gone, having been told where I can go and what I can do
with my money, and then one day, when the terrace or the
bar is crowded, he suddenly keels over with a heavily loaded
tray — and that's the end of Good Old Charlie at Abbey
Lodge or perhaps anywhere."

Judy scowled at nothing in particular and pushed out her
lower lip. "It still sounds silly to me. And you *are* complicating it. Isn't he, Alison?"

But Alison, getting up, wasn't listening. "What time is
it? Nearly nine o'clock? All right. You two clear away —
but don't bother washing up. Make some coffee. I shan't
be long, I hope. I'm taking the car. We're nearly out of
whisky and we need some."

Both of them protested but she waved them away and,
without another word, went out. "It's no use," Judy said as
they began to clear the table. "Once she's decided to do
something, she just does it. No argument. Finish."

"She told me in her letter that *you* were very obstinate."

"Me? Compared with her, I'm just a helping of jelly. Besides, she oughtn't to go out at night in that horrible little
old brute of a car. You'll hear it in a minute. I don't believe
it's got anything a car's supposed to have — except an engine. Listen — there she goes! You didn't tell her last night

you must have whisky, did you? All right, of course you didn't. Sorry! Then what's she playing at? Oh!" And as she checked herself, she flashed a glance at him and then looked away.

"Oh — what?"

"Nothing. I'll get the tray." Then later, in the kitchen: "I'm very keen on this Hilda Neckerson idea."

"He likes women," Tom began rather slowly. "They seem to like him. And he's been here some time now. He may have already found somebody."

"Wait — I must concentrate on the coffee. Let's take it straight in. No, you go ahead." After she had put down the coffee tray in the sitting room, she said, "Naturally it occurred to Alison and me that he might have somebody round here. What do you think we are — a couple of professors? But we soon guessed he hadn't. He came here whenever the bloody Hewson-Smarts gave him a little time off. No doubt about that. And finally he told Alison there wasn't anybody, while admitting there usually had been in the past. So your Hilda, his Hilda I hope, hasn't to face any local competition."

"I'm glad to hear it. Hello — isn't this Alison's car?" He made a move towards the door but she stopped him.

"No, Tom, please! Stay here. I'm sure that's what Alison wanted. Easy now, boy, easy!" She took his hand and squeezed it hard.

Alison burst in, followed by a man. It was his father.

"And I didn't forget the whisky either. Here it is." Alison was talking rapidly, almost at the top of her voice. "And don't think Judy and I are going to leave you two. We wouldn't dream of it, would we, darling? Charles, this is your son, Tom. And don't stand there looking at each other like two strange dogs."

Tom and his father grinned sheepishly. They shook

hands, not unamiable but still silent, struggling with their embarrassment.

"God — I'd hate to be a man," cried Judy. "Great wooden dummies!"

"I'm sorry about this morning — in the bar. It was stupid of me — Father. I'm not usually as stupid as that."

"I was a bit on edge, Tom. I'd had about as much as I could take — on the terrace. And now I'll answer your question properly. No, I don't like what I'm doing. But I also know I've been lucky — for once — just to be able to do it."

Tom had been taking a good look at him. He was wearing a dark suit, quite trim but obviously old and now beginning to shine. He looked both older and younger than he'd done at the hotel: older because his general appearance suggested his sixty-nine years and a dignified elderly man; younger on closer examination because there was no longer the shocking contrast between the waiter's white jacket and the shaking hands. And now of course his face was different; not Good Old Charlie's but his own, belonging to Charles Adamson, former painter and actor. All that remained of the Abbey Lodge bar-and-terrace character was the horrible black dye that ought to be washed out of his hair as soon as possible.

"I'm delighted that Alison was able to bring you up here," Tom said, watching his father carefully lower himself into an armchair. "I never expected it. I had the idea they made you work all hours down there."

"They do. But tonight I'd had it, whatever the Major felt like saying. I'd done drinks before lunch — you saw me — then coffee after lunch, helped with tea, then drinks before dinner and coffee and liqueurs after dinner. It's nearly as bad as a cruise."

"Oh — you know I've been trying to find you, chasing up people you'd worked with —" Tom began eagerly.

"Yes." He looked and sounded sour. "And I must say, I wish you hadn't —"

"Then I'm sorry. But when you mentioned a cruise, I wanted to tell you that I was talking on Saturday night to Jimmy Fetch of the *Coralla* — who said how much he'd enjoy seeing you again."

His father's face lightened as quickly as it had darkened. "Jimmy Fetch — eh? Don't tell me he's still at sea."

"No, he retired. Now he runs a bingo show at a place called Pontisford, not far from Bristol. He showed me a poster you'd done for the Captain's Dinner."

"He did? I'd like to see Jimmy again. He became a friend when I badly needed one. There were just a few of them turned up along the road — but not many, not many."

"I can tell you about some, if you'll let me —"

"Oh, don't worry about that, Tom. I'm too curious to stop you." He nodded and then produced a curious twisted little smile, quite different from his professional grin on the terrace. "Australia doesn't seem to have done you any harm. You're a bigger man than I ever was — and better-looking, I imagine. Mind you though, thirty years ago, when I was still playing in the West End, I used to be told I looked quite dashing. When she was driving me up here, Alison said you were lecturing at a university — and not married yet —"

"He's going to marry me," said Judy, breaking in, "though he doesn't know it yet. And Alison thinks you boys need some whisky. Here!" She handed them their glasses. Then she sat on the floor between their chairs. As they drank, she looked hard from one to the other, comparing them. Alison, glass in hand, came across and stood behind her. "You look to me a pair of very nice men," Judy continued. "But quite different."

"There's a resemblance round the eyes and the mouth," said Alison, using a painter's eye and tone, as if they were two objects.

"You two are making us feel self-conscious," Tom grumbled.

"We're here to do the opposite."

"And anyhow," said Judy, "Tom can walk Charles back to Abbey Lodge, and then they can tell each other all their secrets."

Tom looked enquiringly at his father, who nodded. "Yes, Tom, downhill all the way I can manage all right. And I must be going soon. I've had a long day. And it's hell on your legs and feet at my age. Even the young men complain. Though some of 'em would still complain if they did all their serving and waiting in a bath chair."

"How do you get along with them?" Tom asked.

"Not as badly as you might think. I have to take a lot of *Dad* stuff from them of course — they're all cheeky young squirts — and they're lazy and greedy and don't know very much and don't care — but they don't pretend and most of 'em are really good-hearted. They've saved my bacon more than once when they've seen I was ready to drop. I prefer them to the Hewson-Smarts and most of the guests."

"What about the girls?" This was Judy.

"Which girls — the waitresses or the girl guests? The waitresses mostly come from Ireland — willing if clumsy, and all human. The girl guests — and thank God we don't get a lot of 'em — are nearly all spoilt, bogus, and without any consideration for the staff, a bad lot. Half the time I'd like to throw something at 'em."

"That's what Tom did to the novelties man," cried Judy. "Tell him, Tom."

"Who's this? Not Joe Stane? My God — you did get

around, didn't you?" His father appeared to be divided between pleasure and annoyance.

"I lost my temper with him in the end," Tom explained, almost apologetically. "And I scooped up a pile of his novelties from a chair and threw them at him. Then walked out."

To Tom's surprise, his father suddenly roared with laughter, which Tom somehow had thought him incapable of doing. "I'll have to hear more about that." He finished his drink, and then, not without effort, got out of his chair. "If you don't mind, Alison, I'll have to be going now. No car, please. Tom can walk me down the hill as Judy suggested. No objection, Tom?"

"Just what I'd like to do —" and then he slipped the *Father* in again. And as he followed Alison and his father out of the sitting room, Judy, close behind, squeezed his forearm hard, and when he turned she winked at him. He wasn't quite sure what all this was meant to convey, but he felt ready to face the walk and talk with his father with more confidence. Judy understood, he decided, that the talk mightn't be easy.

It was a warm and windless night, with a moon. They set out slowly, and for the first minute or two his father kept silent. Tom didn't want to talk. Whatever could be said would be either too much or too little. They weren't in a sitting room now, with its close patterned walls, its artful lights, its feminine influences, but out in the huge wide night, which said only one thing, Tom felt, to anybody walking in it — that men live and have their being in a mystery.

But then his father not only spoke but asked the very question Tom had been dreading. "Coming from a university and comfortably off, you can't have enjoyed the sight of me on that terrace this morning. Did you tell yourself it had been a mistake to find me?"

"No, I didn't. Of course I didn't. I knew you'd been in prison, that you'd tried or had to take all manner of jobs, and I hated to think what might have happened to you after you left the *Coralla*. You might be down-and-out or mouldering away in some old folks' home. You might even be dead. But down there this morning you were alive, trim, alert, holding on to a difficult job — not drifting any more — holding on. I didn't like what you were doing — I didn't think it right for you — but I respected you — no, I *admired* you — for doing it. And I wondered if I'd have the guts at your age. But you haven't to stay there — and I hope to God you won't."

"No, my boy, and I'm not going to be too proud to take a lift out from you. Alison says you can afford it. And I'd like to get back to some painting while I can still stand up and hold a brush. I never expected this. I'm half-dazed yet. And I don't deserve it. Not a penny of mine have you seen since you were three." He checked Tom by a touch on the arm. They stopped and looked at each other. Tom thought his father's face in the moonlight looked worn, hollow, very old. How extraordinary they should suddenly be talking like this — in the silvered green and indigo of the night, an extraordinary night too, not quite in familiar space and time, as if from mythology!

"You must have been told, Tom, how I left you to go to that bloody bitch of a woman, Nelly Coping. I was a fool of course. But she'd promised me a one-man show and I didn't want to act again, just paint. Though I won't pretend that was all. She still had a bed hold on me then. She was a woman who excited you by being excited herself but then left you feeling you hadn't possessed her this time but might the next — a kind of will-o'-the-wisp in bed. I was a fool. But I wrote letter after letter to your mother, telling her it would be all over soon, begging her to hold on and be patient. Not a word came back from her — and the next thing I knew she'd taken you and your sister to Australia. Finish! That's how it was, Tom. Like to move on?"

"I'd better explain what really happened first, Father." And he went rapidly from his mother in hospital to the afternoon when he talked to Nelly Coping's old dresser, Agnes, and tried to talk to Nelly herself, now Lady Truskmore and a monstrous ruin. "So it was neither entirely your fault nor my mother's. Though I don't think either of you was quite blameless. I was brought up to hate or despise my father. My sister Joan — who's now a nice dull woman married to a nice dull man — wouldn't listen when I tried to explain to her over the phone just why I was coming here to find you. I'm afraid she's one of those people who refuse to change their opinions: their likes and dislikes fit them like old shoes. What about moving again?" He put an arm out and his father rather shakily took it as they began to walk.

They must have gone a hundred yards or so — they were still a little distance from the main road and had the lane to themselves — before his father said anything. Then when he did speak, he had to make some effort. "No, I blame myself. Though I certainly paid a hell of a price for it. I'd some ability, perhaps talent, but I was split up and confused from the start. And watching the mincing machine at work in the First War didn't help. Straight out of school too, don't forget." He cleared his throat. "Couldn't decide what I ought to be doing. A painter when I acted, an actor when I painted. A great talent for what I wasn't doing. And always a bit lazy and always a bloody sight too hopeful. If you've been running round for weeks, trying to find me, you've probably been told a lot about me. Not much to my credit — eh?"

"It's been mixed. Not as bad as you think, I imagine."

"We'll go into that later. I want to hear your story, but not now of course. But now I'll tell you about me — and no nonsense. It seems a bad luck story. First blow — wife and family gone, when I need 'em. Second blow — prison. Ah — you know about that — good! After that I'm hit all round the ring — sagging on the ropes half the time, a bleeding mess. And I'd be rude to the wrong people. And I drank too much — and I rogered too often, not always caring what I'd got. But that's not why I was nearly down and out, which I was just before I landed here. My trouble was — I believed things would sort themselves without any help from me. No effort when some was needed. Everything'll work out all right. When your mother didn't seem to reply to my letters, of course I ought to have gone to see her. But no, not me. I was given a prison sentence as a cool calculating swindler when in fact — though of course I was leading a life I couldn't afford — I thought, when I did think, I'd be able sooner or later to meet every cheque —"

"I guessed that when my cousin Leonora told me —"

"Those two! God help us! I'm lucky they've never stayed here, asking for two small dry sherries. What's my dear niece like now?"

"Dried up and worried to death about a beatnik son."

"No wonder! One thing I've learnt is not to bother about people like that any more. They think they're on top and very important when nearly everybody they're patronising is laughing at 'em. We get hundreds of 'em here, and though they keep us running around, we're still laughing at 'em."

They crossed the main road and were now in sight of the

269

hotel, long and low and so illuminated at this hour that it looked not unlike a ship. "There it is, Tom. The ring, the stage, where I perform as *Good Old Charlie*. I don't like it. You don't like it. But it's where I really took hold of myself for the first time, didn't trust things to come right for me, made a real effort and kept on making it. Sixty-seven years of age then, when most men are letting things slither and go, I'd either to take charge of myself and my life or soon be slobbering in an old men's home. And — by God — I did it."

"I know you did. Father, I really understand all this. In fact I told Judy and her aunt earlier tonight that I wasn't sure you'd welcome a son telling you he'd come to rescue you. I knew you felt you'd rescued yourself."

"You've more insight than I ever had, my boy. And I think if Alison Oliver hadn't decided to break the news herself and to take me to you, we might have been snarling — not talking. But that's women for you — real women — who are always wanting to bring people and things together, to join up where we men, half out of our wonderful minds, are always wanting to fly apart."

They were nearly apart themselves now. Not thinking, Tom had turned towards the front entrance of the hotel. "Hoy!" his father called. "You're forgetting, aren't you? The help uses the back entrance. This way. Now you've seen and heard the Hewson-Smarts —"

"Yes. And I'm against them."

"Well, to hear the Major talk — and, by the way, he's had no more army service than I've had — you'd think he'd found me in a ditch, carried me here, then dished me out with a white jacket and a tray. But in fact it was his wife who took a chance and offered me a job. What the Major did was to make sure I worked non-union hours for non-union wages. And as soon as I was *Dear Old Charlie*, he knocked off paying me a cent during the high season, I just keep my tips, those I don't split with young Phil, the barman. His wife's not so bad except she's such a ridiculous bloody snob. Nearly all the middle-aged women who come here are just the same, and getting worse not better. They've turned me into some kind of radical republican. That is, when I think about it, which isn't often. What I chiefly think about, Tom, is painting. I've got a theory about objects lighting up other objects. And if you really can afford to give me enough to live on, I'll take it gladly — and stay clean and sober — no trouble to anybody — to see what happens to my theory on canvas and hardboard."

"You can depend on that," Tom told him. "We'll go up to London early next week and arrange for an annuity —"

"London, eh? Years and years since I was there. They tell me I'll hardly know it." They were now round at the back of the hotel. "Better stay here for a minute. We won't hear ourselves speak near that open doorway there. Hell of a clatter when the kitchen staff are clearing up. What's tomorrow — Wednesday? My time-off."

"You could walk out any moment now —"

"No, I'll work the week out. But tomorrow I could be up at Two Cottages by teatime. Then you can tell me your story and I'll tell you mine." He hesitated for a moment or two. "A silly question, I suppose, but I can't help wondering. Who among the people you've talked to seemed to like me best?"

"Hilda Neckerson," Tom replied promptly. "She slipped away from the shop and we talked in a café, got along tremendously. She admitted she was very much in love with you once. She'd kept the letter you wrote to her from Trinidad. And she made me promise to tell her all about you if I did find you."

"Hilda, eh?" he said slowly. "Yes, it would be Hilda. I

might have known." Then he laughed. "Dam' queer conversation this, between a father and a son he's not seen for thirty-odd years! Tom my boy — you're a bit too stiff and I'm a bit too loose — but it'll work out. Must go in now. See you tomorrow. And don't bother about a car. I can walk up, taking my time. Tomorrow then."

After Tom had recrossed the main road, where cars were still passing, again as if fleeing from one catastrophe and hurrying to the next, he saw a figure sitting on a pile of stones a little way up the lane. It turned into Judy.

"You still look good," he told her, "even in the moonlight."

"I ought to look better. Alison went to bed. She wants to get up early and work. So I came down, curiosity gnawing away, to meet you and hear the latest. How did you and Father Charles get along? Any proud and angry words?" She entwined her arm with his and gripped his hand as they began to walk.

"Chiefly thanks to Alison — fetching him like that was an inspiration — no, there weren't. He did say at the end I was a bit too stiff —"

"So you are — and more than a bit."

"He didn't mean it seriously —"

"Neither do I —"

"And added he was a bit too loose —"

"So am I. All the nicest people are. All right, all right, I'll stop this. Seriously now, Tom, and I promise not to interrupt."

They were home before he'd done telling her all that he remembered of what his father had said. "Alison and I had already guessed most of that," Judy told him, "but then so had you. I never think you're going to be perceptive and then you are — a nice surprise. Perhaps it'll go on like that, endless nice surprises. Really the Hilda Neckerson bit was the most important. One of us ought to ring her up tomorrow."

"I don't quite see how *you* can, Judy. Too much explaining for a long-distance call, going to an office too, perhaps with Husband Neckerson listening in and interrupting."

"We can fix that — or at least you can — by simply saying it's about Charles and giving her this number, leaving her to pop out and ring you. She's up to all that, our Hilda — look at the way she met you in that café. Then when she does ring you, perhaps I could listen in somehow and tell what she's really feeling. And don't imagine that's very clever. My God — the number of females I've had to listen to — both at the other end of the phone or at theirs, in the flat! What it must have been like when they could only write notes all the time!" She indicated the drink tray. "Do we have some whisky? One for the road, the golden stairs, Bedfordshire, or whatever the same idiots say in Sydney?"

"I don't think so, Judy. And as I seem to have had a long day —"

"Not too long a day, I hope?" She gave him one of her smaller scowls. "Bed then — um?"

Upstairs, just outside her door, she kissed him lightly, patted him on the shoulder, and then was gone without even saying goodnight. Puzzled, feeling rather depressed, he went slowly along to his own room. Undressing almost in slow motion, he heard her go into the bathroom and then come out again. It was now his turn and he took it. Five minutes later, he was sitting in his pyjamas on the edge of the bed, staring at the wall between him and this oddly disappointing girl, when the door opened. Above the gauzy nightdress, her face seemed especially clear, bright, wonderful.

"You said this afternoon you needed a woman — though not this way. I didn't believe you, Tom darling, though I didn't think you were lying. Then later I stopped you just when — you remember? Not the right time and place. And this *is*. My room, though. I'm a great leaver-behind of things and Mrs. Honeydew may be dim but she can put any bedroom two-and-two together. This way, Dr. Adamson."

"It's Alison not Mrs. Honeydew you must be afraid of," he said as he followed her.

"Alison, Mrs. Honeydew, Mrs. Hewson-Smart, Mrs. Thing, almost anybody — except you, my duck." And she turned and came into his arms.

About an hour later, she said sleepily, "We're going to be good at this, don't you think?"

"My God — we are! But you'll have to marry me."

"Of course." She nuzzled closer and her hair tickled his chin. "I decided that when you were driving me home on Friday." Still nuzzling she contrived to distribute some little kisses, like tiny prizes at some Lilliputian speech day. Then, sleepier still, she went on: "One thing . . . we haven't to settle it tonight, though. . . . We don't stay here. . . . We don't go to Australia. . . . Good. . . . But with four children, starting as from tonight . . . does it have to be Ghana or Cambodia or Ecuador? . . . Couldn't we make it Austria or Thailand or Mexico, my darling?"

22

It rained all next morning and they never left the sitting room until it was time for lunch, just talked and talked and sometimes argued, having plenty of raw material for talk and a certain amount of ammunition for argument. Pressed by Judy, who demanded action, he rang up Hilda Neckerson, only to be told she was away for the day and wouldn't be in her office until five o'clock. The question then was — and they kept presenting each other with questions — would it be better if they let Charles ring her? Or was that rushing him before they were sure about her? And wouldn't they have to fetch Charles in the Allerton-Fawcet if it still went on raining? And if so, then at what time? And on top of all these questions, there was a keen argument about Tom finding himself as well as his father. Judy maintained that Dr. Firmius had said it first; Tom declared — and would not be budged — that he himself had pointed this out, and after all — what the hell! — he'd been doing the finding, not Dr. Firmius; and Judy retorted that he oughtn't to be too cocksure about that, because you never knew with Dr. Firmius. But all this was a mere prelude to the telegram that came when they were clearing up after lunch.

The telephone rang and Judy, answering it, was away some time, and then returned, rather giggly, holding out a

page torn from a pad. "It was for you. Telegram. Here —
read it."

It said: *Congratulations from Ashtree Place. From Chas
and Helga and Firmius.* He stared and muttered and then
looked at Judy.

"Nice, don't you think?"

"But it doesn't make sense. Congratulations?"

"Yes — on finding your father. And me perhaps," she
added demurely.

"But have you been talking to them?"

"Darling, don't be silly. Dr. Firmius isn't on the phone,
and I wouldn't talk to the other two."

"Well, then, how could they know anything? Where do
the congratulations come in? I tell you, Judy, it just doesn't
make sense."

"Never mind. It's a nice telegram." She was calm, smiling.

"Yes — but —"

She put a hand to his mouth. "Not to worry, Dr. Adamson my duck. You're not in Australia now. You're in one of
the old countries."

He moved the hand away but didn't release it, held it
firmly, and now took a long hard look into her eyes. They
were quite clear — a stream going over grey pebbles with
perhaps a flash of green in it — but wasn't there somewhere
in their depths a flickering like a trout in that stream, a
knowing, derisory, mocking *something*, not to be caught
and analysed probably, belonging to some impenetrable
world of feminine magic?

"What are you staring at, darling?"

"I don't know. But I hope I'll spend the next thirty years
trying to find out, Judy."

"Well, you're the finding man, aren't you? Kiss me."